THE
SECRETS
WE LEFT
BEHIND

OTHER TITLES BY SORAYA M. LANE

THE
SECRETS
WE LEFT
BEHIND

SORAYA M. LANE

LAKE UNION
PUBLISHING

Text copyright © 2021 by Soraya M. Lane
All rights reserved.

Published by Lake Union Publishing, Seattle

www.apub.com

Amazon, the Amazon logo, and Lake Union Publishing are trademarks of Amazon.com, Inc., or its affiliates.

ISBN-13: 9781542025904
ISBN-10: 1542025907

Cover design by Plum5 Limited

Cover photography by Richard Jenkins Photography

Printed in the United States of America

For my mother, Maureen.
I hope you love this book as much as I do.

PROLOGUE

"Come on, Cate! We don't have long."

Cate followed Lilly down the pretty streets of the seaside town. She was far more interested in sitting outside one of the quaint little restaurants, and as she admired the striped awnings and rows of tables as they passed, she vowed to convince Lilly to stop on their way back. Her friend and future sister-in-law was so enthusiastic, and Cate hadn't the heart to say no to shopping with her.

"Do you think we could send a little gift back home?" Lilly asked as they entered a store with a tiny bell above the door that jingled when they walked inside. It was full of treasures, knick-knacks that Cate knew her mother would love, and she suddenly felt overwhelmingly homesick. It was Christmas, and the first time she'd ever spent it away from home.

"Maybe," Cate replied, gently brushing her fingers across a porcelain figurine. "But they'd most likely break in transit, if they ever made it back at all."

She saw postcards on a small rack by the counter, and she left Lilly's side to take a look, smiling at a picture of Dunkirk showing the beach with the village in the background. No one back home would believe just how beautiful France was.

The lady behind the counter smiled at her and Cate smiled shyly back, her fingers finding their way to the ring looped on to her necklace. It was always her default when she was nervous; feeling the weight of the ring always grounded her. She wished Charlie were there with them, choosing postcards to send home, his shoulder bumping against hers. She always felt so safe with him, relaxed in his company and knowing he'd look after her, which meant that going on such a big journey without him was even more daunting.

"I'm going to buy these earrings," Lilly called out. "How about you?"

Cate spied some chocolates in a tin and reached for them, deciding she might need a treat over the coming days. Dunkirk might be pretty, but she had no illusions about what they were heading into. No matter how well their British soldiers were faring, war was war, and she couldn't imagine how many wounded she would soon be tending to.

Once they'd paid, Lilly linked arms with her, and they went straight back out into the bright sunshine. Cate forced herself to put Charlie from her mind and just enjoy the day. Worrying about his whereabouts or wishing he were there wasn't going to do her any good.

"Which restaurant?" Lilly asked. "We could drink wine and eat snails if you'd like?"

Cate laughed. "Trust you." She giggled, never having had so much freedom in her life before, and certainly never imagining she would be travelling abroad.

"What, are you nervous about the wine or the snails?"

Cate shrugged before they burst into laughter again. "Both!"

2

They bent their heads together as they walked and Cate couldn't wipe the smile from her face as they marched up to the first restaurant.

"Table for two?" the maître d' asked them from the door in heavily accented English.

"*Merci*," Lilly said, and Cate noticed the way she smiled, fluttering her eyelashes at the handsome Frenchman.

"I think you wanted to come here for more than the food," Cate whispered as they sat down.

"We're not all engaged to be married," Lilly teased. "Although I won't tell my brother if you decide to enjoy the view a little."

Cate just smiled at Lilly, happy to be in her shadow. Lilly was like the brightest flower in a garden, always radiant, her smile easy and her eyes always alight with mischief. And as their wine arrived and the smell of French fries wafted from the table beside them, Cate wished she could capture the moment on film so she never, ever forgot it. Because even with Charlie miles away from her, it was one of the best afternoons of her life.

Dunkirk, she thought, as soldiers strolled past in small groups, talking and laughing as if they didn't have a care in the world. *I've never seen anywhere so beautiful.*

3

CHAPTER ONE

CATE
CALAIS, FRANCE, MAY 1940

Cate stared at the scene around her, wishing her head would stop pounding. She'd never heard a noise like it; German planes were roaring in the distance now, but when they'd flown over less than a minute earlier, the sound had been deafening.

There were men everywhere; some were running with their rifles raised, some were sitting on the ground rocking as if in disbelief, and then there were the dead, littered like rubbish, strewn here and there. But it was the rumble of approaching tanks that scared the life out of her; who knew what would happen if they were still there when the Germans arrived en masse?

"Let's go!" The command was loud and Cate leapt into action, searching for Lilly and finding her within seconds. Her friend's blonde hair had escaped from its pins and was wisping around her in the wind, and her eyes caught Cate's. Months earlier, Cate would have received a wide smile the moment their eyes locked, but now Lilly's face was drawn, no doubt a reflection of the way Cate looked, too.

"We're to go on foot for part of the way," Lilly said when she caught up with her.

"On foot? That's ridiculous."

"Try telling them that."

Cate wasn't even sure who she meant by *them*, but she knew Lilly was right. They were expected to take orders, not question them.

"Do you think it's true that some of the nurses have already been evacuated? One of those soldiers back there said an entire group were evacuated from the port here days ago."

Cate looked back at her and replied with a shrug. "Why would they evacuate some and not others?"

"Honestly, none of this makes sense to me," Lilly muttered. "No one tells us anything, do they?"

A whir above them sent them both diving for the ground, and Cate tucked tight to Lilly as a German plane flew low, the ground rumbling beneath them. A bomb tore through a nearby building. It was like an earthquake, everything shaking, and Cate grabbed for Lilly's hand as smoke curled into the air around them. The dust choked her almost instantly, burning her eyes, and as she looked back at the broken town behind them, someone yelled, "Get in!"

"Finally," Lilly murmured, keeping a tight hold of Cate's hand as they ran to a lorry, climbing up as it slowly rolled forward.

"Where are we headed?" Cate asked one of the soldiers on board.

"Dunkirk," he said.

Cate smiled, remembering the village they'd spent time in when they'd first arrived in France. She turned to Lilly, about to speak, when loud shelling sounded out nearby and the screams of men scolded her ears. Instead she just clutched Lilly's hand and folded it into her lap, thankful she still had her friend beside her.

Please let Dunkirk be better than this.

CHAPTER TWO

CATE
DUNKIRK, FRANCE, MAY 1940

Cate stood in the middle of the enormous room and turned, slowly surveying the narrow beds and the last remaining patients lying in them. She shivered, instinctively wrapping an arm around herself as rain started to tap an erratic beat on the roof overhead. There were barely a dozen soldiers in the room, and it was strange to see so few men. For months, they'd faced an endless stream of men passing through their clearance hospitals, so seeing their numbers dwindle was almost more unsettling than the constant injuries she'd had to deal with. Until now, she'd been so busy she hadn't had time to pause for breath, and that was how she'd liked it. At least then it stopped her from thinking about what might have happened to Charlie. Now the tremor of fear she'd mostly staved off was starting to take hold. She looked down at her hands, balling them to stop the tremble.

They'd arrived at the beautiful chateau in the early hours of the morning, running on little sleep and even less food, and by the time they'd finished setting up, there hadn't been time to rest. They'd arrived in lorries full of surgeons, orderlies and nurses, as well as patients and supplies, and although it was vastly superior being in a house rather than a tent, or the old school building in Calais, it wasn't helping her to settle. They were a clearance hospital, and they'd been told it would only be so long before they were inundated with men. Cate looked around again, surveying the room, so at odds with the canvas tents she was used to operating under. The walls were painted a soft duck-egg blue; luxurious drapes were still hanging, pulled back with elegant gold, plaited ropes. It was the most beautiful room she'd ever set foot in. She turned, imagining it filled with immaculately dressed couples, perched on sofas as they sipped wine, waiting to rise and be called to dinner, before the war.

As more and more orderlies arrived to assist with the evacuation and filed into the room, she forced herself to continue with her rounds, forgetting the possible past of the beautiful chateau and checking on her last remaining patients instead. It was the calm before the storm, because she knew instinctively that ambulances would start to arrive in their droves sooner rather than later, perhaps before she was even able to take her break. Her shifts seemed to merge together now; there was never enough time or enough orderlies or nurses to deal with the influx of men.

It was impossible for there to be so much gunfire nearby and *not* end up with countless casualties as a result, and so Cate started to hum, doing her best to block it all out, to stay focused on what she was there to do. The irregular popping of guns, blasts from bombs and German aircraft sporadically flying and firing overhead had become a background noise that no longer startled her, but today, knowing the Nazis were likely coming as the British troops started to lose ground, she couldn't help but be frightened. They'd placed a large red cross made of fabric on the grass outside the chateau, and so far the Germans had respected it as they'd avoided being bombed, but it hardly made their makeshift hospital invincible and they all knew it.

"How are you holding up?"

Cate paused at the sound of Lilly's voice. Her friend's flushed cheeks and red-rimmed eyes made Cate wonder if she looked the same: equal parts exhausted and terrified of what was to come next. She longed for a good night's sleep and a bath, anything to quell her nerves and create a sense of normalcy again. But she doubted that was going to happen, despite the elegant rooms upstairs almost begging to be filled. What she wouldn't give to tiptoe upstairs and fall into one of the beds, or draw herself even a few inches of hot water in the bath.

"I honestly don't know," she replied, forgetting her fantasy as quickly as she'd thought it. "One minute I feel oddly calm, and the next I'm a nervous wreck. How about you?"

"I just want to know what's happening," Lilly said, her voice low. "Surely they'll start to evacuate us soon, if it's really that bad out there? One of the other girls thinks they'll just leave us behind, but I don't believe they'd ever do that to us."

Cate started. *Surely they won't leave us?* "I'm sure they'll get us out of here soon," she said. "Or maybe they're still hoping to turn this battle around and that's why we haven't received orders?" She shuddered. Now that she thought about it, maybe they would have to stay regardless, to keep tending to those left behind. Perhaps the nurses were simply the last to know?

Lilly gave her a quick hug and continued on towards her patients, and Cate stared after her for a moment, remembering how excited and positive they'd been when they first arrived. Those first days at sea and then walking arm in arm through the streets of Dunkirk seemed a lifetime ago now; then, she'd thought they'd spend a few months working as nurses before she was reunited with her fiancé by Christmas. How wrong she'd been. And why was it that no one was telling them what was happening? Everything they knew came in snippets from the soldiers arriving, and although she'd pieced together as much as she could, she still had no idea how long they'd be staying, or what was going on. Besides, it couldn't really be as bad as rumors had it; she was convinced the direness of the situation was being exaggerated. Could the German army really defeat the British, French and Belgium forces combined? She picked up the bandages she'd come looking for to give her hands something to do, hoping she wasn't being overly naïve in her thoughts.

"Nurse Cate?"

She glanced over her shoulder and saw one of the injured soldiers watching her. Cate had been nursing since the very beginning of the war, and she'd tried so hard not to form attachments to any of her patients. She'd felt pain and sadness for them often, and held more hands and tended more wounds than she could count, but it wasn't until recently she'd been in danger of developing feelings for one of the men in her care. Before, Charlie had always been so clear in her mind, but lately, he'd started to fade, and she no longer saw his face in the soldiers who passed through her hospital every day.

Now, she could barely walk past without this particular man turning her head, and she went to great lengths to make sure Lilly didn't see. After the news they'd received about Charlie . . . She gulped, forcing the thoughts from her mind, not wanting to remember. It only made her feel worse about her growing attraction for her patient. And sitting with him through the night as they'd traveled in the lorry hadn't helped her feelings any, either.

"What can I do for you, Lieutenant?" she asked.

"Get me out of here?" he joked.

She sighed. "You and me both." She wondered if he would be evacuated before the end of the day, and she selfishly hoped not. "Would you settle for a drink instead?"

Jack's grin was infectious, and she wondered how on earth he'd remained so upbeat amongst the chaos and devastation around them. But she wasn't complaining; the day he'd woken from his surgery in Calais had been like a gust of fresh air blowing through the place, keeping her on her toes and somehow lifting the gloomy cloud that had settled over the hospital. Catching his eye, or his smile, was the one thing that seemed to keep her going each day, and she was dreading the morning she walked into the ward and found him gone.

"Water would be great, if it's no trouble."

She set down the bandages she was carrying and went to fetch some water, filling his cup and standing beside him. She didn't let go of the cup until his hand had settled firmly around it, long fingers steady as they brushed hers and clasped it. It was only days ago that he'd been too weak to hold anything, yet today there wasn't so much as a shake. It had been well worth all the extra hours she'd spent tending to him.

"Has anyone ever told you what beautiful eyes you have, Cate?"

Her cheeks ignited as she met his gaze. She very much doubted her eyes looked beautiful right now, not when she was so exhausted from all the long hours working. "I think you're hallucinating, Lieutenant."

"Jack," he said. "How many times do I have to tell you to call me Jack?" He laughed. "And it's polite to say thank you when someone pays you a compliment."

"Thank you," she said, feeling less exhausted nurse and more blushing girl than she had in a long time. "But that'll do with the compliments. I don't want anyone overhearing us and thinking something improper is going on."

"Heavens no, what a *scandal* that would be," he teased, his smile contagious as he grinned at her and patted the small empty space on the bed beside him.

11

Cate shook her head, even though she was sorely tempted. "You know I can't sit with you," she said, almost giving in and to hell with the consequences. But she was used to following rules, and she wasn't about to turn rebel now.

"Well you *could*," Jack said, passing her back the water but not letting go. "We're at war. If we can't break the odd rule now, when can we?"

She ignored his fingers against hers as she clasped the cup, falling forward when he pulled it back closer against his body. Cate steadied herself, but not before Jack caught hold of her wrist with his other hand. He was so different to Charlie. Charlie would never have broken a rule, would have followed every protocol to the letter, whether it was war related or ensuring that they always had a suitable chaperone with them when they went out together. It had made her feel safe, that he was a decent man who followed the rules. But Jack . . . Well, she didn't expect Jack to do anything by the rule book, especially if it came to them being alone.

"Gotcha," Jack whispered, his face far too close to hers.

"Let go of me," she hissed, trying to sound cross with him and glancing up to make sure Lilly hadn't returned. The last thing she needed was her friend thinking she was disrespecting Charlie's memory. "You know it's forbidden for patients to touch the nurses."

His fingers slowly left her skin and she righted herself, checking to see if anyone had noticed their little exchange. But there was no stern-faced matron or surly over-tired surgeon waiting to give her a telling-off.

"I was only trying to steady myself, ma'am." His grin was all kinds of trouble.

"That's not the way to my affections, if that's what you're trying to do," she scolded, crossing her arms over her chest. "You forget that I have brothers, so I'm well versed in dealing with rascals like you."

12

"Rascals, huh?" he laughed. "You do realize I'm stuck in this bed with nothing to do other than watch you walk through the room, right? If we'd met elsewhere, I'd be courting you with flowers and showering you with attention, but somehow I have to impress you from this bed, and it's not exactly easy."

"Stop it," she said, her face heating to what she was certain must be a shade of dark pink. Part of her had thought he was only showing interest in her because he was bored, not in a million years that he would actually be interested if they weren't stuck in the middle of nowhere. "It's just that you haven't seen any other women for so long, you suddenly don't know what to do with yourself. Your affection for me will pass the moment you're on a ship out of here."

"Really?" he murmured back, one eyebrow raised in such a comical fashion she couldn't help but laugh. "Well, to me you're like a ray of sunshine amongst the grey, Cate. I doubt I'll ever forget about my pretty little guardian angel until my last breath."

She shook her head at him, at a loss for words, as one of the doctors called out, summoning everyone to join him. There were only a handful of nurses left with the clearance hospital now, and barely twice as many doctors, but it appeared that they were all being called over for an impromptu meeting. Even the orderlies were being summoned.

"I don't think you realize how the world sees you, Cate," Jack said as she started to back away. "You're so beautiful and capable, and it's like you don't even know it."

"Enough of the flattery, Jack," she said, dismissing him as she turned. "I'll come back and see you soon, I promise." His words echoed in her mind though. Was that truly the way he thought of her? It certainly wasn't how she'd ever thought about herself.

"Cate," he called.

She pivoted, the sudden somberness of his voice making her pause. The way he'd said her name, so serious, so deep, wasn't a tone she was used to from him, especially after him teasing her.

"You'll tell me if they're coming, won't you?" he asked. "I'm not waiting here like a sitting duck if the rumors are true. I won't die like a coward in this bed."

"You really think . . ." She didn't want to finish the sentence, didn't want to admit her fears. But it was clear what Jack suspected: that they were going to be overrun by Germans, which would mean certain death or capture for them all.

"I saw it first-hand, Cate. We're out of our depth here fighting the Nazis," he said. "We were unprepared and they know it, and they'll show us no mercy if they find us here."

Cate nodded, suddenly as cold as ice, frozen in place as she stared back at Jack.

"You promise you'll tell me?" he asked.

She took a deep, cautious breath. "I will," she replied. "Jack, I promise you, I will."

She gave him one last glance, a knot forming in her stomach as she digested what he'd said. Although she tried to remain as positive as possible, his words cut deep. She'd hoped that the evacuation was as much a precaution as anything, but the tension amongst the doctors had been taut enough to cut with a knife earlier, and it had her worried. And now hearing Jack reiterate what she'd already heard . . . She squeezed her eyes shut for a beat, trying to push the thoughts away.

Were they going to be sitting ducks for the enemy? Why was nobody telling them the truth? Or were the doctors in the dark, too?

She crossed paths with Lilly as she followed the doctors to one of the makeshift operating theaters downstairs in the chateau. As she stepped into the room, a parlor from the looks of it, with most of the furniture pushed to the sides and stacked to make space, she saw a soldier with medals on his jacket standing there, clearly someone highly ranked.

She gulped, knowing instinctively that the news would be bad. *Jack's right.*

"Everyone, this is Captain Beaumont," Doctor Connor, who'd summoned them all, said as he shut the door behind them. She doubted it would give them complete privacy, knowing his booming voice would probably carry to the patients in the adjoining room. "Unfortunately he has a rather sobering message to share with us all."

Lilly's fingers suddenly caught hers, and Cate leaned into her, their shoulders pressed together and hands clasped as they listened. They would have heard a pin drop, despite the number of nurses, orderlies and doctors crammed into the small space. She caught another nurse's eye across the room and gave her a small smile; the other woman looked even more terrified than Cate felt.

"As some of you may have heard, the urgent evacuation of British soldiers from France has begun," the captain said. "As I speak, soldiers are gathering on the beach at Dunkirk."

Cate saw the shake of his hand as he held a piece of paper, about to read to them all. She hated to think what would make a soldier of his rank tremble.

"Unfortunately, the port and beach are now full of men waiting to be evacuated to the point of overflowing, and the situation is only going to get worse. There is provision for some of you to leave; however, we will not be taking any patients who cannot make their own way to the beach. In short, many of them will have to stay behind despite our best efforts to accommodate everyone, and we need medical personnel to look after our injured. A minimum ratio of one doctor and ten orderlies for every hundred patients will be enforced."

Cate held Lilly's hand tighter as she heard her stifle a sob. She didn't look at her, not wanting to see her tears or be confronted by her friend's pain. It was the only way she could hold her own emotions in check.

So it's true, it's over for us in France.

"While it is realized that this will mean inevitable capture for you, it is hoped that you will uphold the traditions of the Royal Army Medical Corps. More men will be sent to you as they arrive, and we thank you for your service. The work you are doing is essential during these trying times. God speed."

That was it? That was the message for them? Cate went to open her mouth, to say something, *anything*, but it was so dry she couldn't make a sound. *We're going to be left behind? Surely it can't be true?*

"You're going to leave nurses here? *Women?*" one of the doctors cried. "We might be able to survive behind barbed wire until the end of the war, but do you think the Germans are going to play by the rules with our women? It's barbaric!"

Lilly started to cry again and Cate took her into her arms, holding her and rubbing her back in large circles. He was right; what would become of them if they were taken by the enemy? She swallowed away her own emotion as she listened to the captain continue.

"There's no need for hysteria. I want you all to remain calm," he said. "I suggest drawing straws to decide who remains, but there will be no more patients transported for evacuation; the only way they leave is if they can walk themselves. Their fate has been decided, so straws are only needed for medics, orderlies and perhaps a couple of nurses. You should expect at the very least a few hundred patients, so I suggest three or four doctors and at least thirty orderlies."

"So what you're saying is that the British army has given up on us?" the same doctor asked. "We're bloody well stuck here, with only the grace of God to count on?"

Cate could read between the lines—the British army had as good as given up on the *war*, not just them, if they were going to leave their men behind and admit defeat on French soil. How could this have happened? What if the evacuation wasn't successful? How many of them would be left behind then?

The captain frowned, but there was something in his eyes, something about the way he went still and stared straight at the doctor who'd asked the question. *He's right.* They *had* given up on them.

"We've been outnumbered and outwitted at every turn, and there is no way we can hold the lines," Captain Beaumont said, rubbing his chin. "The French army will hold them off for as long as they can to enable our evacuation, and the success of this war depends on us getting as many men out as possible. We are facing the biggest evacuation imaginable to get our troops home, and our focus is on getting those men waiting in lines on the beach into vessels."

"What of the other clearance hospitals?" another doctor asked.

"Some were evacuated at Calais a few days ago, before the situation there became untenable, and others are being evacuated immediately, including one located in a hotel by the beach." The captain's expression was grim. "French medics are faced with the decision to either run home immediately or remain at their posts, and that will be their personal choice, but there will be no other British medical personnel staying behind. You are the last remaining hospital, which means the fate of all our injured will rest entirely on your shoulders. I dare say the adjoining French clearance hospital will be available for use by this afternoon, and you'll no doubt need the extra space."

The doctors and orderlies around them either erupted into dissent or went strangely quiet, and the other nurses came closer to stand in a huddle. There were six of them still left, and they'd all become as close as sisters during their time together.

"They're not really going to make us stay, are they?" one of them sobbed. "I didn't sign up for this! I want to go home!"

Cate swallowed, not sure what to say in reply. In truth, they *had* all signed up for whatever conditions the war would bring, although it had always been a given that the vivid red cross on the side of a tent or ship would supposedly offer protection from a direct attack. That had been something they'd prepared for—an unexpected bombing, for instance. But if they were simply left behind for the enemy? A shiver ran through her. There would be no one left to protect them if that happened, which could mean a bayonet or bullet for any of them. Or *worse*. All these hours of trying to stay positive, of trying not to listen to the rumors swirling amongst the men as they'd traveled to set up their new hospital, and the decision had already been made to leave them behind. Jack had been right; they were going to be sitting ducks for the Germans. They didn't stand a chance.

As the room fell silent and the captain took his leave, Cate slowly let go of Lilly and stood straight, watching Doctor Connor who, up until that moment, had run a very tight, smooth-sailing ship. Their hospital had been chaotic at times, filled with more bodies than she'd ever imagined possible, but he'd always managed to keep things running in an organized manner. They'd been treated fairly, he was tireless as a surgeon in his efforts to save both limb and life, and she knew that he had a family at home waiting for him, which meant that he'd do anything to get them all evacuated if he could.

"I'm sorry to be the bearer of bad news, but as you heard it has been decided that we draw straws to see who stays behind," he said, before lowering his voice. "Nurses included."

Lilly gasped beside her, and one of the other nurses sobbed loudly. Cate just wound her arms tightly around herself again, waiting, trying to calm her breathing.

"Those of us who stay behind will do what we've always done, and that is to carry on as before. We shall ease the pain of the dying and do what we can for those we can save." His eyes shone with tears. "I'm sorry. I'm truly sorry."

Cate found herself nodding, even as her teeth chattered and her fingers inched tighter around her body. There would be no last-minute change of heart; some of them would be staying. Their fate had well and truly been decided for them.

She watched as he fumbled for a splint, usually used for broken bones, and she listened as he snapped part of it into small lengths.

This is actually happening. We're being left behind.

The doctors went first, and they all stood in quiet solidarity as they picked their lengths. Two of the doctors were ashen-faced as they held the small sticks, and Cate's stomach suddenly twisted into knots as she watched relief on the faces of some and terror in others.

Then Doctor Connor moved to the orderlies, and the same process was followed, until it was finally time for the nurses.

"Let's make this quick, ladies," Doctor Connor said, and Cate smiled at him as he wiped tears from his eyes. He was old enough to be her father, and she wondered if his daughters were a similar age to them, if that was why he was so upset about any of his nurses being left behind. "Only one of you has to stay, orders be damned. I want the rest of you to have the best chance of getting out of here."

"I'll go first," Cate said bravely, stepping forward, wanting to get her turn over and done with.

Her hand shook as she reached, pulling out a stick, her breathing ragged as she slowly looked down at it.

No.

Oh my God, no!

She stared at the short, stubby stick, at the doctor's palm as he slowly opened it to show her that all the rest were long.

"Cate, I'm so sorry," he said.

She heard someone speak, but suddenly there was a loud whooshing sound in her ears, like the ocean roaring right beside her, the waves crashing into her eardrums. Blood rushed to her head and she swayed as the reality of her luck hit hard. Not the first stick. The first couldn't be the shortest!

It's me. I'm the one who has to stay behind.

Suddenly all she wanted to do was run.

A loud bang echoed out then, the explosion so close she almost felt it rattle her teeth, followed by shouts. She walked quickly, following the crowd of orderlies, and saw one of the doctors, a fellow drawer of a short straw, lying in a pool of his own blood in the kitchen of all places, half of his head blown off by the gun he'd used to take his own life. And just like that, he'd sealed the fate of another doctor who'd thought he was about to be evacuated.

That was all she needed to see to tell her how bad it was going to be. To see a doctor in his prime kill himself rather than be left behind . . . She swallowed and looked away.

"Those of you leaving, go now with Captain Beaumont. I'm staying behind," Doctor Connor muttered. "I'm not making another one of you pull a goddamn straw to take that man's place. And Captain, I'm making the executive decision that no nurse will be left behind! I don't give a damn about that particular order, and you can either have me arrested or accept my decision."

Cate paused, heart pounding, as she looked between the two men. They were facing off like two roosters, both with a steely glint in their eyes, determined to win the fight.

"It's fine, I'll stay," she finally said, when the captain refused to answer and Doctor Connor appeared to refuse to back down. "My patients need me, and I want to stay and help. I drew the short straw and I accept that."

Doctor Connor looked at her, and she forced herself to look away before she started to cry. "You're certain? Because I'm not

20

going to make any woman stay. You can walk out that door with the rest of them and I won't be calling you back."

She breathed deeply, forcing herself to nod. If not her, then another orderly would have to stay behind, and she didn't want special treatment for being a woman. Perhaps she was naïve, but she refused to believe they would be overrun with the enemy. "Yes sir, I'm certain."

Cate walked numbly back to the large room where the patients were, ignoring the other nurses as they scurried around her and walking straight back toward Jack instead. Chaos erupted as injured men suddenly started to fill the room and the hallway, as shooting and more explosions echoed out much closer than she'd ever heard before, constant booms like fireworks in the sky. If it was this loud inside a building, she hated to think what it would have sounded like from a tent.

Soon, she would have so many casualties to deal with that it would at least take her mind off her predicament, but for now, she was still in shock.

"They're coming for us, aren't they?"

She reached for Jack's hand when she got to his bed, winding her fingers tightly through his. "Yes," she whispered back, not about to hide the truth from him. "They're coming, and we're being left behind."

His face told her everything she needed to know. Jack had seen war; he'd been left bloodied and broken from his time fighting the enemy. He knew better than anyone else what was in store for them.

"You can't stay," he said, squeezing her hand so tightly that it hurt. "You need to find a way to go. Cate, you have to go!"

Cate shook her head. "I can't." Tears flooded her eyes and she quickly blinked them away, not about to break down in front of him. "I'm staying, and that's just the way it is."

Jack had tears in his eyes now too, but he was even faster to blink than she was. "There's no way they'll get all those men out. They won't have enough time. They'll be slaughtered on the beach."

A loud rumbling seemed to reverberate through the chateau then, rattling the roof, and Cate pulled her hand away and hurried to the front door to look out. As the other nurses fled to gather their things, most with an embarrassed backward glance to her, and the rest of the orderlies and doctors followed, a convoy of ambulances and lorries rolling in an unexpected group down the road started to pull up, more than she'd ever seen all at once. Dust rose in the air, the light rain not yet enough to dampen the ground, and she held up her hand to stop the grit getting in her eyes.

"Cate, you can't stay. I won't let you." Lilly was suddenly behind her, linking their arms as if to force her to move.

"I'm staying," she said firmly. "Those orderlies, so many of them have families at home waiting for them, and I'm not going to leave and make one of them have to stay in my place."

Lilly shook her head, jutting her chin up defiantly. "Then I'm not leaving, either."

Cate took her in her arms and held her tight. "Yes, you are. Your mother needs to have at least one of you safe, Lil. You need to go home." She took a deep breath, remembering the way they'd held one another when they'd received the news about Charlie. *Missing presumed dead.* Which meant the pair of them had never, ever stopped hoping, even if that hope had started to dwindle of late.

Lilly had always been so cheerful, so happy and full of life, but Cate could only see pain in her eyes now. It was like they'd both made a silent pact not to talk about Charlie or even think about him after receiving the news, as a desperate way of coping, simply to make it through each day. It never got any easier, but they'd at least always had one another. Until now. "Cate, *please*. Don't make me leave you. I can't go home without you."

Cate took a deep, shuddering breath before she let Lilly go. "You can, and you will."

Lilly's eyes searched hers before she finally pulled away. "You promise me you'll make it home, Cate. Promise me."

Cate knew better than to make a promise she couldn't keep, but she could see that Lilly wasn't going to leave if she didn't. "I promise."

Lilly pressed a hasty kiss to her cheek before backing away. "You come home, you hear me? Or I'll come back looking for you myself."

Cate watched her go, feeling like time wasn't moving as she stared at her friend. They'd been through so much together, and Cate knew it might be the last time they ever saw one another again. Her fingers found the ring at her throat, and she clutched it, taking comfort in her link to the past.

But there was no time left to stare and wallow in sadness, as the front door to the chateau was thrust open for the first ambulance, and she watched as the first stretchers were carried out. *So this is what defeat looks like*, Cate thought as a procession of orderlies started running inside with men in all stages of death and injury. Her stomach, which had been so strong despite all she'd seen and done, lurched at the sight of the injured soldiers; before, they'd been patching them up to go home, but these poor men were either going to die or end up prisoners of war, and she didn't know which was worse. The smell of defeat was as heavy in the air as the metallic tang of blood that immediately filled her nostrils.

She ran inside after them, no longer thinking about what was to come, what her fate might be. Her job was to ease the discomfort of these men as best she could, and that's what she was going to do until her very last breath.

She'd see Lilly before she left; right now she had lives to save.

So much for the last supper we all had planned for the evening, downstairs in the cellar with a few bottles of the chateau's finest wine.

CHAPTER THREE

ELISE
LE PARADIS, FRANCE, MAY 1940

Elise reached for her sister and pulled her closer, slipping her arm around her shoulders. They both stared down at the basic white cross that marked their father's grave. She instinctively touched Adelaide's hair, her fingers brushing against the long tendrils that fell down her back.

"I still can't believe he's gone," Adelaide whispered, and Elise dropped her cheek to her sister's head. She squeezed her eyes shut, forcing away the tears, refusing to break down when she was trying to be strong for the both of them.

It was only months ago that they'd all gathered together, under the tree that now marked their family's small graveyard. Her father had sat, surrounded by them all, the smile on his face bright enough to power the sun itself, as her mother had poured wine for lunch.

"The Germans will never defeat the might of the French army," he boasted. *"The French and British forces will annihilate them, just you wait and see."*

Elise exchanged glances with her mother, stifling her smile at how certain Father was about their success. She saw the familiar twinkle in her mother's eye, knowing that she too thought he was overconfident. But it didn't seem to matter. The sun was shining, they had a feast spread out on the table to enjoy, and the wine was crisp and delicious. And while her father might be prone to exaggeration, they all believed they would win the war. Defeat seemed unlikely, if not outright impossible.

"How are you feeling?" she asked her brother, Louis. "Are you nervous?"

"He'll be fine!" her father announced, slapping him on the back. "Our strong boy's going to do our country proud, aren't you, son?"

She laughed along with her brother as he flexed his bicep, passing him more cheese and slapping at her sister's hand when she tried to take some of it.

"You leave it for Louis, we don't know what he'll be eating when he leaves here."

The next day they waved him off, so certain that he'd be home before Christmas. Their fearless, handsome, fun-loving brother.

She swallowed, as if she could somehow force the memories down, bury them deep inside her so she never had to think about them again.

So much could happen so quickly. Now it was just the two of them. Louis had been dead within weeks of leaving home, their mother had died of what Elise guessed could have been a broken heart, and their father had succumbed to influenza only months after that beautiful lunch under a perfect, cloudless sky. The last day before everything she knew had changed forever.

Three white crosses were all that was left of them now, and it made her want to hold her sister even tighter to her side, to protect her from all the evil in the world, and shield her from any more pain.

"Elise—" Adelaide's voice died away as shouts and gunfire suddenly echoed out nearby.

"Quickly, grab Oscar!" Elise scrambled with her sister to catch their wayward little terrier, and when Adelaide had hold of him, she positioned herself slightly in front of her.

"What's going on?" Adelaide asked.

Elise's heart was pounding as she stood, listening to the shots and knowing they were getting closer. The fighting had come terrifyingly close lately, which meant that some of their neighbors had chosen to move away; many of the houses had been left deserted in the wake of war. It was deceiving sometimes, the way noise echoed through the trees and from the nearby farmhouses, but there was no denying this was moving toward them now, and fast. There had been activity in the very near distance all day, and in previous days, but this was different. Hot bile rose in Elise's throat as fear threatened to paralyze her. *Are we about to be in the middle of it all?* They should have evacuated days ago!

"We need to get back to the house," she said, launching into action and clutching her sister's hand. "Quickly!"

They started to run, but no sooner had they started to move when soldiers suddenly appeared, running directly toward them with their rifles raised.

"Get back!" Elise shouted, yanking Adelaide with her. "Behind the tree! We need to hide." She knew the big, gnarled oak wouldn't save their lives if they were caught in the crossfire, but it felt a lot safer than standing away from any shelter.

"Are they British?" Adelaide asked as they crouched down, partially hidden from view.

"Yes," Elise whispered back, staring at the large group of soldiers as they ran past. "It must be an entire regiment!"

Please don't stop at our house. Please don't stop.

The last thing she needed was to deal with soldiers commandeering their home. Gunfire echoed again and more soldiers appeared, and she looked across to their house, wishing they could make it; so close yet still so far away.

The fighting had been near enough to hear up until now, especially if the wind was blowing toward them, but this was the first time she'd felt as if they were in the thick of the war. And she hated not knowing whether they should make a run for it, or hunker down where they were to stay safe.

"What are they running from?" Adelaide asked.

Elise glanced at her. "German soldiers, I'd suspect," she said. From what she'd heard, the war wasn't exactly going in their favor, but there'd been so much to deal with after their father had passed that she hadn't given it too much thought. Perhaps, like almost everyone else, she'd secretly believed that there was no way one army could defeat the British and French armies combined, not to mention the Belgian and Polish troops fighting alongside them. Perhaps she wasn't so dissimilar to her father—his optimism had always been too far-reaching.

"They're going past our house," Adelaide whispered. "What are they going to do here? *Why* are they here?"

Elise's stomach knotted. She hoped they weren't about to be stuck in the middle of all-out fighting. "I don't know. But we need to get back to the house soon."

She looked at Oscar in her sister's arms, her fingers tight across his muzzle to stop him from barking, and reached out to touch his wiry fur. He'd been their brother's dog, and had sat on the doorstep every evening for almost a year, as if waiting for him to arrive home, and she knew she'd protect the animal almost as fiercely as she'd protect her sister if it ever came to it.

As she turned her focus back to the British soldiers, she estimated there were eighty, maybe even a hundred of them as they continued on, passing their house and disappearing through the clearing on the other side. She leaned out, taking a few tentative steps to see if any more followed. There was movement; she could hear it in the trees but she couldn't see anything, and something told her it might be their only chance to make a run for it.

"Quickly, let's go!" she urged her sister, grabbing for her hand and letting her go on ahead.

Elise kept looking over her shoulder, praying they'd make it safely inside before gunfire erupted again. And just as they made it, as her foot connected with the bottom step leading up to their house, she heard something that made her blood run cold.

German voices. German shouts.

"Get in!" she yelled at Adelaide, roughly pushing her up the stairs and fumbling for the door.

They fell inside, stumbling over one another as Elise slammed the door behind them. Her hands were shaking as she fumbled for the lock, making sure it was securely fastened before running through the house to check the kitchen door, too.

"Make sure all the windows are closed," she called to Adelaide. "And pull all the curtains."

She had no idea if she was even doing the right thing, but it seemed safer to close everything. German soldiers could easily storm the house and kick down their doors, but it was all she could think to do, and it felt better than doing nothing.

Her breathing was ragged, coming in short, sharp pants as she positioned herself by their kitchen window, slowly lifting her finger to part the curtain and peek out.

"Those British soldiers have gone into the barn next door," Adelaide said, standing on the other side. "They're hiding in there!"

"All of them?" Elise opened her mouth to speak, but the words barely formed a stutter in her throat as she saw German troops marching toward the barn, rifles at the ready.

"Oh my God, we're going to be in the middle of it!" she gasped, as loud booms shook their house. Gunfire erupted from the barn, and it was only a matter of seconds before the German army started to fire back. "Take cover!"

She dropped to her stomach and crawled beside Adelaide to the foot of the stairs, her stomach scraping along the ground as she squirmed across the floor. They stood only to run, taking the stairs two at a time as the house seemed to shake with the constant booms.

"The bath?" cried Adelaide. "Will we be safe in there?"

"We won't both fit," Elise said. "Let's go under the bed."

They dropped low again and crawled to their parents' room. Elise waited for Adelaide to crawl under first before following her, shutting her eyes for a minute as she caught her breath and fought against the intense claustrophobia she was feeling the moment they were beneath it.

"Where's Oscar?" Adelaide cried.

Elise's eyes flew open as she heard barking, and her hand automatically shot out to stop her sister from going straight down to find him. Instead of moving she whistled, short and sharp, just like Louis had, and within minutes the little dog was darting across the room toward them. She reached to grab him, hauling him under with them as they lay silently, listening to the cries and shouts of men, and the incessant sound of shelling.

"What are we going to do?" Adelaide asked, as they lay on their stomachs, shoulder to shoulder, thigh to thigh.

"We stay here until it stops," Elise said, surprised by how sure her voice sounded. "With any luck, they'll move on as quickly as they arrived."

Or more than likely, they'll stay. She pushed the thought away, not about to let her imagination take hold.

"And if they don't?" Adelaide asked.

"Then we cross that bridge when we come to it."

—— ⚜ ——

"It's stopped."

Elise lifted her head, groggy and tired from lying in the same position for so long, listening to the fighting. She'd resorted to pressing her hands tightly to her ears to try to block the sounds out, the anguished cries as men were injured or maybe even killed too much for her to stand. But now, after hours or maybe not even that long, there was suddenly silence.

"Should we look?" Adelaide asked.

Elise took a deep, shuddering breath. "Yes." She should have said no, but she needed to look, needed to see to know what they were dealing with.

Were they going to have to run? Were they in danger? Or would no one care about two women living alone?

She pushed her body forward and wriggled out from under the bed, crawling slowly, as if she were in danger of standing on a mine. She raised a hand to the curtain, holding it open slightly. Adelaide was at her side, leaning in, both peering through the same gap, squinting as the light faded, night starting to creep across the sky.

Elise gasped as they watched the German soldiers, rifles raised, their steps slow and deliberate as they inched toward the barn. The big wooden doors were shut and there was no sign of movement; no sound, nothing.

"What do you think is happening?" Adelaide asked. "Why did the shooting stop?"

"I don't know," Elise replied. "Where did all those British soldiers go? Are they still in there?" She didn't understand what was happening, and she'd expected to see German soldiers dead, not still advancing.

"If they're in there, why aren't they still shooting?" Adelaide asked.

Fear danced through Elise. Something wasn't right. It was hard to see and she squinted as she stared into the fading light, but the barn was on the adjoining property and it was hard to make out what was going on.

Adelaide moved closer, nudging her aside slightly as they pulled the curtain back further. Maybe they shouldn't be watching, but Elise couldn't have dragged her eyes away if she'd tried.

"Addy, they're surrendering." Elise gasped as one of the big doors opened and something white was thrust out. She pressed her nose to the glass, transfixed, realizing it was a rifle with something fluttering on the end, possibly an undershirt. *Oh no.* "The British soldiers are surrendering."

"Why would they do that?" Adelaide asked. "Why would they just surrender to the Germans like that? There were so many more British than German troops!"

Elise shook her head. All she knew was that something had gone horribly, horribly wrong.

She blinked away tears as she watched one soldier step forward, holding the makeshift white flag high, his movements slow and steady. Even from such a distance, Elise could almost feel the tremble of his knees, and the rapid stammer of his heart as he faced the enemy in defeat.

Another soldier followed, and they watched as one of the Germans marched forward, yelling something and gesturing. And slowly soldier after soldier filed out of the barn, their hands all raised, no weapons visible as they gave themselves up.

"I don't understand!" Adelaide cried beside her. "Why are they doing this? Why aren't they fighting back?"

"They must have run out of ammunition," Elise whispered, her voice catching, not letting herself speak any louder. "There's no other reason they'd be walking out without guns." Or at least no other reason she could think of.

She counted them slowly in her head, trying to keep up with their movements and struggling once they started to stand in front of one other. "There has to be almost a hundred men there!"

"I lost count at ninety," Adelaide said. "Why would an entire regiment be here in Le Paradis, without any backup? Where is the rest of the army?"

"I don't know, but they'll all be taken prisoners of war now," Elise told her. "They'll spend their days in a camp until the war is over."

It had been her worst nightmare, worrying whether Louis could be taken and end up in an enemy prison camp, but in the end she'd decided that it would have been a better fate than death on the battlefield. At least he would have had a chance at surviving if he'd been captured.

Elise was just about to let the soft fabric go, not wanting to watch as the men were rounded up and marched off, when Adelaide's hand gripped hers.

"Look," Addy whispered.

Elise tightened her fingers against her sister's, not breathing, not blinking as she stared at the scene unfolding in front of them.

The German soldier, the one who'd strode forward originally and marched the British troops out, was gesturing to his men. She wasn't certain, but she thought his uniform was that of an SS officer, and she watched in horror as a handful of the Nazis lifted their weapons. They all had their backs to her, but she saw the lift of their arms, knew exactly what they were about to do. She strained to see the officer's face, but couldn't.

"They're machine guns," she whispered.

"*Feuer!*" The order was yelled so loud that they heard it from their window.

Fire.

"What did he say?" Adelaide gasped. "What does that mean?"

Elise's hand flew to her mouth, unable to answer her sister, a silent scream choking her while she watched the surrendered soldiers, their bodies ricocheting and falling as they were machine-gunned at close range.

"It's murder!" Adelaide cried. "We have to do something! Elise! We have to help them!"

Elise let go of the curtain then, shutting her eyes, trying to block out the images that she knew she'd never forget for as long as she lived. When she opened them, fear at what they'd just witnessed had her heart racing. What they'd just witnessed went against the simplest rules of war.

"Elise! We have to do something!"

"No," she said firmly, pulling her sister away from the window. "We do nothing. We go about our evening, we cook dinner, that's it."

"You can't mean that." Adelaide's eyes were wild, tinged red and staring.

"If they know we saw that, what do you think they'll do to two women on their own?" Elise asked. "If they do that to men who've surrendered, do you think they'll even hesitate to rape us and steal all our food? To murder us, too? They'll see that pretty face of yours and—"

"Enough," Adelaide said, her hands over her ears. "Stop, please just stop."

Elise opened her arms, drawing her sister in and holding her. She pressed a kiss to her blonde hair, wondering at how she was barely three years older than her, but felt more mother than sister sometimes.

"This is war, Addy," she whispered. "Nothing is fair, nothing is just. But we have to be careful if we want to stay alive."

"I thought it would be over soon. I thought we were going to be safe," Addy sobbed.

So did I. Elise nodded, knowing she should be soothing her sister with calming words, but not even knowing where to start.

33

When she finally let her go, she stepped toward the window again, braving one last, final peek. Elise froze. There was movement. Not all the troops had been killed.

She pressed herself against the wall, fingers trembling as she kept the curtain parted just enough to watch, not wanting to be seen, not after witnessing such a violent massacre. Was she imagining the movement?

No. She wasn't imagining anything, because it wasn't only her who'd seen them.

Elise could hear shouts, but they meant nothing to her in German, and suddenly those British troops that had survived, who were staggering to their feet or writhing on the ground, were being roughly pushed and kicked to get them to move. As she watched, she saw them being yelled at, presumably to empty out their pockets, which they did, some of them bleeding and stumbling, and suddenly they were all marched away.

"What if someone's still alive down there in that pile?" Addy asked from behind her.

"They've taken all the live ones," Elise replied, taking a few deep breaths to calm herself before she turned. The urge to vomit was overwhelming now.

"Do you think they'll kill them too?" Adelaide whispered.

Elise nodded. "Perhaps."

But as they walked down the stairs, hand in hand, ten minutes later, the repetitive thud of machine guns made her legs buckle beneath her. She landed on the stair with a thud, narrowly missing the dog, and dropped her head between her knees, hands over her ears.

Every single one of those men was now dead. She just knew it. And she had no idea how she was going to protect her sister from an enemy who knew no bounds.

CHAPTER FOUR

CATE

Cate had never seen anything like it. It was horrendous. One minute she'd been terrified for her own fate, the next they'd been inundated with men crying out for help, and she'd barely spent another second worrying about what was going to happen to her. Time was a luxury they didn't have. It was a race to save lives, patch up wounds, administer morphine and assist the remaining doctors. Even with their usual staff, it would have been a tall order to deal with so many casualties; there were men being rushed in by the dozen.

Her fringe clung limply to her forehead, her skin clammy as she ran between beds, trying her best to drown out the sound of men dying, wishing she could cover her ears. She whispered to the soldier lying on the bed in front of her, his head bandaged and a tourniquet around his leg, waiting for a surgery that would most likely never eventuate. She silently shuddered at the thought of the rot setting into his limb if he didn't get the operation he needed, which was probably an amputation.

"This will help with the pain," she said, forcing her smile, knowing that he needed to see her appear outwardly calm. It always surprised her, the change in some men who were gravely injured, close to death even, when they had a nurse touch them and take care of them. She supposed it reminded them of someone from home; a wife or even their mother or sister perhaps, and as she gave him morphine and then wrote a hasty M on his forehead bandage in red, she touched his hand and gave it a quick squeeze. The light in his eyes at her touch made it worth the effort, and she thought of the men regaining consciousness who were being told they'd had the surgery they needed, simply to placate them and put an end to their hysteria. They were being lied to just to keep them calm.

She turned to the next patient, her smile still fixed, but froze in place as she saw the distant, glassy look in his eyes. Cate shuffled forward and pressed two fingers to his neck, feeling for a pulse, even though she knew she wouldn't find one. She'd been nursing long enough to recognize those eyes, as if she were looking at a house with no lights on inside. He was long gone.

Cate gently brushed her fingers over his eyelids, closing them before saying a quick, silent prayer. She'd lost a lot of men over the past year, and it never got any easier. She cast a glance around her, at the room that had once seemed so elegant, the first reminder she'd truly had since stepping foot in France of what life had been like before the war. This was now a place of hell, the old-world elegance gone, replaced with splattered blood and bandages, with cries and profanities as men fought to live and doctors fought to save them. One man had been strung up by straps, suspended above his mattress, his skin so badly burned that if he touched anything it would adhere to him. Cate knew she'd never, ever forget his howls of pain as they'd stripped his clothes off before realizing the extent of his burns, before plying him with morphine as orderlies worked fast to do something, *anything*, to avoid placing him on a bed.

"Help!"

The call wouldn't have surprised her usually, not when so many men called out to her so frequently in the hospital, but the fact that it was a woman's voice made her turn. Cate scanned the room, finding her balance again, looking for where it had come from. There were no other nurses left behind, which meant that as far as she knew, she was the only woman.

And then she saw her. The woman was a similar age to her, maybe early twenties, and her eyes were so wide as she stood in the open doorway they reminded her of saucers. She was clutching something, a case of some description, but it was the desperate look on her face that caught Cate's attention the most.

She ran over to her, reaching out. "Are you injured? Where have you come from?" She searched her face. "I'll help you, just tell me what you need." Cate glanced past her and saw that the rain had started to fall with more urgency now, the front door wide open at the end of the hall.

"I'm Ruth. I, I . . ."

Cate reached for her arm and grasped her, holding her firm. "You're safe here, Ruth. I'm a nurse and if you're injured I can help you." She looked over her, not seeing any injuries other than scratches on what skin she could see.

"No, we're not safe," Ruth said, leaning in closer, so close that Cate could feel her warm breath against her cheek. She instinctively went to take a step back, but stopped when the other woman started speaking again.

"The Nazis are coming. They're right behind me," she cried. "I came here because I thought there might be soldiers, I thought maybe they were protecting the hospital when I saw the red cross on the ground outside, but . . ."

As Ruth's voice trailed off, Cate turned slowly and looked back at the injured soldiers, all thinking they had a chance at survival now they were in a hospital. But she could see now that they were little more than a target.

"Surely they're not so close yet," Cate said, focusing her attention back on Ruth. "We were assured they were some way off, at least a day or more. You've seen them with your own eyes?"

Ruth nodded, backing away slightly, like a cornered animal. "I'm with the ATS, I'm a telephone operator," she said. "We were amongst the last to be evacuated, and when the order came it was too late. We all had to make our way as best we could to the beach, but there's no way they're going to get us all out of here in time. It's impossible." She shook her head. "The Germans are only a mile or so away, maybe less."

Cate touched her hand to her chest, feeling her heart as it hammered away. She took a slow, deep breath, knowing she should be attending her patients instead of talking to this woman. But she managed to block out the shallow groans and cries of the troops behind her for another moment.

"What are you saying?" she asked. "That we don't have any time left?"

"I'm saying you need to go, and you need to go now," Ruth said. "It's every man, and woman, for themselves."

Cate stood and watched as Ruth backed further away down the hall, not able to take her eyes off her.

"Run!" Ruth yelled, as gunfire echoed outside, so close that Cate half-expected to smell the gunpowder in the air. "You need to go now!"

Panic threatened to paralyze her, but it was a sudden surge of fear that made her lurch forward as shouts and more gunfire became audible from outside. Ruth had been right: they weren't just coming—she was guessing they were already well and truly here.

Cate ran to the door, bustling past orderlies who were making their way in with more patients. Only it wasn't the enemy who caught her eye, but Lilly. She would have recognized her blonde halo of hair anywhere.

"Lilly!" Cate screamed. "What are you doing here?"

Lilly looked around. Cate could see that her face was blurred with dirt, and as Lilly gestured with her hands, wildly, she saw they were stained with blood. She only hoped it was someone else's blood, not hers.

"Get Jack!" Lilly screamed. "I have space for one more!"

"What? Why aren't you at the beach?"

"Had to come back for them," Lilly called back, as another boom shook the chateau and made Cate duck. "You're not the only one who can save lives, Cate Alexander!"

Cate laughed, despite the horrors, despite the shuddering and squealing of war so close to them that all she wanted to do was curl up in the bathtub upstairs and pretend none of it was real. But it *was* real. Painfully, viscerally, bone-chillingly real.

Hours earlier, she'd watched as the walking wounded had shuffled, limped and hobbled alongside nurses, doctors and orderlies, headed for the beach. Soldiers who should have been bedridden had managed to haul themselves up to their feet, not about to be left behind if there was even a chance of being on a ship headed for home, one using a garden rake as a crutch. And Lilly, who had been part of that procession, had somehow ended up back at the hospital to transport an ambulance full of men who obviously hadn't been able to walk even as far as the gate. Had she already taken men to the beach and bravely returned for more? She hadn't thought even Lilly would be so brave. Or stupid.

But if Lilly had space for one more man, then she was going to make sure that Jack was the one who made it. She would do anything to give him a fighting chance.

She cringed as she heard a cry and then yelling, both British and German, and fear raced through her.

"Cate, hurry!" Lilly screamed.

Cate lifted her skirt and raced to Jack's bed, slipping on the floor as she grabbed hold of the metal railing. He was pushed up on his elbows, the sheet thrown off him. She held out her hand and gripped his arm to help him sit up properly. He hadn't joined the walking wounded because the doctors had told him he wouldn't make it, but now she regretted not encouraging him to go.

"What the hell's going on?" Jack asked.

"The Germans are here already," she whispered. "We need to go. There's space on an ambulance for you."

"Go?" He stood and she grimaced at the way he wobbled, unsteady on his feet after so long lying in bed. "We're leaving *now*?"

Cate dropped low and looked for his things, knowing she'd stored his boots beneath his bed for him. She fumbled with the laces and put them down, tapping on his right leg for him to lift it and struggling to get the boot on, then doing the other. He was only wearing a shirt and some long pants, but as the commotion outside the chateau became louder, she knew there was no time to look for anything else. Cold was better than dead.

"Quickly," she ordered. "We don't have long." She prayed that Lilly was still outside, that she hadn't already been shot waiting for Jack.

"No, Cate. You go," he protested, pushing at her, the desperation in his eyes only adding to her terror. "I'll only slow you down."

"Move!" she cried, clutching at his shirt, not about to make a run for it on her own. "This is your chance to get out of this hell-hole!"

"Cate—"

"I'm not leaving you, so either get moving or we're both as good as dead!" Boots echoed down the hall, like booms of thunder during a storm. It was too late. There was no way they were making

40

it to Lilly. They had seconds before they wouldn't be able to move an inch without being gunned down.

She didn't look over her shoulder as Jack gave up arguing and started to hobble. There was no time to look back, and as guilty as she felt at running away from the doctors and those who needed her, and her colleagues, nothing was going to change their fate.

Yells erupted behind them, another gunshot, but still Cate refused to look as she dragged Jack through to the next room, scanning, panic clawing at her throat as she realized she'd mistakenly gone into the wrong room. There wasn't another door to the outside from here. Her hand was firmly woven around Jack's arm, hauling him along with her, cringing every time he tripped and almost took her down with him.

"Through here," she cried, lurching forward and grabbing a footstool that was in her way. She threw it straight through the glass window, shattering it with one insistent swoop, heart in her throat as she half-expected a Nazi to be waiting with a gun on the other side for them, or to find one behind her ready to stop them in their tracks as she pushed herself up and out of the large, low window. Glass snagged on her clothes and cut her skin, digging deep as she leaned in to help Jack, pulling him so hard he hit the ground with a thud before clawing himself upright, his hands bleeding as she took hold of him once again.

But there was no one waiting to execute them. No soldier, no patrols, just the carnage that had been left behind in the wake of the battle and a commotion from around the other side of the chateau.

Lilly!

She watched in horror as the ambulance started to move, hoping on the one hand they could make it to her, but knowing there was no way. Lilly was going, and Jack wasn't leaving with her.

As she looked to the other side, it was like the British army had just abandoned the fight; they were nowhere to be seen, and she wondered what the beach looked like and how long it would take them to make a run for it. Could they evacuate? Would the ships have left or were the soldiers in danger of being massacred where they waited? She had no idea what to do, where they even were in relation to the beach, what direction she should be propelling them in to find safety.

"Under there!" Jack said, doing a long, stretched-out kind of limp ahead of her. She ran with him, relieved that he'd taken charge, seeing what he was going for—there was an abandoned ambulance with the rear doors left open, just sitting out in the open.

She turned, running backward to see if anyone was following them or was watching, but there was no one. But the noise in the chateau behind her stole away any relief she'd felt at making their escape.

"Cate, get under."

Jack had already dropped to the ground, and even though he was injured he waited for her to get under first. It wasn't too bad for her, although being on her stomach and sliding across dirt that was fast turning to mud wasn't her idea of fun. But if it meant they could stay hidden, she'd have crossed an alligator-infested river to get away.

She almost felt Jack's pain as her own when he winced, grunting as he forced his way into the space beside her, and she only hoped his stitches would hold with the exertion. The last thing she would be recommending for him was to be walking or running, let alone crawling on his belly to fit beneath a vehicle.

Cate shivered, positioning herself better so she could watch the chateau. But then she had an idea as her teeth started to chatter from the cold. She'd been worried about Jack freezing in what he was wearing, but her white dress wasn't exactly any better. They needed something to protect them from the elements, and fast.

"I'm going to check what supplies are in here," she said. "There might be keys inside."

"You're not moving," he ground out.

Cate reached for his hand and bravely gave it a quick squeeze. "I am," she insisted. "If we manage to evade capture, we need to stay warm. God only knows how long we might need to survive for, and I need medical supplies in case I have to treat you."

When I have to treat you. It was definitely not a case of *if.* He was silent for a moment, his eyes searching hers until he finally spoke again.

"Fine. But if I tap twice on the side, you stay hidden. It means someone's coming."

She nodded and wriggled backward so that she came out at the rear of the ambulance. Her heart was pounding and she could barely breathe, but she forced her feet to move, shuffling as quietly as she could, moving to the driver's door. Cate paused, listening for danger, but she couldn't hear anything close by, and she quickly opened the door and looked in. *Dammit!* There were no keys in the ignition. She moved back around the vehicle and stepped up into the back, immediately seeing a grey wool blanket. There was only one, and it was in a heap on the floor as if it had been accidentally discarded. She scooped it up, sticking it under her arm. There wasn't really anything else of use except some bandages, so she grabbed them and then carefully, silently, lowered herself to the ground.

Cate was still expecting to hear the click of a rifle trained on her, to be grabbed roughly and marched back to the chateau, but nothing happened. She lowered herself and wriggled forward, side by side with Jack again, conscious that her right side was pressed almost along the length of his left now. She'd touched him before— skin to skin, nursing him—but it felt different to have her body against his. Too intimate, almost, for someone she didn't know that well, but intimate or not, she wasn't about to move away from him. She felt safer against him, his body warmth comforting.

"What do you think's happening in there?" she whispered.

"I don't know," he murmured, his eyes facing forward, chin in the dirt as he stared out. "We haven't heard any more gunshots, so that's good. But who knows what they'll do to them next?"

"Aren't there rules about this sort of thing? I mean, they have to take them as prisoners of war, don't they? They can't just . . ." She couldn't bring herself to say it.

"Kill them?" Jack turned, his face inches from hers, his eyes glinting with unshed tears.

Cate looked into his eyes and wondered what he'd seen, what he'd been through out in the field before he'd come into the hospital. She had so many questions for him, but she wasn't sure she wanted to ask them, or know the answers.

"Would they?" she asked. "Kill them, I mean?"

He slowly shook his head. "I honestly don't know. I've heard stories about their cruelty, about what they're doing to the Jews, and if they can do that to them, then I don't know whether they'll abide by the rules here or not."

Just then, there was a flurry of movement and noise, and Jack lifted his finger to his lips. He hadn't needed to silence her, though; she had no intention of making a sound. Cate instinctively moved back as far as she could without allowing her feet to stick out the other side, eyes glued to the scene in front of her.

Her heart was pounding hard, and her breathing was coming in shallow pants. There was Doctor Connor, and the rest of the men she'd worked with for months, slowly lining up outside the chateau. Cate couldn't have looked away if she'd tried, and she was certain they were going to be seen, given that she could see them so clearly.

If our hiding place is discovered, that'll be me lined up there. That'll be my fate too.

Her breath sounded too loud to her, even though she knew it wasn't possible for anyone to actually hear her from such a distance.

"What are they saying?" she asked.

"I'm not sure," Jack whispered. "My German is fairly basic."

As one of the Nazis yelled, Cate's hand covered her face, half-shielding her eyes as she waited for the inevitable. The Germans' guns were raised, and as she watched the doctors and orderlies stand, hands held high, some of them crying and almost all of them visibly trembling in fear, she waited for the first shot.

Only it never came.

Two of the German soldiers stepped forward, prodding at the doctors and saying something. She couldn't hear what they were asking, but she could hear one of the doctors repeating over and over that he was a doctor.

And then suddenly they were being yelled at to move as the ground vibrated through her fingers, the dirt moving as a rumbling sound came closer. Cate pressed her ear to the ground, her head at an angle to get a better view of what was coming. She half-expected to see tanks, but instead there were two large trucks rolling in.

Patients were walked out then too, some barely able to hobble along. Jack glanced at her and they exchanged a look of disbelief. She'd been so certain they were going to kill them all, and instead they watched as patients and doctors alike were loaded into the back of one truck. It was covered with a big canvas awning, so she couldn't see inside.

"The doctors and orderlies are too valuable to them," Jack said quietly, shuffling further back against her. "They must need them."

Her lips were so dry she had to moisten them before speaking. "So they're going to force them to treat German soldiers?"

Jack didn't bother to hide his grimace. "It's better than the alternative."

Cate knew he was right, but she couldn't help but wonder why they'd taken the patients. Why not leave them behind? She hadn't been able to count them, so she didn't know if any might have been left, and she certainly wasn't going inside to see for herself.

As the trucks finally rumbled away, the ground vibrating once more, Cate let out a breath she hadn't even known she was holding. They'd left behind two Nazi soldiers by the looks of it, the rest either going in the convoy or leaving on foot in the opposite direction, and the two who'd been left were patrolling around the perimeter of the house.

"What are we going to do now?" she asked Jack, her voice so low it was barely audible. She wondered what had happened to the ATS girl, whether she'd made it safely to the beach or not, or whether she'd simply found somewhere to hide. If only they'd stayed together, if she hadn't left in such a hurry like that. Whatever the case, Cate knew she owed the girl her life. Without the warning, she would have been rounded up and taken on that truck, too. She gulped. Or just as easily gang-raped by all those soldiers and discarded before the truck had even left.

And Lilly . . . She fought the image of Lilly screaming at her from the ambulance she'd obviously commandeered. How on earth had Lilly ended up back at the chateau, and transporting injured soldiers on her own at that? She only hoped she'd made it all the way.

"You all right?" Jack asked, his hand catching hers.

She nodded, quickly blinking away her tears. "I'm fine. I just keep thinking what could have happened to me, that's all." *What could still happen to me.*

The knowing smile he gave her in reply made her wonder if he could read her mind, or perhaps he was just worrying about the same thing.

"We're not safe yet," he said. "And heaven help us if someone decides they want to drive this ambulance."

Cate hadn't thought about that possibility. "What if I somehow found the keys? What if we found another vehicle we could drive?"

Jack's fingers interlaced with hers, both of them ignoring the drying blood streaked across their skin, and she watched, hopeful, as he stroked his thumb across her hand before finally meeting her gaze.

"No, Cate, we can't," he said. "We'd be dead within minutes, maybe an hour at best. There's a reason no Allied soldiers are left standing here. It's too late to make a run for it."

Jack was right. Defeat was obvious now; it was stale in the air, clinging to them and everything around them like a corpse amongst the living. But what did that mean for Lilly? She hoped her friend had made it to the beach in time and hadn't been caught by a German patrol.

"So if our army has left us behind, and we can't steal a vehicle, what do we do?" She tried to disguise the panic in her voice, but she couldn't quell the feeling inside her.

Jack let out a low, shuddering sigh. "We wait until nightfall, and then we start to walk."

"In the dark?" she asked.

"In the dark," he confirmed. "It's our only hope if we want a chance at survival."

"Where will we go? How is that a safe option?" Terror rose like bile in Cate's throat. "Do you not think we'll make it?"

"Cate, we're lying in the dirt beneath an abandoned ambulance, surrounded by the enemy," he said. "There is no safe option, but it's our best bet. Trust me, I want to live just as much as you do."

"And where are we going to go? Do we try to make it to the beach?"

"No," he said quickly. "We don't even know if the evacuation was successful. The Germans could be attacking our soldiers right now, while they wait on the beach. We could be heading straight into a trap if we do that."

"You think they might not make it home?" Surely hundreds of thousands of soldiers couldn't be killed as they waited to evacuate?

"At this point, I honestly don't know," Jack said. "But when you think about that many men and how fast everything's moved since then . . ."

Cate nodded. She understood. She wished she didn't, but she did. As she stared at the hospital and wished she could sneak back to the house to collect her warm clothes and personal items, a sense of calm settled over her. They had a chance. If nothing else, they had a chance to make it to safety. What would happen after that, with France under German occupation, she had no idea, but she did have hope, and that was better than nothing.

Rain started to pelt more steadily now, making gentle dinging sounds on the vehicle above them, big plops soaking into the dirt around them and slowly turning it to thick mud. At least they were dry while they were hiding.

"We're alive, Cate, and for now, that's something," Jack whispered, grunting as he shuffled back and reached for the blanket.

She should have asked about his pain, offered him the blanket, but she didn't. Because there was nothing she could do to ease his suffering, and for the first time in almost a year, it was nice to have someone pull a blanket over her, take care of her, for a change.

"We're going to hunker down here until it's safe to leave," he murmured. "We stay warm, we rest, and then we walk for Le Paradis or St. Venant. The Nazis will have already passed through there, so if we can make it . . ." His voice trailed off.

Cate was grateful for the blanket, and she pressed her face against her hands as she lay, not wanting Jack to see her tears. She had no idea where Le Paradis was, but if Jack wanted to go there, then she didn't exactly have any better ideas.

She only hoped Lilly could make it to safety too.

48

———— ❧～✦❧ ————

Cate hadn't intentionally fallen asleep, and when Jack woke her, she wondered how she'd ever managed to relax enough to slumber. Her hips jutted into the unforgiving dirt, and when she lifted her head to stretch she banged it on the undercarriage of the ambulance.

"Ouch," she muttered.

And then she realized that Jack's body was curved to hers, the blanket over both of them, and embarrassment heated her cheeks. That certainly hadn't been planned.

"Is it time to go?" she asked.

He grunted, his voice rough from sleep. "Yeah. Let's go."

She pulled the blanket up and attempted to ball it, given she couldn't fold it in such close quarters. And she stuffed the bandages into her pockets, desperate to stretch her legs and her back as claustrophobia crept up on her.

"Let me go first," he said.

Cate was happy for him to take charge, knowing that her knees would be knocking as soon as she hauled herself out. She waited for him to give the all-clear, and within seconds he was telling her to join him.

The rain had reduced to a thick drizzle now, but she knew it would only be a matter of time before her nurse's uniform was soaked through, leaving her shivering and wet. And Jack wasn't exactly going to fare much better in what he was wearing, not to mention being only a handful of days post-surgery, and should have been on strict bed rest to recover.

"Do you know the direction we're supposed to be going?" she whispered.

"Yes, I've been there before," he said. "It's fifty miles, give or take."

Cate decided to spread out the heavy wool blanket and draped it over her shoulders, offering the other side to Jack.

"Here, let's walk with this over us. It'll keep us dryer for longer."

"I'm fine, you take it," he said.

Cate watched him limp beside her as they started walking, and decided not to take no for an answer. "Take the blanket, Jack. If you don't, you could die on me. You shouldn't even be out of bed walking, and I don't want to have to add hyperthermia to your list of ailments."

That stopped him in his tracks. He took half the blanket and draped it over his shoulders, meaning it lifted off one of hers as he was so much taller. But she didn't care. They were as dry as could be, given the circumstances, and for now, they couldn't see or hear the enemy. It wasn't dark yet, but she knew it would be soon, and she strained to adjust her eyes to the fading light. Cate's foot slid from beneath her on the mud, but she managed to quickly right herself.

"I have no idea how long it takes to walk fifty miles," she confessed as they set off slowly, side by side.

"A long while," Jack replied, but from the grunt that came along with it, she realized it wasn't going to be easy for him and they hadn't even walked a quarter of a mile yet.

"Lean on me," she offered, ignoring his protest as she slipped an arm around his waist. Cate refused to be embarrassed about touching him or pressing her own body so close; surely they were past that by now. They were two people doing their best to survive, and she needed to forget any romantic thoughts she may or may not have had about him in the past.

"We can do this, Jack," she whispered up at him. "We're not dying tonight. Not here. We're going to make it."

She was answered with silence, but when his arm slid around her shoulders, letting her take some of his weight, it was all she needed, just to know that he believed the same. They'd survived so far, and that was all the evidence she had that they could stay that way. And so they kept walking, connected at the hip, as they bumped along in the dark toward Le Paradis, wherever that might be.

CHAPTER FIVE

ADELAIDE

Adelaide couldn't stop shaking. It had started when they were upstairs under the bed hiding, and ever since her body had trembled as if she were shivering from the cold. She glanced over at her sister, who was busying herself in the kitchen, preparing a meager meal for the pair of them, and even though she knew she should help, she couldn't seem to move.

She shut her eyes for a moment then quickly opened them, the sight of all those men walking out with their hands held high coming straight back to her, their little white flag on a stick. *Boom.* She kept hearing that, too, the loud explosions as they were gunned down, one after the other after the other.

"You need to do something to keep your mind off it all," Elise said.

Addy looked up at her sister and nodded. She was right—Elise always was.

"Set the table for me," Elise suggested. "The soup is almost ready."

Addy did as she was asked, taking out place mats and spoons, and then sitting to wait for her sister. She placed her palms flat on the table, pleased to see the shaking become slightly more controllable.

"What are we going to do?" she asked.

Elise set two steaming bowls on the table and sat down across from her. Addy watched as she folded her napkin on her knee and reached for her spoon before looking up and finally acknowledging her question.

"We're going to eat our soup and then do the dishes," Elise said matter-of-factly.

"About the men! We can't just leave them out there, Elise!"

Elise gave her the same fixed, firm kind of look her mother had always given her. It was as if her mother had passed away and Elise had somehow morphed into her.

"There is nothing we *can* do, Addy. Don't you see? If we go out there, the Germans could be watching, and the only way to stay safe is to keep our heads down and not draw attention to ourselves."

Addy wiped away her tears with the back of her hands. "I can't stop thinking about them," she confessed.

Elise set down her spoon and reached across the table. Her palm was warm and she linked their fingers together. "I can't stop thinking about it either, Addy. It's running through my head over and over. But there's nothing we can do. They're already dead, so the best thing we can do is force our minds on to other things."

Addy squeezed Elise's hand, holding on to her for a moment longer before they both picked up their spoons and began to eat. She was so sick of soup, especially given their limited ingredients, but at least it temporarily quieted the growl in her stomach.

There was a noise outside, then a sudden thump, and it made Oscar bark.

"Enough!" Elise scolded.

When he didn't stop straight away, Addy scooped him up and kept him on her lap as she ate. His warm little body was like a heater, and she liked the weight of him against her, even though her mother would have rolled in her grave to see a dog at her dining table. And it was also nice to hold him when she was scared; he always helped to calm her down.

There was another thump then, and Elise's eyes met hers across the table. She could see that her sister's spoon was shaking now, as if her tremble had been contagious. There was something, *or someone*, out there.

"Keep him quiet," Elise said.

Addy nodded, not about to make a noise herself. Her heart was starting to beat fast and she could barely stomach another mouthful of her soup. They had so little, though, so she wasn't going to let it go to waste.

Her imagination was working overtime, thinking of all the things that could be making that noise. Had some of the British soldiers miraculously survived? Were the Germans out there hauling the bodies away? Were there more men being killed? She shuddered at the last thought, willing it to go away.

"Is it morbid that I want to look outside so badly?" Addy asked.

Elise sighed and stood, taking both their bowls and walking them to the sink. "No, it's not morbid at all. I'm going to go mad sitting in here with the curtains drawn, wondering what on earth is going on out there as we listen to every noise. But it's dark and we don't want anyone out there to see us in here, so for now, we pretend nothing has happened. And we ignore that god-awful noise."

Easier said than done. Addy tried to take a leaf out of her sister's book and busied herself with wiping down the table and going to dry the dishes, but it was a job that only took ten minutes between the pair of them. Soon they were both exchanging glances without saying anything, and both trying to ignore what could be going on. She only wished she had some of her sister's strength.

When the rain started to fall more steadily, pounding out a constant beat on their old roof, Addy finally felt her nerves start to settle, and she snuggled up on her favorite chair, the one that had been her father's until he died, patting her knee for Oscar to jump up.

Elise sat down beside her, and although they'd usually read a book or knit, or something other than just sit, tonight that was all they did. Hand in hand, side by side, they sat, listening to the rain, not a word said between them.

Knock, knock, knock.

Addy almost fell off her chair as Elise leapt to her feet. Her sister immediately took their father's rifle from the wall where he'd always hung it, holding it out in front of her and checking it was loaded. An involuntary shiver peeled down Addy's spine as Elise pushed the bolt forward before lifting the rifle high so she was staring down the barrel, the butt pressed into her shoulder.

The knocking echoed out louder this time, more like a loud thump, once, then twice.

"Keep the dog tight under your arm and slowly open the door," Elise said.

Addy rose, obeying her sister's orders. Her legs were like a newborn colt's, knees knocking and wobbly as she inched her way across the room.

"Who could it be?" she whispered.

Elise didn't reply straight away, moving behind her, the rifle positioned between them, like Addy's own personal protection.

"I don't know, but I'm not letting anyone storm into our house without a fight."

Addy reached for the handle, extending her hand, fingers clenching around wood as she took a deep breath. If someone was determined to get in, she reasoned, then they would have simply kicked the door in, and it was that sudden realization that gave her confidence.

"We either wait in here, afraid, or we open the door and see who it is," Elise said. "But if someone forces their way into our home, I *will* shoot."

Addy nodded. She didn't doubt her for a second, and when Elise nudged her with her shoulder, she knew it was a now-or-never moment.

"On three," she whispered. "One, two . . . three!" She yanked it back, and then almost fell straight out the door, she was so taken by surprise.

"Oh my God!" she gasped.

She'd expected German troops demanding to be fed, watered and put up for the night, but this . . .

She bravely stepped forward, using her right hand to press her sister's rifle down and out of the way as she stared at the scene in front of her.

It's nothing short of a miracle.

CHAPTER SIX

ELISE

Survivors. Elise almost dropped her rifle, she was so surprised by the scene in front of her, and she put a hand on her sister's shoulder to steady herself as she looked down.

The two men wore what was left of their British army uniforms, and they were on their knees in a bloodied, muddy heap on her front doorstep. Their faces were thick with dirt, but one pair of eyes glinted up at her, searching her face, as she had the sudden and impulsive thought to haul her sister back into the house and lock the door. She tentatively pulled Addy back a little.

"Elise, we have to help them!" Addy cried, dropping down, her hands hovering over the closest man, the one who'd been so intently staring up at Elise.

Elise stared a moment longer before panic set in. She frantically, futilely scanned the darkness, wondering who could be watching, who might see the two men who'd somehow hauled themselves to her house. *Why us? Why did they have to come here?*

"Get inside," she said, catching Addy's wrist and pulling her back. "Now."

"What? Why?" Her sister's face was a picture of confusion. "We have to help them!"

"No, we can't," she said, surprised by how firm her own voice was. "It's too dangerous."

The men were groaning, one more than the other, and she watched as one of them crawled forward, like a broken dog hauling himself across the doorstep on his hands and knees. Her heart broke and her stomach churned uneasily at the sight of him, but she had to protect Addy. There were only two of them now, and she wasn't about to lose her sister or risk being taken herself for helping strangers. It was a luxury they couldn't afford.

"Elise!" Adelaide begged. "We can't turn our back on them! They have nowhere else to go!"

Tears streaked down her little sister's face, but Elise stood straighter, not about to give in. Addy was the soft one, the one who always followed her heart, which meant that she wasn't the right person to be making the decisions for them. She'd never had to be the one taking charge.

"Adelaide . . ."

"Please," the man closest begged, pulling himself up to his knees, holding up his bleeding hands. "*S'il vous plaît.*"

His French was heavily accented, his words slow. But she'd understood him in English anyway.

"Help us." His voice was more of a choke, the words dragging out as he reverted to English. "You can't leave us out here."

She looked from him to Addy and back again, so close to dragging her sister inside and standing in front of the door with her gun trained on her just to keep her safe. But for every second she stood staring down at the broken man in front of her, her willpower diminished tenfold.

"Elise, *please*," Addy begged, her voice almost childlike. "We can't turn our back on them!"

Louis. She could suddenly see his face as clear as day in her mind. What if this were her brother, begging for mercy, for someone to show him some compassion, as he cried on his knees, moaning in pain, smeared with blood? What if her brother had been given that same chance to survive, and the one person who could help had turned him away? Something inside of her started to soften.

"Elise!" Addy cried.

"Fine. Bring them in," she muttered, reaching down and pulling the first man up. His eyes were so bright, despite the state of his face and his broken body, and she kept hold of him tight, arm around his waist, as she helped him into the house.

"You speak English?" he asked, sounding surprised.

"We do," Elise replied, before scolding the dog as he almost tripped her up, no longer in Addy's arms. "Go away and sit down."

The stench coming from the soldier told of death, and she forced herself to breathe through her mouth so her stomach didn't churn. They had a modest fire burning, and she knew that one of them would have to go looking for more wood if they were going to keep these soldiers alive. The one she was helping was starting to shake almost uncontrollably, and she wasn't certain whether it was from shock or from getting so wet out in the rain.

"Sit here," she instructed, lowering him into a wooden chair. It wasn't the most comfortable, but she'd never get bloodstains off the fabric sofa.

She gave him a long, cautious look, wondering if he'd even make it through the night, but there was something about the way he sat, proud even in defeat, that made her think that if anyone could make it, maybe he could. And with that, she dashed back to the front door, seeing that Adelaide was having a much harder time getting the other soldier off the ground. He'd half-crawled, half-dragged himself with Addy's assistance, but she needed him inside and hidden from sight immediately.

"Grab him under the arm," Elise said. "I'll take this side. We need to get him to the table, next to the other soldier."

She saw Addy grit her teeth from the exertion, the man a deadweight, and they hauled him up so he could stumble forward. What she hadn't been expecting was the sudden howl he let out the moment they had him upright.

"Shhh!" she hissed.

"Elise, he's in pain!" Addy scolded.

"Pain or not, we don't need anyone else coming here looking to see what's happening, do we?" Elise snapped back. "We could be killed for hiding them here!"

Adelaide gave her a sharp stare but Elise ignored her, cross with her naivety, kicking the door shut behind them as they helped the soldier across the room. One of his legs was useless, dragging behind him, and she could tell that was the primary source of his pain.

When they finally had him next to his comrade, she instructed her sister to lower him. "Carefully does it, nice and slow."

They both grunted with the effort as they levered him into a chair. Then, as his eyes closed in relief, they stood back for a moment. Elise caught her breath, looking at both the men now sitting at their table and wondering what on earth they'd done. Inviting them in was one thing, but these men looked close to death and she was no nurse. What were they going to do?

"Addy," she said, beckoning for her to follow. She walked into the kitchen, leaning her head closer to her sister. "I need you to scrub the blood off the doorstep. We can't have any evidence that anyone injured came here tonight, do you understand?"

"Yes, of course."

Elise glanced back, shaking her head that she'd so easily given in. She didn't even want to think how long they'd have them for. "You need to clean it as best you can, then check for marks from where they dragged themselves and come in and help me."

Addy's fingers brushed against her arm. "Do you know what to do for them? I mean, they're so badly injured . . ."

Elise swallowed, not wanting her sister to see how rattled she was. It was her job to keep their little family together, to make sure they were safe. "I'll be fine, I have a very strong stomach. You just worry about your job, and I'll worry about mine."

Addy suddenly threw her arms around her neck, and Elise embraced her back, not used to her sister being quite so affectionate. "Thank you, Elise. We did the right thing opening our door to them."

Elise gave her a quick squeeze back before retrieving her father's rifle from where she'd dropped it, carrying it with her and putting it on the table within easy reach, as Addy disappeared to clean the step. If either of those men thought they could lay a hand on her or her sister, she planned on teaching them a very fast lesson.

"Where did you learn to speak English?"

Elise turned at the sound of a raspy, deep voice. She could see that the first soldier had tried to stand, holding on to the table for support. He was the leaner and taller of the two, his eyes a warm brown and the dirt smearing his face doing little to hide how handsome he was. His hair was a dark blond, but mud clung to the tips and made it stick up at the front.

"Sit down," she ordered. "Our mother had a love of languages and our grandmother was English, so it was important to them that we learn."

He smiled, and she was surprised how white his teeth were, or maybe it was just because of the contrast against his dirty cheeks.

61

"Need t-t-to s-s-surrender," the other soldier chattered, his teeth audibly clanging together as he stuttered. "Help me surrender. Please."

"That didn't go so well for you the first time, so I'd say that option is off the table," Elise said, setting the water to boil and finding some old towels that she kept for cleaning. She scooped them up and marched back to the table, touching a hand to the soldier doing all the jabbering. He looked like he was about to slide straight off the chair.

"You saw what happened, didn't you?"

She met the gaze of the more coherent of the two again. "Yes, we did see," Elise said gently. "I'm so sorry."

"Those bastards, they just massacred us! We tried to surrender and—"

"I know," she replied, taking a deep breath. "I know what they did, I saw all your men, and you're right, it was nothing short of a massacre. I'm so sorry."

She wanted to touch him, to even just put a hand on his shoulder, but it felt too intimate for someone she didn't really know. Instead she turned to go and fetch the water, not sure what else she could do for either man other than clean their wounds with warm water and apply bandages where needed.

When she returned, she cleared her throat and looked between them. The one who'd been babbling away like a madman was silent now, just rocking gently back and forth in his chair, and she wondered if perhaps he was no longer right in the head. He was sizeable, broad-shouldered and heavier than his friend, and she didn't know how they'd restrain him if he wouldn't let her tend to his wounds.

"Your friend, is he . . ."

"In shock, I think."

She nodded. "All right, well then, shall I help you first?"

"No, help him. His leg seems pretty bad."

Elise's stomach churned as she considered what she might be about to deal with, but she tried not to let it show on her face. She forced herself to put one foot in front of the other, wondering whether her measly bowl of hot water was going to do her any good.

"Do you have any medical training?" she asked the soldier.

"No. Do you?"

She sighed. "None. But I'll do my best."

"I'm Harry," he said. "We are part of the"—he paused, grunting as he adjusted his weight—"we *were* the Royal Norfolk Regiment."

Elise was grateful that he was talking, because it was taking her mind off what she was about to do, although she could hear the rasp of his voice and knew that he must be in terrible pain. "I'm Elise, and that's my youngest sister Adelaide out there."

Speaking of Addy, what was taking her so long? There must have been more blood ingrained into that doorstep than she realized.

"Were you really thinking about leaving us out there?" He hissed out a breath as he adjusted himself, and she winced for him, hating that he was hurting so badly. "After what you saw them do to us?"

Elise bristled. "And here I was thinking you were about to thank me."

He dipped his head then, and she hoped he had the good sense to keep his mouth shut.

"I just didn't expect a woman to turn away injured men. Especially Allies."

This time she did more than bristle. "I'll have you know that the life of my sister, and protecting her, is more important to me than anything else in this world. So instead of judging me, how about you thank me and then sit quietly."

His nod told her that he'd heard her, and she took a deep breath and refocused. There was so much Elise wanted to know, wanted to ask, but after their little exchange, she decided to sit on her questions until later. She was curious to know how they were still alive. Had they been hiding elsewhere or had they just miraculously survived the slaying outside the barn? Where was the German army stationed now? And what had happened to the French army?

But instead of asking, she dropped to her knees in front of the other man, hoping he could tell how badly she wanted to help him. In between his rantings he was moaning, *groaning* as he moved, big tears raining down his cheeks. She'd never seen a man look so broken; not even her father had looked like that when her brother had died.

"Soldier, I'm going to roll up your trouser leg and take a look," she said, in the softest voice she could muster. "I'm going to see what I can do for you."

"His name's Peter," Harry said. "I think his leg might be badly broken."

Elise carefully lifted his trouser leg, fast realizing that she was either going to have to cut the fabric off or figure out a way to get him out of his pants. The sight that confronted her was heartbreaking, and as she stared at his lower leg, she felt the most helpless she'd ever felt in her life.

No wonder his foot had been dragging. She stared in horror at the piece of bone sticking out from his lower leg, jagged and sharp. Elise sucked in a breath, hands hovering, not knowing what in God's name she was supposed to do.

"You were right about the break," she said, her voice low as she angled her body for Harry to see past her, forgetting her anger toward him. "It's bad."

Peter was moaning and still mumbling to himself, and Elise was loath to touch him, knowing that whatever she did was going to cause him so much pain.

"How's it all going in here?" Addy's warm, sunny voice was at odds with the gruesome sight Elise was still staring at, and she stiffened as she felt her sister standing behind her.

"What the . . ." Addy gasped, before making a sudden retching sound and turning around, one hand on her stomach and the other covering her mouth.

"He has a very badly broken leg and we're going to have to do something to keep it still," Elise said, trying to sound like she knew what she was doing even though inside she was floundering. "Addy, is the doorstep clean?"

"Yes," Addy called back from the kitchen.

"Well, wash your hands and pull yourself together then," Elise said. "I need another pair of hands in here."

She wanted to walk away and vomit herself; she'd never had to deal with anything like this and she'd never felt so physically sick before either, but they'd opened their home to these men, and that meant they were as good as responsible for them. If she had to go for help, it would mean involving someone else, and she couldn't risk it.

"Am I right that you need help?" Harry asked.

She fixed him with her stare, not liking his tone. "The last thing I need is you collapsing in a heap, so you just stay put."

He nodded. "Fair point. But can I ask you something?"

Elise waited. "Of course."

"Do you have any alcohol?"

She hesitated, seeing the anguish on Peter's face and the pain in Harry's as he tried to get comfortable on the small, upright wooden chair she'd sat him on. "Yes, of course," she eventually said, before calling out to Addy. "Bring Father's whisky."

"How many glasses?" Addy called back.

"Just the bottle," Harry replied for her.

Elise turned back to Peter, knowing she couldn't put it off for much longer. She stared at the bone, wondering if he even knew that his lower leg was as good as snapped in half.

"Peter, can you hear me?" she asked, placing a hand on his forearm and giving him a little shake. He was tipped back, his shoulders slumped and his head to the side, his body still trembling. What was she thinking? She should have wrapped them both in blankets straight away, stopped them from becoming hypothermic, and started to give them small sips of something, *anything*, hot as well.

Addy was standing by her side now and she held out the bottle of whisky. Elise took it from her, passing it to Harry. He took a few big gulps that made her cringe just watching, but when he passed it back to her she decided to take a sip herself for courage.

The burn in her throat was instant but she stifled her cough, inhaling through her nose and wondering if it would, in fact, help her. The only thing she knew for sure was that it had landed in her stomach like a pool of liquid fire.

"So what can I do?" Addy asked.

Her sister was as white as a sheet and Elise took one look at her and knew she wasn't going to be the best hands-on assistant. "I need you to get blankets to wrap both men in, and boil more water. I need them sipping something hot to warm them up from the inside, so you could make coffee." She doubted they had enough ingredients to make more soup.

"Anything else?" Addy asked, already backing away.

"A broomstick," Harry added. "To splint the leg."

Elise cleared her throat as she prepared to lean forward and touch the leg. "Good idea. Get the broom, it'll be the straightest length of timber we have."

Elise looked at Harry, hoping he would give her more instructions. She didn't usually like being told what to do, but in this case she was as good as blind.

"Give him the alcohol first," Harry said. "Before you touch him again."

She leaned forward and cupped the back of his head, but his arms started to flail around then and she only just ducked out of the way before he connected with her, his fists flying.

"I need to surrender! Let me go!" he cried.

It was the liveliest he'd been, and Elise had no idea what to do with a violent patient—or any patient for that matter.

Harry was by her side almost immediately, gripping the table with both hands as he inched forward. She didn't even know what his injuries were, but she wasn't about to scold him for moving when she needed his help.

"Peter, that's enough!" he said, grabbing hold of his friend's arm as it flailed once again. "She's trying to help you!"

"Should I just start?" Elise asked, not even sure what to start with.

"Pass me the bottle," he said. "We need to get a good few slugs of this into him first, to help with the pain."

"Surrender! I surrender!" Peter cried, and Elise was tempted to slap her hand over his face to keep him quiet, worried that if there was anyone lurking outside they'd hear him. What if they thought *she* was the one stopping him from surrendering to the Nazis?

"You need to find a way to stop him from yelling," she said.

"You want me to knock him out?"

Elise didn't reply. Instead, she took a deep breath and placed her hands on Peter's leg, surprised at how little blood there was despite such a gory break. She did her best to straighten it, hating how flimsy and weak the limb felt, when it should have been so strong.

"Argh!" The yell was loud and fast, and then suddenly there was silence.

She looked up and into Harry's eyes.

"Well, look at that. You knocked him out all by yourself," he said.

Elise's stomach turned as she touched the bone, wanting to work fast now that he was unconscious, hating that she'd caused him so much pain he'd blacked out. When he woke up, he was possibly going to be in even more pain than before, though, and she didn't want to still be working on him.

"Should I try to push the bone back in?" she asked Harry, swallowing down bile as she felt a part of a human that was supposed to be hidden on the inside behind flesh and muscle. "Or just try to straighten it as best I can?"

Harry was silent, and she didn't think anything of it until she looked up, expecting that he was just thinking over the best option. But he fainted so fast and so hard, she didn't have a chance to save him, his head whacking on the table before he hit the floor.

"Addy!"

She appeared almost immediately, the broom in her hand and a bucket in the other.

"What happened?" Adelaide dropped the stick and ran to Harry, hands fluttering over him as if she really had no idea what to do.

That makes two of us.

"Just make sure he's breathing and put a blanket around him to keep him warm," Elise said. "Then come here and help me splint this leg before this one wakes up." He might have been condescending, but at least Harry had known a little about patching his fellow soldier up, and she wished he'd held on a bit longer before passing out.

She had no idea how they were going to attach Peter's leg to the stick, or whether she was supposed to clean it or not, but the only thing worse than doing it wrong would be to not do anything at all.

Elise grimaced as she looked at both men, unconscious, knowing she was completely, utterly out of her depth.

An hour later, Elise sat beside Harry on the floor. He was propped up against a chair, and she was sitting cross-legged as she carefully wiped at his wound. Addy was sat quietly beside her; Peter was still asleep, albeit lying flat out on the floor now, where they'd managed to put him after securing his leg. It was only a temporary fix and she had no idea what she was actually going to do with him long-term, but for now she'd done her best. Incredibly, although he'd managed to sustain a shocking injury, perhaps from men falling on him, he hadn't been shot at all.

Harry was another story, though.

"I'm going to have to get the bullet out," Elise said confidently, as if it were something she'd done before. "If I don't, I suspect an infection will eventually set in."

Harry's breath seemed to whistle through his teeth. "Just get it over and done with."

"Should I get you a stick to bite on or something?" she asked.

"Just more whisky," he said. "I'll be fine."

She had tweezers that Addy had found for her, and although they'd already been cleaned in boiling water, she tipped a little alcohol on them for good measure. And as Addy passed Harry the bottle of whisky, Elise shuffled even closer to him, one hand pressed to his chest, the other ready to dig into his shoulder.

"Ready?" she asked.

He took a quick sip. "Ready as I'll ever be."

She carefully inserted her tweezers, being as gentle as could be. Harry grunted.

"Tell me what happened," she asked, wanting to keep his mind off what she was doing. "Where did you all come from?"

"So now you want to chat?" he asked, wincing.

Elise gave him a sharp stare before going back to work on his wound.

"There were ninety-nine of us in our regiment," he eventually rasped, groaning as she dug deeper into his flesh. "We were trying to stall the Nazi advance, so the rest of our soldiers had a fighting chance of making it."

"An advance toward the coast?" Elise asked, leaning even closer to see the bullet as she pulled.

"Yes," he gasped. "Trying to delay them as long as we could so the evacuation could go ahead. The entire British army is going home, if they make it, that is."

She cringed as her tweezers slipped off the bullet. If only she had pliers or something sturdier to use.

"And do you think they did? Evacuate, I mean?" She couldn't believe the British were leaving France.

He went silent, and she wasn't sure if it was from the pain or whether it was more telling of what might have happened to the troops trying to evacuate.

"We were watching what happened in the barn, from upstairs," she continued, squeezing tightly with the tweezers and finally, slowly extracting the bullet. "Why did you surrender?"

He yelped as she did one final pull, triumphantly holding up the bullet as Addy gave a little clap from behind her. Elise passed her both the bullet and the tweezers, before picking up the whisky and pouring some in the wound.

"Jesus Christ! Why didn't you warn me?"

"Sorry." She gave him the bottle by way of apology, and then tried to figure out how to bandage his shoulder.

"We defended until the bitter end, but we were out of ammunition. There was no way we were getting out of there alive if we didn't surrender, and so that's what we all decided to do."

She slowly looked up at him. His eyes were swimming with tears. Up until now, he'd seemed so angry with the world, but now he just looked plain sad. And vulnerable.

"But they killed most of you, anyway," she whispered. "We saw."

Elise took in his thick brown hair, pushed off his forehead, the blueness of his eyes that shone so brightly despite his filthy face. As she finished bandaging his shoulder, she reached for a cloth and dipped it in the small amount of clean water she had, still warm, then wiped it across his cheeks. She suddenly needed to wipe all the grime away, as if by doing so she could erase some of the horrors they'd both witnessed, but she had barely started when he pushed her hand away.

She didn't let him deter her, straight away starting to clean his skin gently again, and this time he didn't stop her.

"I survived beneath the bodies of my friends," he murmured, and she could feel his eyes searching her face as she carefully wiped, moving over his forehead now. "I lay there, feeling the weight of them and smelling the stench of death, until it was dark. Until I couldn't hear anything any longer and lay buried beneath them all."

"And that's when you crawled to our front door?" she asked.

"I could hear something, but I wasn't sure if it was my imagination or not. Turned out to be Peter, writhing in pain beneath a pile of men too," Harry said, as she moved back and smiled at his now-clean face. "I managed to haul him out, and I knew we had one chance to pick a friendly house."

"Why did you pick ours?" Addy asked, taking them both by surprise when she spoke after being silent for so long.

Elise sat back so Addy wasn't blocked by her body, surprised at how brave her sister had been through it all. Her face was still ashen white, and her blue-green eyes were wide, but there was an open curiosity there that told Elise she wasn't completely traumatized by what had happened. That she was genuinely interested in the men in their house, or maybe at having anyone in their house at all.

"Because I saw you when we ran past, just a glimpse, but I saw you both scurrying into your home as we holed up in that barn."

Elise froze. "You didn't see us watching, did you?" What if the Nazis had seen them too? What if they knew there were witnesses to what they'd done? Her pulse started to race.

"I saw two young women as we passed, that's all. And I figured you might take pity on us." His eyes met hers, the unspoken words reminding her that she almost *hadn't* taken pity on them, and they both knew it. "I didn't see you watching, and to be honest, I doubt anyone could have."

Elise breathed a sigh of relief as he sank down to the floor, his eyes shut and his breathing heavy. She rose to her feet and reached down a hand for her sister, hauling her up beside her. She was so tired that she felt like her eyelids were drooping; her feet like lead as she moved.

"We did the right thing tonight, Elise," Addy whispered, staring down at the two men.

Elise embraced her, dropping a kiss to her hair, and wondered if she'd been too soft in opening their door to them, despite what her sister thought. But if she'd turned them away just because she was scared, she would never have forgiven herself. And she doubted Adelaide would have ever forgiven her, either.

CHAPTER SEVEN

ADELAIDE

The past year had brought so much pain with it; such soul-deep, gut-wrenching pain that Adelaide had often wondered how she'd ever survive beyond it, but today she'd seen pain on another level. Today she'd seen men massacred when they should have been taken prisoner, and she'd also witnessed the aftermath of injuries that would have challenged even the strongest of constitutions.

"What are we going to do with him?" Addy asked her sister, tucked up beside her in bed. It was cold, and they were both feeling so uncertain about what had happened, not to mention the fact that there were two strange men sleeping in their home, that they'd decided to curl up in bed together. They were propped up with pillows behind them against the metal headrest, blankets pulled up almost to their chins, and despite the warmth, Adelaide still had a regular shiver run through her.

"I don't know," Elise said, angled to face her now, so close that their knees were bumping under the covers. "If he keeps blabbering on about surrendering and trying to leave, we can't exactly stop him, can we?"

Adelaide blinked away tears at the thought of giving him to the Germans. "What if he does surrender, and they just shoot him like they did all the others?"

"I know. I keep thinking that they expected all of them to be dead. I mean, they massacred those soldiers, so they certainly didn't mean to leave any witnesses behind, did they?"

Addy gripped the blanket and pulled it up even higher, snuggling deep into it. *Witnesses.* That word terrified her, because that was exactly what they were; they'd witnessed the entire thing from start to finish.

"I tend to think that he's not right in the head, or perhaps that he's just in a state of temporary shock," Elise said. "But I don't know how to stop a grown man from doing something, other than by forcibly restraining him."

Adelaide had never seen anything like it before, was still in shock herself at seeing anyone behave that way. She'd felt the terror inside him as if it were a real, breathing thing.

"I don't want you to get upset with me, because it's the last thing I want to do, but if it comes to it, and he seems sound of mind, we might not be able to stop him from leaving."

Addy could tell from the gentleness of her sister's words that she expected her to be upset about it. But if she were entirely honest, it was something she'd already thought about. Peter had terrified her when he'd kept insisting he be allowed to surrender, muttering like he was actually demented, the whites of his eyes flashing the moment he'd gained consciousness. How could they help him if he didn't want to be helped?

"What if we do, though, and then he tells them what we did? About Harry?"

Elise sighed. "I know, I've thought of that, too. But short of knocking him over the head or shooting him myself and burying him in the garden, I don't see what our other options are if he still feels that way next week, or next month even. And we can't exactly keep him hidden if he doesn't want to be here, he'll jeopardize our safety either way."

Addy shut her eyes, wishing they didn't have to consider something so horrid. "What's going to happen to us? If we're found out?" she asked. "What would the Germans actually do to us?"

Elise caught her hand. "Listen carefully to me, Addy. If we're discovered, we say that we helped them because they were on our doorstep in the middle of the night and we felt vulnerable as two women here alone. We feared for our safety. As long as we both stick to the same story, we'll be fine."

"You're certain that will work?" She couldn't tell if her sister was simply trying to make her feel better.

"We're two young women on our own who were put in an impossible situation. We simply say that we were scared, and we weren't able to physically restrain two men with brute force, or defend ourselves against them."

Addy laughed, despite it all. "Maybe not, but after seeing you in action today, I think you would actually do it if you had to. I was actually pretty impressed with you."

Elise laughed back, and within seconds they were both laughing hard, heads bent together. It had been an awful day, but laughing made Addy feel so much better, even if only for a few minutes.

"I can't believe I took a bullet out of a man," Elise said, head in her hands as she groaned. "Somehow I just did it."

"I can't believe any of what you did! All I managed was to scrub the doorstep. Honestly, I would have fainted if I'd had to so much as touch either of their wounds."

After a few minutes, as Addy sank down in the pillows and felt her breathing start to slow, Elise whispered to her.

"So we're agreed then?" she asked, her voice somber now, not a trace of humor left. "We look after them as best we can, but if we're discovered, we stick to our story?"

"Yes," Addy whispered back. "We're agreed."

She'd saved injured birds and found stray cats all her life, not to mention rescuing Oscar as a puppy from a farmer who was about to drown him in a sack with rocks. So it shouldn't have surprised her sister when she'd been so insistent on saving the two men. They would do their best, but if they were discovered, they needed to save themselves and plead for understanding.

"I'm really proud of you, Addy."

Addy should have told Elise how proud she was of her, too, but instead she just let her draw her close and hold her, almost able to imagine it was her mother holding her, instead of her big sister.

The next morning, after waking up snuggled tight to Elise, Addy rose and quickly got dressed. She roused her sister, not used to being the first up, which told her that the events of the night before must have really taken a toll on her.

Thump.

She cringed. It was a very weird feeling hearing noises downstairs, knowing that they were being made by men; men who were essentially strangers to them. As their family had slowly become smaller, she'd grown used to it being just the two of them, and that also meant having a very quiet house most of the time.

Oscar had already jumped off the bed to go down and investigate, and Adelaide pulled on a thick woolen cardigan as she waited for Elise to drag herself out of bed.

"What time is it?" Elise croaked.

"Seven," she replied. "And it sounds like there's a large animal downstairs, so I think we need to get down there."

Elise groaned, swinging her feet over the edge of the bed and rubbing at her head. Adelaide decided to leave her and go down on her own, although the second she stepped into the living room, she wished she'd waited for her sister so she wasn't alone.

"Oh Lord," she muttered, as she surveyed the room.

Somehow Peter had dragged himself almost to the front door, his broken leg outstretched and with the makeshift wooden splint miraculously still attached. There was a small trail of blood, which she supposed must have come from another wound under his shirt that they hadn't yet found, because his leg hadn't been a source of blood despite it having a horrendous injury.

"What does he think he's doing?" Addy asked, horrified as she moved closer to Harry.

"Apparently he's going to surrender," Harry said, shaking his head as he stared at his friend in what she imagined was disbelief. "I've tried to talk sense into him, but he won't listen."

"Is there anything I could say?" Adelaide asked.

"Honestly, he's just so fixated on trying to surrender again. Other than tying him to a chair—"

"Maybe he just needs someone to be patient with him," she said. "To talk to him instead of telling him why he's wrong."

"You're suddenly an expert on talking soldiers down from the ledge?" Harry asked. "There's nothing you can say that I haven't already said."

"Or perhaps you could show a little respect to the women of the house," Elise said, the final stair-tread creaking as she walked toward them. "If she wants to talk to him, let her talk. There are worse things a man could be subjected to than my sister's kindness."

Addy shielded her mouth with her hand to hide her smirk. She doubted Harry could have missed the condescending tone in her sister's voice. She chanced a quick glance at him and saw that he was less than impressed, but he clearly knew what was good for him because he didn't say anything else.

"Harry, I'm going to lay some ground rules," Elise said, coming closer. "We all show one another kindness and respect, and you remember that we're not your troops. This is our home, and I'd say you're very fortunate to have been given refuge here."

Peter cried out, silencing them all, and Harry looked like he'd just received a blow to the stomach, his face drained of color as he watched Peter writhe across the floor. Addy felt herself flood with pity for both men.

"If we can't keep him here, then we'll be forced to let him go at some point, but for now, I think we should let Addy talk to him," Elise continued.

"Wait, you actually want to let him go?" Harry spluttered.

Addy watched as Elise shook her head. "That's not what I said. But you've said it yourself—there's only so long we can physically contain a man who doesn't want to be here. If he's still wanting to surrender another week or month from now, I don't see that we have any other choice."

Harry turned, and Adelaide wished she could comfort him, the pain in his face so visceral as he processed what Elise was saying. "They'll probably kill him if he surrenders. They've already shown what bloody barbarians they are."

"I know," Elise said softly. "Harry, please don't think this is what I want. I'm just being honest about how I see the situation."

"He's not just a fellow soldier to me, he's my friend," Harry said, his voice cracking with emotion. "He's all I have left at this point."

"Then we force him to stay," Addy said, joining the conversation. "We can keep him in the attic, one of us can watch the door when the other goes in with food, and . . ."

Elise gave her a sharp look.

"He's not a child or a prisoner," Harry said, his voice firmer all of a sudden. "Maybe your sister's right. He's a grown man, and if he wants to surrender, then none of us can stop him. But I'll fight with him tooth and nail as long as I can, because I'm not letting him go without a damn good fight." He cast Peter a sad look. "Because if he walks out that door, he's as good as dead."

Adelaide looked from her sister to Harry and then over at Peter. He seemed more lucid now, even though he was clearly as determined as ever to get out of the house. But where on earth did he think he was going to go on his own? Was he going to crawl to the Nazi camp?

"Peter, it's Addy, from last night," she said, bending down low and reaching out to him. She touched his arm, gently holding him for a moment before rubbing in small circles. "I need to talk to you for a moment."

He looked up at her, and the desperation in his eyes broke her heart. Here was a man who'd fought for his country, who'd bravely tried to hold off the Nazis to let others evacuate, crawling on his belly as if he were a wounded animal. She smiled down at him, hoping he could see how much she cared, that she wanted to help him if he'd let her.

"I want very much to look after you," she told him.

"Thank you," he whispered.

She could see then, from the way he looked at her and said those two small words, that he was in fact very lucid now. She could see the agony, the pain, within him.

"We can keep you hidden here, with your friend Harry," she told him. "Do you understand that it's just the two of you left? There's no one else. If you try to surrender again, we can't keep you safe." She gulped. "Harry truly believes you'll die trying to surrender again."

He blinked at her, but never said a word, and she remembered what Elise had said to her about him being in shock. Perhaps he didn't truly grasp what had happened? Maybe he didn't remember it all, didn't recall the true horrors? Regardless of what Harry had said, she believed that kind words and love might be able to change his mind, or at least make him understand the situation better.

"We have to try again, we have to surrender," he stammered. "We can't hide here, they'll find us and kill us. Surrender is our only option."

The thought sent a shiver through Addy, but she tried to hide it. "Peter, the Nazis killed your entire regiment. Do you understand that?"

If for a second she'd thought he didn't remember, the tears in his eyes, the anguish written all over his pain-etched face, told her she'd been wrong.

"I have to try. Please, help me to try," he begged.

Adelaide nodded and lifted from her haunches. Elise and Harry had been silently watching, but now they were both moving closer. Harry was well patched up, and although he'd lost a lot of blood and had a hefty wound, he was at least able to move easily now.

"Pete, you really want to do this?" Harry asked. "You really want to surrender again? We tried that twice yesterday, remember? We surrendered once, and then again after they'd shot half our regiment? They put bayonets and bullets into the rest of them, too."

Peter had fallen silent now.

"They slaughtered them all, Pete, when we were holding a goddamn white flag!" Harry choked out.

"I can't stay here, I have to try," Peter cried. "We have to surrender, we have to. It's the only way! They'll find us here and kill everyone!" He clutched at Addy's sleeve, frightening her when he wouldn't let her go. "Please, you have to help me!"

Harry turned then, gesturing to both of them as he stared down at Peter, his eyes as cold as ice. "Maybe locking him in the attic isn't such a bad idea after all."

"Harry, I want you to go up to bed and get some rest," Elise said softly. "You must be exhausted, and we can look after Peter."

"I'm fine," Harry muttered, running his fingers through his hair and looking almost as crazed as Peter now, his eyes bloodshot and his skin ghostly white.

"It wasn't a question," Elise said. "It was an order. You need to rest if you're going to heal."

Adelaide didn't hear what he said in reply, focusing on Peter instead and bending to try to help him up. She couldn't stand to see him lying on the floor like that. He yelped, the sort of a noise a dog made if it were kicked, and she knew that with every movement he must want to scream out in pain.

"Here, let me help." Elise was beside her now, assisting Peter to his feet. Or *foot* in this case.

"I need to go," he whimpered. "*Please.*"

Elise let out a loud sigh, clearly frustrated, but Adelaide could only cry. Her cheeks were flushed and her hands were starting to tremble, but she felt the most overwhelming desire to do something. She'd been helpless last night when it came to nursing wounds, but caring for Peter was something she could do—so long as Elise dealt with his wound, because she couldn't so much as look at it.

"Let's make up a bed for him on the sofa," Elise said, as the stairs creaked and Harry followed her orders and went up to rest. "Then I'm going to see what food I can get, and you can stay and look after him."

Addy moved slowly as Peter shuffled between them across the living room. "Are you sure we're doing the right thing?" she whispered. "If he wants to surrender, if he truly thinks it's the right thing to do—"

81

"You stay with him, I'm going to get the food," Elise said, as if she hadn't even heard her. "Are we clear?"

But when Addy glanced at Peter, she knew that he'd heard her, and she also knew that she was the only one truly listening to him.

Adelaide gritted her teeth as she grasped the wheelbarrow handles. She hadn't banked on how impossible it would be to actually push a grown man on her own. Sweat formed on her brow and every footstep made her want to collapse, but she hoped that with every movement, once they got a head of steam up, it would get easier. Twenty painful steps later, though, she decided there was no truth to her theory.

If she'd been able to talk instead of grunting from exertion, she would have kept making conversation with Peter, but he was crying out in pain himself with every bump. And as they passed the barn where he'd almost been shot dead, she knew there was little she could say to him.

Where were the bodies?

She stopped, staring at the space where they'd once been. There was still blood splattered all over the side of the timber barn, reddish-brown stains that were starting to fade already as they dried, but there were no fallen soldiers.

"That's the place, isn't it?" Peter rasped.

"Yes." There was nothing she could say to soften the blow, so she didn't try.

And then she saw the mound of dirt out in the field. They'd buried the bodies. A mass grave that contained . . . She tried to recall how many soldiers had been killed. Ninety-seven. There had been ninety-seven of them killed, that's what Harry had said. How on earth they'd buried that many men so fast, she had no idea.

Adelaide's lower back spasmed in protest as she fought to push Peter again, knees deeply bent to help with the load. She'd discreetly asked one of the few neighbors still in residence where the German compound was, and she doubted she'd be able to take another step by the time she got there.

Thankfully it wasn't too far to go. With sweat making her top cling to her body and her hair damp to her forehead, Adelaide saw movement up ahead. She thought that Peter might have passed out from the pain he was so quiet, but when she set the barrow down and bent forward to catch her breath, he finally spoke.

"Are we there?" he ground out.

She surveyed the chateau up ahead. It looked to her as though the Nazi regiment had set up camp in the old abandoned property, and all of a sudden she felt truly scared for the first time since offering to take Peter.

What if they shoot at me? What if he tells them straight away where Harry is hidden, that we wanted to keep him hidden too? She forced the thoughts away, not wanting to think too far ahead, but it was impossible not to.

Adelaide barely had time to jump off the road before she was retching into the trees beside them, vomiting over and over until there was nothing left in her stomach. She stayed bent over for a moment longer, taking a few breaths before finally standing upright and taking out a handkerchief, dabbing at her mouth, horrified that she'd been so violently ill where anyone could have seen her.

"You're worried, about me, aren't you?" Peter's voice took her by surprise.

"About both of us, actually," she admitted. "But yes, mostly about you." *And what my sister will do to me when she finds out,* she thought.

"I just want to go home." Tears filled his eyes and he started to cry. "If they let me surrender, maybe I'll make it back. Maybe they'll let me go home."

She was no soldier, and she knew very little about war, but she was sensible enough to know that there was little chance Peter was going home; not if he stayed with her, and certainly not if he surrendered. But she had to believe that what had happened yesterday wasn't normal, that it wouldn't happen again.

"Come on then," she said, mustering energy she didn't even know she possessed. "Let's get this over and done with, and don't forget to keep the white flag where everyone can see it as we get closer." She'd given him her handkerchief, because it was white and all she had, and tied it around a little stick she'd found along the way.

Adelaide pushed him a little further before stopping again, this time straightening her skirt and checking her hair was in place. It was still damp, but she hoped that it looked passable, pinned up high off her face.

"I'm going to leave you here and go on ahead."

It's now or never. Adelaide started to walk before she lost her nerve, keeping her back straight and her eyes up. Her breathing was shallow, but there was little she could do about that, given how fast her pulse was racing.

"Help!" she called out, in French. "I need help!"

She approached the gate that led to the chateau, and her stomach lurched as she saw rifles trained on her.

Adelaide forced a smile, despite the terror building inside her. She had a role to play, and she'd rehearsed what to say in her head almost the entire way there. "I have a British soldier with me. I need help."

Not one of the German troops staring at her called back, and they certainly didn't lower their weapons. Her palms started to sweat and she clasped them in front of her, trying to stifle the desperate urge to run back the way she'd come.

"Lower your weapons!" The command came from the front door, which had already been wide open when she'd approached the front gate.

A tall man with immaculately combed blond hair marched out of the chateau and down the steps, his smile lighting his piercing blue eyes as he strode toward her.

"These men have no idea how to treat a lady," he said.

He was dressed in an immaculate, tailored dark uniform, with colors pinned above his left breast pocket and a red band on his arm that bore the Nazi insignia. Addy shuddered just looking at him, as intimidated by the way he looked as by who he was.

"I'm sorry for scaring you like that."

Adelaide was surprised at how handsome he was; even more so as he took off his hat. She'd convinced herself that all German soldiers were monsters, but this man looked anything but a monster. Her tongue stuck to the roof of her mouth as she stared back at him, suddenly at a loss for words. With everything that had happened recently, she'd barely met a man who wasn't family, other than Harry and Peter, and she suddenly wasn't sure how to behave.

"Forgive me, I'm Commander Wolfgang Schmidt. This is my company."

"Adelaide," she replied, clearing her throat. "I'm Adelaide DuPont."

His French was perfect, as if it were his native tongue. "You said something about a British soldier?"

Adelaide forced a smile, made herself take a slow, deep breath. "Yes, sir, I did."

"That is him over there? In your wheelbarrow?"

She didn't miss his smirk, or the grunt of laughter from the men behind him, although one sharp stare from their commander put an immediate end to their sniggering.

"Yes, sir, that's him. He tells me his name is Peter."

She received a warm smile in response, and the commander gestured for her to walk with him, which she did. Every step was filled with fear, her eyes downcast as she studied her small feet compared to the large black boots that belonged to the German.

"Miss DuPont, may I ask if you've seen any other British soldiers near here?"

Fear was like an arrow through her stomach, threatening to fell her. But she refused to drop the smiling façade she was trying so hard to perfect.

"No, sir, I haven't," she said, shaking her head and praying that Peter wasn't going to give her away and declare her a liar to try to save himself. "I brought this one straight to you, and he says he would like to surrender."

They kept walking until they were beside the wheelbarrow. When the commander stopped, so did she, and she slowly, bravely raised her eyes.

"Did you make this for his leg?"

Adelaide gulped. "I did. I had hoped he would be able to hobble along, but his injuries were far worse than I originally realized." She lowered her eyes, not wanting to look guilty but having the most overwhelming feeling that he was trying to catch her out in her deception.

When the German smiled at her, it reached his eyes, lighting them as his gaze found hers again. Warmth flooded her cheeks and she fought the urge to wrap her arms around herself, knowing she should be feeling self-conscious and ashamed, but instead being strangely drawn to the handsome man standing before her.

"I surrender." The pained whisper made Adelaide turn, and any warm thoughts she'd mistakenly had for the commander disappeared as she looked at Peter. Poor, poor Peter. The small flag was clasped tightly between his fingers, his knuckles as white as his face, terror written as plain as day all over it.

"What happens now?" she whispered. "To him?"

The commander simply gave Peter a curt nod before moving to stand in front of the wheelbarrow and blocking her line of sight.

"Don't worry yourself. You did the right thing in bringing him here."

She wanted to ask more, but her words stuck in her throat as she slowly looked up at the man demanding her attention, watching as he reached into his breast pocket. For a moment she froze, terrified of what he was about to produce.

"Cigarette?" he offered, as she exhaled in relief.

"Thank you, but no, I don't smoke."

He nodded and put them away, surprising her that he didn't light one for himself. He was still smiling, watching her, and she nervously ran her hands down her skirt before clasping them in front of her just for something to do.

"I should be heading home now," she said. "My sister will be getting worried."

"You have a sister?"

Adelaide swallowed. "I do. Her name is Elise."

He gestured past her and barked an order in German, and she felt a familiar shiver run through her, the same one she'd felt as they'd hidden beneath her mother's bed the night before.

Within seconds two soldiers were at his side, and she listened uselessly and wished she'd taken more of an interest in the German language when she'd been at school. With his men, he was a complex blend of intimidating and commanding, but the moment he turned back to her, the smile that had lit his eyes returned, a softness there that scared her. Because any other time, she could have fallen for that softness, but he was a Nazi. He was her enemy.

"Perhaps we shall cross paths again soon," he said.

Adelaide smiled and agreed with him, too scared to disagree. "Perhaps."

She turned to leave them, cringing as she saw the way the two soldiers roughly hauled Peter to his feet, his yelps of agony as they dragged him along. Adelaide squeezed her eyes shut for a beat, trying to block it out, waiting for Peter to scream out in pain and confess that Harry was alive too, that she'd tried to convince him not to surrender—anything to make them treat him better.

But to his credit, the only noises he made were howls of pain that he couldn't have stifled if he'd tried.

"Miss DuPont?"

Adelaide opened her eyes and slowly turned, waiting to be caught out, waiting to see a gun raised in her direction. But when she faced the German commander again, all she was met with was an amused smile.

"Yes?" It was barely a whisper.

"I think you forgot your wheelbarrow."

Heat flooded her cheeks again, this time from embarrassment. How could she have been so stupid?

"Yes," she replied, not able to come up with anything wittier. "So I did. I think your dashing uniform distracted me, sir."

If Elise could have heard her, she'd have likely whipped her for daring to flirt with a German soldier, but it was the only thing that had come to mind. And it hadn't required a lie, either.

His chuckle was deep. "Wolfgang," he called to her. "You may call me Wolfgang."

Adelaide was incapable of words, but she gave him a quick smile as she pushed her barrow and left the German house behind her.

I need to wash my mouth out with soap and water when I get home, she thought as she forced her feet to slow, not wanting to look like she was in too much of a hurry. *And say a prayer or two for daring to have even one romantic thought about a monster.*

But Commander Wolfgang didn't look like a monster, and that was part of the problem. She couldn't believe that a man who looked like him could ever be part of the massacre she'd seen the day before; so maybe Peter would be all right after all.

"Where's Peter?"

Adelaide stood at the foot of the stairs, backing away as Harry started to descend. His hair was sticking up and his eyes were still bloodshot, but he looked a lot better for the long sleep he'd had.

She moved toward the kitchen as he reached ground level, and she could see how agitated he was starting to become as he scanned the room.

"Where is he?" Harry asked, spinning around. "Where's Peter?"

Addy lifted her head as her heart started to pound, her face burning hot as she met his stare. "I couldn't stop him," she finally said, trying not to stammer. "You said it yourself, it's not so easy to restrain a grown man."

"What the hell do you mean, you couldn't stop him?" Harry bellowed. "Where is Peter?"

The door opened and shut with a bang and Elise came storming in, a paper bag in one hand, her face like thunder.

"Quiet!" she hissed. "You don't raise your voice like that in this house, not if you don't want to be found."

Addy cowered as Harry stalked closer to her, his face inches from hers.

"What have you done?" he asked. "Where is Peter?"

"Get away from her!" Elise smacked the barrel of her rifle into Harry's shoulder, her paper bag of food discarded on the floor. "Back up," she ordered. "Now."

Harry skulked backward, and Elise slowly lowered the gun as he held up his hands.

"What's actually going on here?" Elise asked. "I leave for a few hours and I come home to an argument?"

"Ask your sister," Harry muttered.

"Adelaide?"

Adelaide gulped as tears started to spill down her cheeks. It had seemed so right at the time, what she'd done, what she'd chosen to do when she'd seen Peter in so much agony.

"Where's Peter?" Elise asked, her eyes widening as she stared at her and then around the room. "Where the hell is he, Addy? What's happened while I've been gone?"

"He was so insistent," she whispered, her back pressed against the wall now, her fingers frantically clawing the wallpaper. "I couldn't let him suffer like that, Elise, I just couldn't do it."

Elise set down her rifle and slowly sank into the sofa, head in her hands. "Tell me where he is so I can go get him," she said with a sigh. "Honestly, Adelaide, could you not make things easy for me, just this once?"

"You can't go and get him." Adelaide wiped at her cheeks, summoning her courage. "I fell asleep," she confessed. "I was sitting with him and watching him for so long, and the next thing I knew I woke up and he was gone."

"And then what happened?" Harry asked, his voice strained, *pained*, from across the room.

"I saw the front door was open, and I ran outside looking for him," Addy said. "He'd dragged himself all the way down the steps, and I followed the marks in the grass. I could see where he'd been. And then I found him crying, all alone, just lying there."

Harry seemed shocked at this, but her sister looked more disbelieving than anything.

"What happened then, Addy?" Elise asked.

She swallowed. "At the time it seemed like the right thing to do. He was so adamant that I help him, so I found a wheelbarrow and . . ."

"Oh Addy, what have you done?" Elise groaned.

"He begged me to take him, and I did," she admitted. "He knew what he wanted, Elise, and I wanted to keep him safe, I did, but all he wanted was to surrender so he could go home."

"Go home?" Harry thundered. "If by go home you mean receive a bullet through his head? You sent a lamb to slaughter, Adelaide. That's what you've done."

Elise didn't even seem to hear Harry, because her eyes never left Adelaide's. "You pushed a *wheelbarrow* containing a British soldier into a German camp?"

Adelaide looked at Harry and then back to her sister as the reality of what she'd done came crashing down around her. "It seemed like a good idea at the time," she whispered.

"A *good* idea?" Elise choked. "A good idea to hand a man over to the Nazis, not to mention put yourself in that kind of danger?"

"Elise, I'm sorry—"

"Are you a child in a woman's body?" Harry interrupted. "Of all the ridiculous, reckless, *stupid* goddamn things—"

"Enough!" Elise shouted. "You don't talk to my sister like that."

"Are you saying she's not a child?" Harry asked, shaking his head. "Because what she's done . . ."

"I'm sorry," Addy cried. "I'm so sorry but he begged me and I just couldn't keep saying no."

"I thought I could trust you," Elise said, shaking her head. "Adelaide, this has compromised us."

Addy shook her head, defiant, not ready to accept her sister's scolding. "It seemed like the right thing to do at the time. If you'd seen him, if you'd listened to him, truly listened to him—"

"Adelaide," Elise said, rising and reaching for her gun, putting it back on the table. "I did listen to him, and he wasn't capable of making that decision."

"And I can tell you right now," Harry said, tears shining in his eyes, "that you've just sent Peter to his death."

CHAPTER EIGHT

CATE

It had been harder than she'd thought to stay hidden. German soldiers were everywhere, and every voice whispering to her on the wind or sound of footfalls or vehicles had Cate's heart pounding and her teeth chattering. Darkness was their friend, though, and as the German army continued to force the British soldiers toward the beach at Dunkirk, the closer they got to Le Paradis, the easier it became—although Cate knew that the area was probably crawling with the enemy, which meant she could never relax, not even for a second. Every noise forced her to swallow away a tide of anxiety, and every time she felt a vibration through the ground, she thought of the buildings they'd seen reduced to rubble, some of them half-blown apart and exposed like the insides of doll houses. It was horrific.

"Do you think there's much further to go?" Cate whispered to Jack as they leaned against a tree to catch their breath. What she wanted to ask was how long he thought they could continue, because she was within an inch of collapse, which made her wonder how on earth he kept putting one foot in front of the other.

Her stomach growled; she hadn't eaten since Dunkirk, and she was beyond hungry.

"Not far," he said with a grunt.

Cate could hear the strain in his voice, and she inched closer to him. "How's your pain?"

"I'm fine."

Liar. She doubted very much that he was fine, but she chose to ignore it. For now, they had to keep moving; it was the only way they had a chance of survival. Cate had no idea how they'd managed to stay alive for so long. Under the cover of darkness, they'd managed to silently amble along, but now, as the sun was starting to lighten the sky again, she knew they had to find somewhere to keep themselves hidden.

"Jack, don't you think we should find somewhere to rest?" she asked. "I have no idea how far Le Paradis is, but we're moving so slowly and . . ." Fear laced her voice, and so she shut her mouth, not even sure what she was trying to say.

"Yes," he said, surprising her. "We need to find somewhere we can survive until nightfall again."

Cate's heart sank. Agreeing was one thing, but where would they go? They hadn't passed anywhere safe for hours, although it had been dark and they hadn't exactly been able to scan their surroundings, and with the exception of climbing a tree, she was out of ideas. Even if Jack managed to climb high enough with her, come daylight they'd easily be seen if anyone looked up, like ripe fruit waiting to be plucked. She shuddered at the thought. Where was another barn when they needed one?

"Where will we hide this time?" she asked, trying to disguise the shake in her voice.

Jack reached for her hand, his palm warm to hers as they shivered beneath the blanket together, still draped across their shoulders. "We keep moving until we find somewhere," he said. "Trust me."

She did trust him, but it wasn't helping her deep-seated fear. They started to walk again, and Cate found that her eyes were able to adjust more readily as the sky began to turn pink and give them the smallest amount of light to move by. But as welcome as that was, it also signaled how little time they had left to hide.

She looked around at the trees and bushes, seeing nothing that looked suitable, but then she heard a sound that put the fear of God himself inside her. Jack's hand shot out to stop her from moving.

"Get down," he ordered, and they both dropped low, crawling on their hands and knees. As she looked down, she caught sight of the criss-crosses of blood welded across her skin, and for a fleeting moment she wondered if there were tiny bits of glass stuck there from when they'd jumped out the window. She was so tired, and suddenly she became fixated on the glass she couldn't see, wanting to pick at her skin to remove it, to give her something else to focus on other than staying alive and surviving the gut-deep pain of starvation.

The familiar sound of gunfire made her ears prick, pulling her from her sleep-deprived thoughts, but it was the sound of a vehicle that jarred her the most.

"Could it be friendly?" she whispered to Jack, worried that she could see him too clearly now. It was far too light for them to be out in the open; they needed to be well-hidden already.

"It could be a dispatch driver, but more likely it's the Nazis," he said.

They kept crawling in the grass, heads down, although Cate secretly wondered if they were equally as obvious as they would have been walking, but she didn't say so. A voice in her head told her that crawling was as naïve as a baby covering its eyes with its chubby hands and expecting to be hidden from sight. When they came to a fence, Jack indicated for her to climb through, which she did, thankful for the long grass to obscure them at least slightly from view.

But there was no barn or farmhouse for them to seek sanctuary in, and her heart sank as she surveyed the land around them.

"There's a ditch down there," Jack said. "It might be the best we can get."

She nodded and followed him, her hands stinging from being used like feet on the ground, palms red-raw already from connecting over and over again with grass, stones and dirt. And her knees were numb as she focused on each movement, moving as quickly as she could despite her discomfort.

The shooting became more intense then, going from irregular pops to a constant barrage of shots, and she stared down into the ditch, her and Jack like two animals frozen in place, surveying the field.

The ditch may have been fine to hide in a day earlier, but the rain had turned it to mud, and there was at least an inch of water for them to sit in. But it would obscure them from view, and she knew that was the only thing that truly mattered. It was hide or die, and a little bit of mud wasn't going to kill them.

"I'm sorry," Jack muttered.

"Don't be, it's not your fault," she replied, trying not to sound too disheartened. "If it keeps us hidden, then it'll be worth the wet. I'll go first."

She shimmied down, the muck up to her ankles and squelching as she braced herself against the wet cold. As a nurse, she knew the repercussions of their decision; they could end up with horrible skin infections from their feet being submerged in mud all day, and Jack was terribly susceptible to infection, but she couldn't see they had any other option.

Jack tucked in beside her, moving closer, tentatively as if he wasn't sure of her reaction, but she did the same, pressing against him and holding out the blanket again. The edges of it were covered in mud now, but it was still their best bet at staying warm.

Rain started to fall again then, and they both huddled down lower, using the blanket as a shield from the wet like a tent canopy above them. Cate shut her eyes and prayed it wouldn't last long, as her teeth started a determined chatter that she had no chance of putting an end to.

She had the most overwhelming feeling that she was about to die, and no matter how hard she tried, she couldn't stop the tears that started to slide silently down her cheeks. Was this how Charlie had felt when he'd died? *If* he'd died and wasn't in fact missing all alone somewhere, or in a POW camp? Had he known it was coming, or had it happened with little or no warning? She squeezed her eyes tighter shut, wishing she'd known how it happened, *what* had happened, whether his death had been fast, or if he'd suffered. She knew there was a small chance he was still alive, although she'd long since given up hope. It had been months now since the letter.

"Goodbye, Charlie," Cate said, her lips whispering a kiss to his warm, smooth cheek.

"Not goodbye," he said, his arm warm around her, protective until the end. "See you soon."

He'd been superstitious about saying goodbye, hating the word and thinking it too final, yet she'd been so upset about him leaving that she'd said it anyway.

"Cate?"

She stared up into his dark-as-midnight eyes, his gaze so familiar and safe. "I'll be back, all right? You don't have to worry about me."

She leaned into him as he pressed a kiss to her forehead, their parents looking on. They'd been friends for years before it had turned into something more, and it was his friendship she would miss the most.

"But if I don't come home . . ." he said, holding her shoulders.

"Don't say that," she murmured back. "Don't you dare say that."

"If I die, I give you permission to fall in love with someone else. Do you hear me, Cate?"

She shook her head, but he caught her chin, his thumb soft as he looked into her eyes. But when he didn't look away, when he wouldn't back down, she finally nodded, the moment more intimate than she'd ever felt before with him.

"You're going to make a great nurse," he whispered. "All those fellas will recover just from you smiling down at them, I reckon."

His kiss was gentle, just the slowest, sweetest brush of his lips against hers before he took a step back and took off his hat, waving to everyone he was leaving behind. They'd hardly ever kissed, and although she'd expected a kiss goodbye, it still surprised her, and her fingers flew to her lips. Part of her thought of Charlie as more friend than anything else, someone who always kept her safe, but she cared deeply about him and couldn't ever imagine life without him in it.

And then he was gone, and she'd been left standing in the crowd, catching her breath as the plumes of smoke from the train rose and circled above them.

Cate sighed, still able to feel his lips on hers, still able to smell the smoke from the train and recall the beat of her heart as she'd wondered if she would ever see Charlie again. She might have accepted his words that day, but she'd never for a moment thought he'd leave her, that one day she'd have to think about what he'd said again. There had only been a few days between him leaving and her completing her nursing training, and the months since then had been a blur. Except for the day when time had stood still, when she'd been summoned to the matron's office soon after they'd arrived in Dunkirk. That day, every second had lasted an hour; every painful moment had cut so deep she'd wondered how she would ever survive it.

But war hardened a person, on the outside, anyway. War had taken so much from her; it had demanded her body and soul every single day, and it had broken her heart a hundred times over. Charlie had only been the beginning of her suffering; there had been so many losses, so much pain, so much trauma every single day since.

"Matron wants a word with you, in private."

Cate looked up from the bandage she was securing around a patient's forearm. "In private?" Had she done something wrong? Matron was so hard on all the girls, always insisting they adhere to the highest of standards, and Cate had thought she was doing so well.

"Would you mind finishing up for me here then?" Cate asked.

The other nurse nodded and Cate waited for her to take over before quickly going to wash her hands. She smoothed her hair down too, checking her pins were in place and her hat was positioned properly on her head. The last thing she needed was to be scolded for her appearance as well as her work.

Cate took a deep breath and squared her shoulders, hurrying to the matron's quarters.

"You asked to see me?" she called out, ducking her head in the open doorway.

"Yes, my dear, come in."

My dear? Matron never softened her words with kind phrases. Cate swallowed and walked to her desk.

"I'm sorry if I've—"

"Cate, you haven't done a thing. Please. Sit." Matron gestured at the spare seat and Cate sat, hands folded in her lap.

It was then she saw the piece of paper, folded in half, and Matron gently nudged it across the desk toward her.

"Cate, I'm so sorry to be the bearer of bad news, but you've just received a telegram. It's terrible news about your fiancé."

A small cry escaped her lips as she reached for it, hands trembling. Her fingers fumbled as she opened it, eyes scanning the page frantically, and then reading it over and over again. It was from Charlie's mother.

Charlie was missing in action, presumed dead.

Tears filled her eyes as Matron rose and came to comfort her, arms cocooning her, shushing her as she might a child as Cate cried.

"He went missing in the line of duty, a hero until the very end," Matron murmured. "We will all pray for you tonight, my dear girl. I'll send one of your friends to spend the rest of the evening with you, and of course Lilly has been notified too."

Cate composed herself, the words from the telegram running on repeat over and over in her mind. He'd been missing for more than a week, presumed dead only weeks after being deployed. The day they'd arrived in Dunkirk, full of smiles, eating lunch in the sun, he'd probably already been killed. The one person who'd understood her, who'd seen what her life had been like after her father's death, had known how damaged she could be sometimes.

All this time she'd been thinking about him, wondering where he was, whether he was looking up at the same star-filled night as her, and he'd most likely been gone.

She pulled herself from her memories and glanced over at Jack, his eyes shut, his full lips slightly parted as he shielded beneath the blanket alongside her. Jack had made her smile from the day he'd regained consciousness on her watch, and despite everything he'd been through, there had been a lightness within him, something that had given her hope all over again. After weeks and months of doing her job because it was her duty, routinely going through the motions with a numbness deep inside her, Jack had brought her back to life without even knowing it, his presence making her feel again. Which was why she'd never have fled the hospital that day without him. If he hadn't agreed to come with her, she'd have been taken along with everyone else; she knew that as clearly as she knew her own name.

But now the man she'd have done anything to save was chattering and shaking from the cold, and as the sky continued to lighten, she realized that his shirt was covered in blood. A deep dark red stain that was spreading across the fabric right before her eyes.

Panic rose within her, its tentacles spreading through her body as she stared at his abdomen, knowing how serious his bleeding could be. If she didn't help Jack soon . . . A cold chill settled over her as she steeled her jaw and fought the tears that threatened to spill. He could be dead by nightfall, and then she'd be alone, in a country she barely knew.

Gunfire echoed close by, followed by the roar of what she supposed could be a tank. It was one hell of a time to be surrounded by the enemy in the middle of a bloody battle.

"I have a feeling I walked us straight into the worst of it," Jack said. He must have seen her horrified stare because he looked down, one of his hands slowly reaching up to touch his stomach. His palm fluttered first, as if he wasn't sure whether to touch himself or not, and she reached for him, pressing it there for him.

"Jack . . ." she started.

When he looked up, he gave her the smallest smile, their eyes meeting. "You should have left me behind. I'm only going to slow you down."

"If I didn't have you, I would still be hiding under that ambulance, if I'd even left the chateau at all," she told him, as the rain began to fall even harder, starting to soak through their blanket. Her uniform was drenched and she suddenly had the most terrible feeling that she'd be recognized wherever she went because of it. There was no possible way she was going to be able to pretend she was a French woman if they were found. *Was there?*

Jack's face had lost its smile, his eyes full of sorrow now, and she wished there was something she could do to bring his spark back. It was why she'd been so drawn to him in the first place, because there was something about him that always pulled her from the darkness of her thoughts. Without it, the doubts would seep in and paralyze her with fear.

"Come on, let's figure out how to stop this bleeding," she said, trying to sound bright and wishing she had hot water, bandages and food on hand, and knowing it could be days before they might have any of those things. "Hold the blanket high for both of us for a moment."

Rain soaked through her back as she tended to him, but she ignored it, even as it trickled right through to her undergarments. She should have been checking his wound regularly through the night, but instead they'd kept pushing on and Jack's condition had deteriorated rapidly.

Despite how cold she was, Cate broke out in a sweat as she examined him, her face suddenly burning hot as the seriousness of his wounds became apparent all over again.

"It's not good, is it?" he whispered, lowering the blanket, his arms shaking from exertion.

Cate glanced up at him, not saying a word because she couldn't lie to him.

"We either need to sacrifice a piece of clothing or rip off some of the blanket," she said, trying to wear her nurse's hat and forget about any emotional attachment she had to him. *Focus on the wound, just focus on the wound.* "I need to do something quickly before you lose any more blood." She was also deeply worried about hypothermia, given how fragile he was.

"Take my shirt," he said.

Cate cringed as she looked at his abdomen. She touched her fingers to the edge of his incision line, worried that so many of the stitches had come loose. She knew how quickly infection could set in, and the worst-case scenario was that he'd need surgery again. That would mean certain death for him.

"I could use part of my dress," she suggested. "I don't want you being any more exposed than you need to be. I have to keep you warm."

Jack grunted. "You need your clothes. You can't go looking for somewhere safer for us without them."

She pressed her hand over his stomach as blood started to seep out again, the warm moistness against her skin so overwhelming she didn't know what to do. She needed a hospital and proper medical supplies! Cate's breath came shuddering out of her just as Jack's head dropped. He was leaning back against the side of the ditch now, but he bent and touched his wet forehead to hers.

"What are you scared of?"

"Losing you." She blurted it out, wishing she could take it back the moment the words left her lips. *I can't lose someone else, Jack, I just can't.*

"Dying here with you sounds a lot better than taking a German bullet, so don't sweat it." She knew he was trying to sound jovial, but he couldn't disguise the painful grunt that accompanied his words.

"Don't sweat it?" Cate laughed, trying not to cry. She punched his arm. "Trust you to crack a joke at the most inappropriate time!"

They sat quietly for a moment longer, as Cate ran through a hundred different scenarios in her head. She had to be strong; she was their only hope now, and Jack was leading her to an area he thought was friendly, so it was up to her.

"Let's take your trousers off," she said brusquely, hoping he had underpants on.

"Aren't you going to at least take me out to dinner first?"

Her hand covered her mouth as she gulped back a laugh. "How are you joking at a time like this!" she scolded. The poor man must have been in a world of pain, but still he managed to make her smile.

"In all seriousness, I don't think that's the best idea."

She blushed but refused to acknowledge it, even as he chuckled. Clearly there were no underpants.

"Your shirt then," she said. "Let's take it off and I'll use it to tie around your stomach to stop the bleeding."

She took over holding the blanket above them, thankful that the rain had eased to more of a drizzle. She watched as he lifted his arms, saw the pain in his face and wished she had something to give him. Even just the smallest amount of morphine would have done so much to ease his suffering. His shoulders and chest were muscular, and she realized then how different he was from her Charlie. Where Charlie was white as snow and skinny, Jack was more tanned and had a build that told of physical work perhaps, and he had a sprinkling of dark hair arrowed down his chest. In fact, she wasn't sure she'd ever even *had* such an eyeful of Charlie's body in all the years she'd known him!

Cate shook her thoughts away, not wanting to start dwelling on Charlie as well as worrying about her growing feelings for Jack. Instead she took the shirt from him and used one sleeve to wipe around the wound. It was impossible, though; she couldn't clear the blood or mud completely, and her fears about infection trebled.

"This is going to hurt a little, but I have to tie it firmly," she explained, reaching to secure it around his back.

He let out a hiss. "It's fine. I've felt worse."

Once she was as happy as she could be with it, she leant against him, drawing the blanket around her other shoulder.

"What do we do now?" she asked, as gunfire started to boom even closer to them. She looked at Jack and saw that his eyes were shut, his pain making his face look so strained and tired.

"We wait until nightfall," he murmured. "Then you go for help."

Cate reached for his hand, linking their fingers as she closed her eyes. *If he even makes it until tonight.*

"I've never been so hungry in all my life," she whispered.

"I'll teach you a little soldier trick," he said, his eyes opening halfway, lids hooded as he watched her. "Here, pretend this is a can of beans."

She frowned, but reached out anyway for the imaginary beans. "You actually do this?"

She shouldn't have asked; it was obvious he wasn't joking. "Once we found one can of baked beans for our entire unit, and when we shared them out, there were three beans each."

"You truly had so little food at times?" she asked.

"We used to sit together, delirious with hunger sometimes, and pretend we were eating steak and mashed potato," he said. "It sounds strange, but it can make a desperate man feel better."

And so Cate sat, crouched in mud that was making her lose the feeling in her toes, using a pretend knife and fork, eating pretend beans and potatoes. Tears spilled then, dropping in plops down Jack's cheeks and spilling fast down hers as she chewed her imaginary dinner and wondered if, real or not, it could be her last.

Cate touched her palm to Jack's cheek. He was cold and clammy, and although she wasn't surprised by the damp or the cold, given the conditions, she was worried about how long he'd been sleeping.

"Jack," she said, giving him a gentle shake. "Jack, wake up."

He grunted, but didn't open his eyes. She pushed his shoulder more forcibly this time.

"Jack! Come on, wake up."

His eyes opened a slither then, and she breathed a sigh of relief. "I'm so tired."

"I know." She crouched down low, cringing at the mud squelching around her ankles. "It's getting dark again, we've been here all day."

They'd both managed to fall asleep after their pretend feast, her far more fitfully than Jack, who'd as good as been knocked out cold the past few hours—she'd checked him every time she'd stirred. The ground rumbling at times had woken her, as had yells and almost constant gunfire that came and went with varying intensity, but she'd still managed to rest. It was a miracle they'd survived so long, and she was determined to keep things that way.

"You look," he said, grunting as he tried to move, "pretty."

"Pretty?" She shook her head. "Trust you to say something nice even when you're at death's door." But she shyly pushed her damp hair from her face anyway, blushing at the unexpected compliment.

"Death's door?" He chuckled then coughed, shaking his head when she reached for him. "I'm alive and kicking, Cate. I'll be just fine."

She seriously doubted it, but she wasn't about to say that. Instead she wrapped the blanket around him, tucking him in tight and hoping she was doing the right thing in leaving him. He was alive, and that was all that mattered to her.

"Should you come with me?" she asked.

"No." His breathing was raspy now, wheezing in and out, all pretenses gone. "Patrols could be anywhere."

"I'll come back for you, Jack. I didn't leave you back at the hospital, and I'm not about to leave you now."

She went to stand then, but Jack caught her hand, stopping her. He pressed the warmest kiss to the inside of her wrist, and she shut her eyes, basking in their brief connection. She would have curled up to him and left the world behind if she could.

"Take the blanket," he said.

"The blanket? No, I can't leave you here with nothing! You don't even have a shirt on!" She sighed.

"And you," he murmured, coughing again, "are wearing a British nursing uniform. You need to wrap yourself in this blanket so no one recognizes you for who you are."

Cate stared down at her clothes, then at him, knowing he was right. She reluctantly took it from him, hating that he was forced to wrap his arms around himself, his shoulders bare and exposed. Part of her thought he'd be dead by the time she returned, which made her think she'd rather give up than be alone in the midst of enemy territory. But she owed it to him, and to herself, to at least try to find help.

"I'll see you soon," she said, gritting her teeth to stop herself crying.

She turned away from him, unable to bear another glimpse of his pained face or shivering, half-naked body. Cate clambered out of the ditch, nails digging into the dirt as she dragged herself up and back into the field. It wouldn't be completely dark for a while longer, but dusk had fallen and it seemed deceptively safer.

Cate focused on putting one foot in front of another, her ears pricked, jumping at every sound, eyes darting back and forth, certain she was about to walk into some sort of ambush or straight-out warfare.

Home, she told herself. *Think of home.* And she did. With every tentative step, she imagined her mother's arms around her, imagined her eldest brother sitting in the coveted chair closest to the fire, smoking his pipe. She remembered hot cups of tea and laughing as she did the washing, chasing her brothers, them shooing her away when she tried to climb trees after them and keep up with their friends as they adventured around the neighborhood as kids. All of it, from childhood to becoming a young woman ready to leave home, came crashing back to her, wave after wave, and the memories settled around her like a warm embrace. And as the long minutes passed, so did the worst of her fears, and she started to relax just a little.

The only thing she still hadn't figured out was what she was going to say if she was stopped. Why would a woman be out on a wet evening on her own, with only a blanket for protection? What reason would she give for being in the countryside as a war raged on nearby?

She was mulling her options over when something rustled. Cate started to walk faster, hoping to leave the noise behind. It could easily be an animal, she reasoned, ears straining now for any noise at all.

The rustle was louder this time, and she wished the moon would rise bright in the sky to illuminate the path ahead better. And then she heard the fall of boots, heavy footfalls, and as she spun to see which way she could run, she froze.

"Halt!"

Cate's heart thudded all the way down to her toes. The thickly accented word rooted her to the spot. This was it. This was her last breath, her last moment, her last chance to do the right thing.

Run. The word was like a bullet being shot through her mind. *Run.*

No. If I run, they'll shoot me.

Cate inhaled deeply through her nostrils, gripping the blanket tighter around herself as her internal argument raged. She could see one faint light up ahead, a house, and she guessed there would be more.

She'd been so, so close.

The voice spoke again, but it was the glowing tip of a cigarette that caught her attention the most, followed by the sound of boots scraping that revealed two more soldiers. German soldiers.

She'd walked straight into an ambush, most likely in place to catch British soldiers, not a girl on her own.

"What are you doing out here?" barked the first voice.

She tried not to quiver as he moved in front of her, another soldier moving behind her. They were close, so close she could taste the tobacco smoke rising off their cigarettes, could smell the damp of their uniforms. Cate could almost feel their hands on her, could sense their intention: a woman out on her own in the woods at night, after dark, was surely an easy target. She gulped. Would anyone even hear her if she screamed?

"He said," the soldier behind her muttered with a snigger, "what are you doing out here?"

Cate hugged herself tighter, terrified of their words, of their hands, of their weapons. Of their sense of smugness at being three men against one defenseless woman.

"I'm looking for my dog," she said in near-perfect French, fighting the tremble in her voice and jutting her chin high as she looked one of them in the eyes. "Have you seen him?"

CHAPTER NINE

CATE

"Your dog?" It was asked with another snigger, with an arrogance that she wished she could smack away with her palm.

Cate had never been so frightened in her life. She nodded, giving the scowling German her sweetest smile. She could only imagine how wet and bedraggled she appeared, but at least it had started to rain again and it wasn't completely beyond the bounds of possibility that she could have become so disheveled searching for a beloved dog. She gulped. A dog that didn't exist, which would be a problem if they decided to help her look, although she doubted that was going to happen. She wiggled her still-squelching toes, the mud caked into her shoes.

"I've been searching for so long," she replied, forcing tears that were easy to conjure, given the circumstances. "I was so worried, with the fighting so close, and I haven't been able to find him."

The soldier snorted and puffed on his cigarette before blowing smoke into her face. Her eyes watered as she tried not to cough, not wanting to give him the satisfaction even as the smoke curled around her skin.

"Your dog, eh?"

Cate fought the tremble that threatened to shake her body as she eyed the gun at his side. She glanced sideways, frantically searching for a way to escape, but there was none. Even if she dropped the blanket so she could run faster, where would she go? They could have dogs nearby for all she knew, dogs who would sniff her out and rip her to pieces if the soldiers didn't shoot her first, a bullet piercing her back or entering the back of her skull. It would be a death sentence for Jack, too, if she was gone.

They moved closer to her, trapping her all the more tightly between them. The one with the cigarette lifted his hand and put his thumb beneath her chin, forcing it to jut upwards as he inspected her face. Cate clutched the blanket tighter between her fingers, clenching her toes as she forced her feet to stay still. She wouldn't show them how afraid she was, just as she wouldn't spit in their faces even though she'd never wanted to do something so badly in all her life.

"I don't think you have a dog," he sneered.

She forced her eyes up, staring back at him, not hesitating. "Why else would I be out in the cold, sir?"

The soldier behind her laughed. "Maybe you were out looking for some company, eh?"

Cate felt fingers against her hair and she bit back a scream, but she was saved by heavy footfalls that echoed out of the darkness from the woods. She strained her eyes to see, her stomach sinking as she realized it was another soldier, and when he stepped out of the dark shadows, her blood ran cold. He was clearly superior to the other three, even the way he held himself, his posture as commanding as his stare. Was that the SS symbol on his hat? If she'd thought the first three were bad, then he was probably pure evil.

I need to get them further away from Jack, she thought in a panic. *I need to put more distance between us.*

She'd been walking for some time, but still, if they were moving in the direction she'd come from, they could end up finding him, and with more soldiers arriving . . . She knew there was a chance she was starting to lose her mind, delirious from so long without food and water, not to mention the sheer terror she'd experienced, but she still needed to lead them as far away as possible. Maybe he'd manage to crawl to a farmhouse if she didn't come back?

The new soldier spoke in German, and although she knew a little of the language, she couldn't make out what they were saying; they were speaking too fast. Although she did make out the word *dog* and perhaps *stop*.

He stepped closer as the other soldiers backed away, and she had the sudden feeling that they'd been less of a threat together than he was alone. Just looking into his eyes, seeing his calm, self-assured arrogance at being superior to the other men, and being superior to *her*, terrified her. She knew instinctively that he was a man she'd never be able to escape from.

"You're missing your dog?" he asked.

Cate nodded and forced a smile. "Yes, I am. He's been missing for some time and I've been out looking."

"Where is your house?" he asked, his head tilted to the side ever so slightly as he considered her, as if he were trying to figure out whether she was lying or not.

Cate inclined with her head rather than pointing, not wanting to lift the blanket from her body. If he saw so much as a glimpse of her uniform, if he suspected her for even a second, if . . . She stood straighter, refusing to start panicking now. Just like she'd pretended to eat beans with Jack, she was going to pretend she was a French woman searching for her dog.

"The first house there," she said, the lie falling from her tongue so easily she surprised herself.

She hadn't been expecting a smile in return, but a smile was exactly what she received. Something about his demeanor changed, and her immense fear of him slowly fell away as his eyes softened.

He said something to his men in German, and then waved them away, leaving the two of them alone.

Cate gulped. Was he staying with her? She liked the way he'd seemingly reprimanded his men, but the way he'd suddenly decided to accompany her wasn't what she'd been expecting. Had she chosen the wrong house? Was there something he knew that she didn't? Suddenly her fear grew and she knew how naïve she'd been to relax around him for even a second.

"I, ah, I can walk back alone," she said. "I don't want to trouble you."

"Not at all." His French was perfect as far as she could tell, and she hadn't expected a German officer to be so eloquently bilingual. "But I'm sorry to say I haven't seen a dog. I hope he comes home to you, but it's not safe for you to be out here looking for him. You shouldn't go out in the dark again."

He's playing with me. He wants to go to this house, and I'm not going to know why until it's too late. Cate fought to keep her head high as they walked together, keeping as much distance between them as she could without showing how fearful she was of him. There was something about him; he was so handsome, but despite his friendliness, he was as cold as ice. His good looks were chiseled and his height was intimidating, especially in such a well-fitted uniform jacket that showed off his broad shoulders, but it was his calm, precise way of talking, as if nothing could ever scare him, that upset her the most. Perhaps it was her overactive imagination, but she could almost sense what he was capable of, and it terrified her. And she had a feeling he was toying with her, the way he'd feigned interest in her missing dog.

They walked the rest of the way in silence until they reached the house, and she glanced at him as he stopped.

"Thank you for your kindness," she said, half-turning, waiting for him to leave. "I'm fine from here."

But he didn't go. He waited, smiling still, and she knew then that he wanted to see for himself. *He doesn't believe that this is my house.*

Cate's knees knocked; she couldn't stand in the drizzling rain any longer, playing this dangerous game. Her fate would be sealed by whoever opened the door, and she knew then that he was capable of killing as quickly as he could squash an insect beneath his boot.

She walked up the two steps and knocked, realizing as she did so that if it were her home, she wouldn't have to knock. She would have walked straight in.

The German cleared his throat behind her, and she knocked again, louder this time, her knuckles stinging. Had he realized that? Was he about to level his gun at her for making such an obvious mistake? But now that she'd knocked, she had to stick with it, didn't she?

This time she heard feet padding on timber from inside, and as the door swung open, she was greeted by a pretty blonde, her brown eyes wide as she stared back at her, followed by a loud yap as the smallest, scruffiest dog she'd ever seen came flying between the blonde's legs.

"Oscar!" the woman scolded, at the same time as Cate took her chance to scoop the unsuspecting canine into her arms and shower him with kisses.

"Darling! There you are!" she cooed, almost using English and giving herself away. "I can't believe you came home on your own! I've been looking everywhere for you!"

"I see your dog was home all along," came a deep voice from behind her.

But as she turned, stepping slightly away from the door, the soldier appeared decidedly less interested in her. His eyes were trained on the other woman who'd answered the door, all the silent menace of before disappearing without a trace as his smile reached all the way to his eyes.

"Miss DuPont," he said, taking a step forward. "We meet again after all."

Cate studied the other woman, taking in the upturn of her mouth but not missing the tense way she clasped her hands behind her back, knuckles interlaced.

"So we do," the woman replied, an obvious waver in her voice. This woman was understandably scared of him too, just as she'd been, but how were they already acquainted? Was this woman a German sympathizer? "What brings you here tonight?"

Cate cuddled the small dog closer to her, burying her mouth against his soft fur and wishing she could scream.

"This is your sister?" he asked.

"Cousin," Cate interrupted, lifting her lips from the dog. "I am her cousin."

To her credit, the other woman didn't miss a beat. She didn't so much as glance sideways at her, when she could have given her away as a fraud within seconds, but she did smile and nod. Cate had taken a risk in trusting her, but it had paid off in spades.

"Your cousin?" he repeated.

"She is. Thank you for escorting her home."

Cate moved beside her, heart racing, the warmth of the home at her back beckoning her in, making her long to curl up beside the fire. But this was only the first hurdle; the minute she was safe, she had to find a way to go back for Jack. To brave soldier-infested territory again and somehow smuggle Jack to safety, whatever that might look like.

"May I call again to see you?" the soldier asked.

Cate watched the tremble in the woman's top lip, and she reached for her hand, standing in solidarity with a stranger as they both faced the enemy. She knew then that he was interested in the woman, and that the feeling was most likely not reciprocated; but he hadn't seemed to notice, or if he had, it certainly wasn't putting him off.

"Yes, Wolfgang, you may," the woman replied with so much warmth Cate wondered if she'd been wrong in her assumption.

How did the woman know his name? Cate's hand fell away, as if she'd been slapped, terror rising inside her for a moment, wondering what kind of situation she'd stumbled into. Was this a friendly house or not? Were they simply playing a cat and mouse game with her? Or was this woman just a tremendous actress?

But as Wolfgang smiled, waved, and finally turned to go, disappearing into the darkness, the other woman's sigh of relief calmed Cate's nerves.

"I'm Adelaide," she whispered, once he'd gone.

"Cate," she replied, passing her the dog she'd been holding under her arm. "Thank you for going along with my story, you saved me there."

"You're playing with fire, lying to the Nazis." Adelaide pushed open the door with her elbow. "I suppose you'd better come inside."

But as they turned, into the warmth, into the type of house that reminded Cate of home, as the door closed behind them, a voice in the dark stopped her in her tracks.

"Oh Adelaide, what have you done?"

The words fell from the shadows, from a woman not quite as beautiful as the other, even though it was clear they were sisters; only this one was pointing a gun at her. And she knew then that if the other woman had opened the door, she may not have readily accepted the lie.

Perhaps this house wasn't to be her refuge after all.

CHAPTER TEN

ELISE

This can't be happening. Elise stared at the bedraggled-looking woman standing in her doorway, hair plastered to her head and clinging to her forehead, and a soaking wet blanket clutched around her shoulders.

"Elise, this is Cate," Adelaide said quietly, her eyes downcast.

"So I heard," Elise muttered.

Cate stood and blinked back at her like a lost child, and even though Elise could see her shaking with cold, her cheeks so white they looked like they'd been touched by ice, she still didn't move. She should have opened her arms and her heart to her, taken her in by the fire and made hot coffee for her, but instead her feet stayed rooted to the spot.

We can't take someone else in. I cannot have another fugitive in my home!

She prayed that Harry wouldn't make a noise. They didn't know who Cate was or why she'd suddenly ended up in their home; for all they knew, she could be a Nazi sympathizer despite the scene on the porch. Did this have something to do with Addy helping Peter? Had someone suspected they could be hiding something or some*one* else? Elise had never been so openly suspicious of people, but something had changed within her since the war began and their family had been reduced to two, and no matter how hard she tried, she couldn't stamp it out.

Adelaide put her arm around Cate's shoulders then, ever-nurturing, and Elise hastily set down her gun. She'd been holding it since the knock at the door, ready to defend them if she needed to, and once again she'd sent her sister to answer it. Thank goodness she had—the German commander certainly seemed to like Adelaide, and he'd been too busy smiling at her to bother checking their home.

"Where have you come from?" Elise finally asked. "Why are you here?"

"Elise!" Adelaide scolded. "Be nice, she's not exactly the enemy."

Elise glared at her sister, her nostrils flaring out as anger pulsed within her. "She's a stranger to us, who's turned up on our doorstep at nightfall in the rain, so no, I will not just be nice. I want to know who she is and why she's here."

Adelaide glared back at her, but she didn't argue. Cate stepped forward, though, slowly opening the blanket she'd been keeping so tightly clutched around her body.

Elise automatically reached for the rifle, but the sadness in Cate's eyes, the way she dropped the blanket, made her stop. This woman didn't have a weapon; she was trying to show them who she was.

"You're—" Elise started.

"A nurse, with the British army," Cate interrupted. "Everyone else was taken, except for me. I'm no threat to you, I promise."

Elise was lost for words, studying the woman's filthy uniform and then her face, trying to tell if she was lying, but she instinctively knew it had to be the truth. The British army had abandoned her? Her heart danced all the way to her stomach and back as reality struck her: there would be no easy defeat of the German forces by the French and British. It was surely as good as over if this were the case.

"Go on," she urged, trying to quell the rising unease within her.

Cate's lips parted, but they were dry and still chattering. There was fear shining in her eyes, and Elise immediately regretted how cold she'd been toward her.

"Adelaide, get her some water," Elise said, not taking her eyes from Cate's face. "And something to eat."

"I can't stay, I have to get back to Jack," Cate said, sounding panicked. "I left him, but he'll die if I don't—"

"Who's Jack?"

Cate looked like she was about to faint, and Elise stepped forward to take her elbow, walking her across the room and forcibly pushing her down into a chair by the fire. She crouched beside her, wondering if the nurse was about to go into complete shock. Elise kept hold of her hand, warming it between her two palms.

"You need to tell me everything so I can help you," she said quietly. "Who's Jack?"

Cate looked back at her as if she suddenly didn't want to tell, as if she were suddenly unsure who she could trust. But when Adelaide returned with the water, holding the cup for her as she greedily gulped it down, she seemed to calm. As they waited, Adelaide standing worriedly by the fire and Elise still crouching, the color slowly returned to Cate's cheeks.

"All the British soldiers are being evacuated from Dunkirk," Cate said, her voice so low that Elise had to concentrate hard to hear her. "We were the last remaining hospital, and we had so many patients being brought in. We were the only ones left to help them, but they were doomed anyway, whether we saved them or not."

"All the British soldiers are leaving?" Elise asked, not sure she'd heard her right. "You're certain? We've lost the war?" Harry had mentioned the evacuation, but she'd found it hard to believe, and she certainly hadn't comprehended the scale of it.

Cate nodded, rocking as she wound her arms around herself. "Yes, they're all leaving, if they can make it out of here," she said. "And the Germans came for us all, they were relentless, but I managed to escape as they took everyone else. All the doctors, the orderlies, and some of the patients." She let out a shallow sob. "I don't know if we've lost the war completely, but it definitely feels that way."

"They didn't kill them?" Adelaide asked, her voice softer than her sister's, pushing between them. "The doctors and the patients, they didn't just kill them?"

Elise frowned at her sister, but Addy didn't seem to notice the reprimand.

"No, they didn't kill them. They loaded them all in a big lorry and they just disappeared."

"And who is this Jack to you? A doctor?" Elise asked. "Why is it so imperative that we return for him? Are you sure he's even alive still?"

Cate was staring into the fire now, arms unwrapped, flexing her fingers as if the feeling were slowly coming back into them.

"Jack, well," she started, shivering now, "he was a patient of mine. I couldn't escape without him, and he's the one who wanted to come here. When I left him, he was still very much alive."

Elise rocked back on her haunches, studying Cate, deciding to trust her words and believe her story. She had no reason not to, and there was no way she could be faking the pain in her eyes. It was reflected in every part of her, that she'd been through trauma, and protective or not, Elise had a heart. She couldn't turn her back.

"Where is he? Where did you leave him?" Elise asked.

Cate slowly turned back to her, as if she were coming out of a trance, lost in her memories perhaps. "We traveled on foot from the hospital because he told me we'd find help here, that it was a friendly village," she said. "We got so close, but then daylight came and we had to hide. I left him in a ditch and then I started to walk, for maybe half an hour, maybe an hour, but—"

As Cate started to cry, Elise stood and gestured for Adelaide to comfort her. She needed to think, and as she paced the small room, all she could think about was how much the past twenty-four hours had changed everything for her. Up until then, all she'd had to focus on was keeping her and her sister fed and safe, keeping them out of harm's way. And now she was faced with hiding two British soldiers in her home, along with a British nurse, with no hope of ever getting them home if Cate was right about the British army fleeing France. In the end, harm seemed to have found them anyway.

Which gave her two options: she could either open her heart and home and try to find this missing soldier with Cate, regardless of the risks, or she could refuse and prioritize her own little family. Which would mean turning Cate away and closing their door to her, or telling her to stay, but on their terms.

"Are you sure you'll be all right?"

Elise had never seen her brother so serious. His face, with the corner of his mouth usually upturned in a smile and eyes shining, held none of his usual humor, and as easy as it would have been to tease him for it, instead she took his hand into hers.

"I'm going to be fine," she said. "We're all going to be fine."

He was silent, eyes searching her face. "It's always been the two of us against the world," he said. "I can't imagine life going on here with me gone."

She wanted to tell him not to go, that they'd find a way for him to stay, but she knew that wasn't true. He had to go. Their father wouldn't hear of him staying, and their country needed him.

"You'll look after Mama and Addy, won't you?" he said. "Keep her well out of harm's way, you know what she's like."

They both laughed, but it was Louis who spoke again before she had the chance.

"Do you remember that day she came home with Oscar?" he asked.

"How could I forget?"

"Mama was furious when she brought him into the kitchen, all wet and bedraggled, and declaring those fleas falling off him were the plumpest she'd ever seen."

Elise laughed. "I remember Mama running around the kitchen swatting at the floor, she was beside herself!"

Louis's smile faded again then, and she squeezed his fingers as the memories faded, too.

"I worry that she'd bring anything home with a broken wing or a grazed knee," he said.

Elise stared into his eyes. "Or an injured German. Is that what you mean?"

He swallowed. He didn't need to nod, because she knew. "That girl is as sweet and kind as they come, but she's also as naïve as a child sometimes."

Elise drew her brother in for a hug, arms wrapped tightly around him. "I'll keep her safe while you're gone, Louis. Don't you worry."

He hugged her back, chin to the top of her as she pressed tight to his broad chest.

"Just make it home," she whispered. "I'll keep everyone safe until you get back."

"Elise," Adelaide whispered to her from behind, her hand closing over her shoulder as she leaned in close to her.

Elise wanted to pull away, her memories twisting with the decision she was facing, knowing that her sister would automatically be on the side of helping anyone, no matter who they were. But she didn't. Instead she reached for Addy's fingers and held on to her for a moment, still thinking, still remembering, still trying to decide what to do. What would her mother have done, or her father?

What would her brother have urged her to do, if he'd survived? Would Louis have thought she was being soft in siding with Addy, or after what he'd seen during the war would he have wanted to help any Allied soldier?

"We have to help her," Addy implored.

"No matter what the risks?" Elise asked, choking back unexpected emotion as she felt Louis's hand in hers, remembering his strength. She angrily swallowed it down, clenching her fists, not used to it and not liking the wash of vulnerability that came with it as the past merged with the present in her mind.

"Elise, I don't see what other choice we have," Adelaide murmured. "I've already told the Nazi captain that she's my cousin, so we can't exactly turn her out in the cold now, can we? And she's never going to leave her Jack behind."

Elise's shoulders were heavy as she slowly turned around. Adelaide was right. And deep down, she knew what needed to be done; she just needed to be brave enough to do it.

"Can you find your way back to him?" Elise asked Cate.

"Yes, I can find him." Cate's voice wobbled, but Elise didn't doubt her.

Elise couldn't believe what she was about to say, but she knew it was the only decision she could make. Or at least the only decision she could live with. "Well, let's get you into some dry clothes and go find him then," she said. "We need to do it in the dark, and we need to do it fast."

"You're going too?" Adelaide asked incredulously.

"Yes," Elise said firmly. "I'm going with Cate, and you're staying here in case your *admirer* comes calling again. At least you can keep him distracted if he does."

She ignored the immediate blush that ignited her sister's cheeks, praying that she wasn't foolhardy enough to actually fall for the charms of a German soldier, albeit an extremely handsome one. Right now it felt like saving soldiers was the riskiest thing she could do, but being entangled with a Nazi? That was a cat-and-mouse game she was not going to allow her sister to entertain, no matter the consequences.

"You're certain it's this way?"

Less than an hour later, Cate's teeth were no longer chattering; she was dressed properly in Elise's clothes and with a warm jacket on, and they were walking side by side, shoulders brushing. It was strange to be so close to a stranger, especially after being with just Adelaide for so long. As the war had raged on, and the situation had become more dangerous, any of their neighbors who could move away had done so, at least for the short term, and Elise and her sister had retreated and kept largely to themselves. So to find herself rubbing shoulders with someone who wasn't her sister was unusual at best. But in the dark and with the constant fear of a gunshot piercing the night air, it was beyond unusual; it was unbelievable.

Elise's ears were pricked as they walked, listening for the smallest of sounds, certain they were going to encounter a German patrol or unwittingly be caught in the crosshairs somewhere, but so far they'd managed to move undetected. What possible excuse they could come up with if they encountered the same patrol Cate had met earlier, though, she had no idea. But what she did know was that they were playing with fire; a patrol had been close enough to flush Cate out in the first place, which meant it was highly likely they could bump into them again. The Nazis might be out looking for Allied soldiers, but she didn't want to come across any.

"I'm sorry," Cate whispered.

"What for?" Elise whispered back.

"For risking your family," she whispered. "For forcing you to take me in. I should never have put that burden on you."

Elise sighed, instinctively touching Cate's shoulder, feeling her brother's palm settling over her, telling her everything was going to work out for the best. "Let's just find your soldier and we can talk later. The quicker we make it back home, the better."

She just wanted to be with her sister, to know that at least they were as safe as they could be in their home, hidden away from the world, hunkered down. At least at home they could speak freely and try to work out a plan for what they were going to do.

"He's over here, I think," Cate said.

They had a small flashlight, but Elise was loath to use it unless they absolutely had to. It was the one thing that would immediately give them away in the dark, but they weren't going to find this Jack if they didn't use it. She wished they could rely on her senses, like when she'd been a little girl out hunting with her father. He'd loved to blindfold her and Louis, making them use their ears and their noses, telling them that one day they'd appreciate how well they could focus on their surroundings. She was certain he'd meant in case she ever wanted to hunt when she was older, not that she'd one day be skulking in the shadows, fearing for her own life, in a part of France her family had called home for generations. And with Louis but a ghost haunting her memories.

"You're certain he's this way?" she asked.

"I'm certain. I didn't travel far before they found me."

Cate had the flashlight low to the ground, and Elise had to move quickly to keep up with her. She was wearing a spare coat and Cate was wearing a shirt, both of which had belonged to Elise's brother. She hated to lend anyone her brother's clothing; she'd kept everything as he'd left it, but she knew he'd want someone in need to have it instead of leaving it hanging and gathering dust.

"He's through here," Cate said, and Elise could hear the haste in her voice, didn't doubt that the other woman was right.

She knew this land, had walked past it countless times, but after ducking through countless fences and crossing meadows, it could have been anywhere on earth. Suddenly Cate left her side and Elise rushed to keep up with her, tripping as she almost fell straight into the ditch that stretched across the field. Cate had already dropped low, on her haunches now, and Elise did the same, not wanting to twist an ankle as she scrambled on the slippery grass that made way for dirt. No wonder Cate's uniform had been so thickly caked with mud.

"He's here!" Cate cried out as she disappeared into the ditch, and Elise followed, the flashlight creating a small pool of brightness around the nurse. She was huddled over a body, the man's bare shoulders and chest smeared with dirt, but it wasn't this that made Elise stop in her tracks; it was the pain etched on his face. It was horrific, it made her shudder, made her want to turn away and run in the other direction. But she didn't, couldn't, *wouldn't*.

She saw Cate's hands flail, as if she didn't know where to touch or what to do, and Elise stepped closer, dropping down and placing her hand flat to her back. She was used to being the strong one, to pushing her own fears aside to be there for someone else.

"What do you need me to do?" Elise whispered, taking in the shirt tied tightly around his waist, blood having soaked through much of the fabric. She was no nurse, but even she could see this man wasn't going to survive without some kind of medical assistance.

Cate's wild, pained eyes met hers, but after a moment of just staring at Elise and breathing, she seemed to find herself. Elise could see her steadying, could see the change in her as she turned back to the soldier and quickly removed the extra coat she'd been wearing to help him into it.

126

"We need to move him," Cate said. "We need to move him as quickly as we can, before he loses more blood."

"There's no way we can carry him between us," Elise said, studying his big frame. "I don't know how—"

"We can't leave him here! We have to try," Cate cried, and attempted to haul him up herself. And then Jack grunted, eyes still half-shut as he slowly rose.

"You're right, we can do this, we're not going to leave him here. I wasn't for a moment suggesting we leave him," Elise agreed, knowing that even if they failed in the end, she had to at least try instead of giving up before they started. This man deserved better than to be left to die in a ditch; she just had no idea how two small women were supposed to haul him all the way back to her house, undetected.

"I can walk," Jack said with a grunt as he righted himself, but Elise quickly positioned herself under one arm as Cate stood steadfast beneath the other. "Let me"—he sucked back a breath—"walk."

"You walk as best you can, and we'll be here for the rest of it," Elise told him, speaking English so he could understand her, and instinctively knowing that there was no way he could even get himself out of the ditch, let alone walk. But she understood pride, and she wasn't going to knock him down.

"Who's she?" he groaned.

"She's the cavalry," Cate muttered as they propped him up and attempted to get him out of the ditch. "There's no one else coming to save us, we're all you've got."

Elise might have been uncertain before, but now that she could see Cate's determination, coupled with her abilities as a nurse, she was fast realizing what an asset she could be. She'd be able to tend to Harry's injuries far better than Elise herself could, which could inadvertently save them all in the end.

A cluster of gunshots cut through the air then, far enough away not to terrify her, but close enough to remind her that they weren't alone out in the dark. As children, they'd run barefoot for miles, exploring and playing without adult supervision. They'd climbed trees and munched fruit out on the grass, staring at the sky and watching as the clouds passed by. Now, the same place she'd grown up in wasn't safe enough for a dog to walk alone, let alone two women after dark.

"Just one foot in front of the other," she heard Cate say, and she looped her arm more firmly around Jack as they started to walk.

He was only managing a very slow shuffle, but he was at least supporting some of his own body weight, which made it easier on them. Elise's arm was against Cate's now, pressed together as they walked, and it was a strange feeling to be touching someone. Again. In the past forty-eight hours, she'd had contact with four strangers, touching each of them: fingers brushing, skin colliding, tending to them, even; and it wasn't natural for her. Two years ago, maybe even a year ago, she'd never have thought about it, but now it was as strange as could be. Although something about touching Cate felt a lot more natural than touching the men.

"You can leave me," Jack said, grunting with every step.

"No, we can't," Cate snapped back. "I won't."

"You're more . . ." he said, before coughing and seeming to struggle to catch his breath. Elise cringed. The cough sounded wet and choking from deep in his lungs, like nothing she'd ever heard before. ". . . important."

Cate seemed to ignore him, not answering him, and Elise was happy to walk in silence. Cate was clearly determined to bring him with her, and although she didn't know if there was a romantic attachment to the man or not, Elise admired her for it. And she suddenly knew without a shadow of doubt that she'd done the right thing in coming to help her with him.

"We don't have that far to go," Elise said eventually. "And we're not leaving anyone behind, not if we can help it."

She couldn't see Cate's gaze in the dark, but she could feel it, and she knew that whatever happened, this woman would fight to save anyone she grew close to, and that could be more useful to Elise than anything else.

"Thank you," Cate said, her voice cutting through the dark that had managed to swallow them all. They were following their noses home now, the sky barely giving them any light to walk by.

Elise stayed quiet, because what could she say? They all knew what a risk she was taking. But, after a moment, she found a reply. "I do have a favor to ask you in return," she said.

There was a pause, a beat of silence between them where Elise could hear Cate breathe, as if she were biding her time before answering.

"What kind of favor?"

"I have another soldier hidden in my home, and he needs medical attention too," Elise said. "Jack can stay, but you need to put as much energy into caring for my soldier as you are this one."

Cate didn't hesitate. "I'm no surgeon, but whatever I can do to help him, you can count me in."

Elise thought of Harry then. He had only been in her home one full night and day now, but there was something about him. He was different to any man she'd ever known, and as much as he'd riled her, she also found herself being drawn to him. She'd felt different getting up that morning knowing he was downstairs, a spark of something she hadn't felt in a long time making her want to rise rather than stay curled in bed all day.

She gulped. Until he was gone. And then she'd have someone else to mourn. Elise steeled her jaw and forced herself to keep moving. *One foot in front of the other.* There was a reason she'd closed herself off to anyone other than her sister. What if she lost another person she loved? She'd be broken for life, and it wasn't something she was ever going to let happen again, not if she could help it.

CHAPTER ELEVEN

CATE

Cate took a moment, palms flat against the table as she caught her breath. Her head was pounding. It was like her heart had found a direct line to her head and was thumping a loud, roaring beat in there.

"Are you all right?" The soft voice belonging to Adelaide soothed her, as did the warm hand that covered hers. "Is there anything I can get you?"

Cate inhaled, keeping her eyes shut a moment longer before answering. She was scared she was about to pass out, her head woozy and her face feeling flushed.

"I'll be fine," she replied, finally straightening. But the second she lifted her hands, they started to shake. She quickly fisted them, but not before Adelaide had seen them. Cate could see the recognition in her eyes, but she didn't say anything and for that Cate was grateful. She didn't need to be told to rest or to sit down, because she had a life to save, with no doctor to ask for help, no surgeon to work miracles. It was just her and a soldier who deserved better than to die like an abandoned, neglected dog.

"When did you last eat?" Adelaide asked gently. "That might help with the, ah . . ." She paused, glancing back at Cate's hands. "With your fatigue."

Cate managed a smile as her stomach growled in response. "It's been a long time, days now, so yes, something to eat would help a lot. Thank you." She pushed away the memory of eating air with Jack, of pretending to use a fork and visualizing real food.

"I'm going to fix you something," Adelaide said. "It'll make you feel better."

She was also in desperate need of a wash, a warm drink to soothe her parched throat and a bed to curl up on, but food was a good start. Food would give her the energy to keep going.

Cate turned back to Jack, but for the first time since they'd left the hospital, she wondered if they'd done the right thing. Would he have had a better chance at survival if she'd left him behind in Dunkirk? Was he going to die because she had selfishly chosen to take him with her? She knew that he would argue with her and tell her that he'd rather die than be taken prisoner, but neither of them truly knew what the conditions would be like. And at least there would have been doctors, surgeons who could have saved his life, possibly without breaking a sweat. Instead, she'd dragged him into the great unknown.

She used her sleeve to wipe her brow, wishing she could keep her hair off her mud-streaked face, but when she reached up she found that almost all her pins had fallen out. She'd always been such a stickler when it came to her appearance, no matter the conditions; until now. Now she couldn't even hastily bundle her hair off her face.

"Do you need help with him?"

Cate started, turning slowly and coming face to face with a man who looked to be about the same age as Jack. But it was his accent washing over her that startled her the most, because it reminded her so much of home. Of her brothers talking and laughing; of roast dinners and crackling fires. She blinked, realizing that he was clearly the man Elise had mentioned. *Another British soldier.* It was almost impossible to believe.

As Cate studied him, she could see he was in pain from the lines that bracketed his eyes, the way he cringed as he moved closer; and the bulky bandage beneath his shirt was another giveaway. But she could worry about him later, for now all she had time to care about, to fight for, was Jack.

"I might need help," she said. "Perhaps you could talk to him? Keep him calm and try to talk him through the pain?"

The man nodded. "I'm Harry," he said, holding out a hand. "I should have introduced myself straight away."

"Cate," she replied, shaking it quickly before moving back closer to Jack. Seeing this other soldier in the house had thrown her, made her wonder how on earth they'd all ended up in the same place, but there would be time for questions later.

She felt fiercely protective of Jack, now more than ever; even though she knew he was in no danger, or *should* be in no danger here, she suddenly wanted to be by his side.

"Has he been shot?" Harry asked.

"Some time ago, yes. But he's post-surgery for internal injuries."

Cate knelt, the warmth of the fire caressing her cheeks. It was the perfect place for Jack's body to thaw out, and as she flexed her fingers, she realized how much she needed it, too. The rain had turned into a thunderstorm the night before, unseasonably wet and cold, and she was certainly grateful for the timber burning beside them.

With Addy crouching beside her, Cate took a deep breath, smiling down at Jack. His eyes were open now, and she was grateful he was still conscious, that his lips were capable of forming a smile still, even if it was a small one.

"Could someone please get me some towels or cloths, hot water and scissors?" Cate asked, remembering her training, focusing on the task at hand. She suddenly remembered the bandages she'd taken from the ambulance and stuffed into her pockets. How had she not remembered them when they'd been lying in the ditch? It was as if her brain was full of fog that she couldn't seem to clear no matter how hard she tried. She went to move then but Jack groaned, and she took his hand, staring into his beautiful brown eyes; eyes that had followed her every movement back at the hospital from the moment he'd gained consciousness.

"I left bandages in my pocket, in my nursing uniform," she said, looking up at Elise, who was standing, hovering now. "Could you find them for me? And a needle and thread would be useful, too."

"A regular sewing needle and thread?" Elise asked, as if she couldn't quite believe what she was being asked for.

Cate nodded. "It's better than nothing, and he's not going to heal if I don't stitch him up." On second thoughts, she added, "Could you boil it all up for me first? The needle and the thread both?"

Elise's smile was warm, and Cate felt the kindness in it. "Of course I can."

Cate had stripped down to her undergarments and redressed in an upstairs bedroom, and Elise had taken her dirty clothes, so she had no idea where to retrieve her belongings from. With both Elise and Adelaide gone now to do her bidding, she was left alone with the two men, but it didn't concern her. She'd spent her childhood joined at the hip with her older brothers, her protectors who'd never let anyone hurt her, and then had been surrounded by men as a nurse, so she was fine. But not knowing Harry's story bothered her, all the same. Where had he come from, and how had he managed to find his way to Elise and Adelaide? Had he just arrived or was he

133

a deserter? The thought was unsettling and she eyed him cautiously as she shuffled closer to Jack.

"What actually happened to him?" Harry asked as she bent low over her patient, gently trying to untie the knot she'd made earlier around his abdomen.

"He's never told me," she admitted, thinking of all the stolen moments she'd shared with Jack, sitting by his bed. Only he'd never let himself be drawn on what had happened, always changing the subject, asking about her, making her laugh even when she was so tired she'd wanted to collapse into sleep until her next shift started. But something about Jack had always drawn her back in. "He had two surgeries to repair internal damage. He was in such a bad state when he arrived that I don't think anyone expected him to make it, there was so much blood pumping out of him." She sighed, remembering how another soldier had come in with him, hand pressed to Jack's side in a desperate attempt to stem the blood. "And yet, here he is still. He's a fighter, that's for sure."

Harry nodded, and she saw in his eyes, in the way he held her gaze so calmly, that he understood. Maybe she'd been wrong to think he could be a deserter; she had the feeling that he might be the complete opposite. There was a steadiness about him that she imagined he deployed with his troops.

"Sometimes we get lucky, sometimes we don't," he said. "It's as simple as that. It's the times you think you'll make it that sometimes end up the worst."

She had so many questions, but she didn't want to press him. If they were going to be stuck in the same house together, hiding, they were going to have plenty of time to talk. And unless he knew something she didn't, they wouldn't be leaving in a hurry unless the Allies magically managed to storm back through France and regain all the territory they'd lost.

"We could give him something to drink, to help with the pain," Harry suggested.

"Might need to save it to use on wounds," she said. But when she glanced down at Jack, at his pale, damp complexion, she relented. "Well, maybe just a little, to ease it. But we need to be sparing."

Harry left her then, no doubt to retrieve the alcohol; and Cate took a moment to hold Jack's hand, whispering to him, "We're safe here, Jack. You're going to make it."

His eyes held hers, but he didn't say anything, and when Harry returned she held his head, cupping the back of his skull as Harry tipped the bottle to his lips. She watched Jack's Adam's apple bob as he swallowed, and after two sips she gently lowered his head back down.

Adelaide and Elise returned with everything she'd asked for, and as everyone sat back and gave her space, she started to work.

"What can I do?" Elise asked.

"Hold the fabric steady while I cut it," she said, having given up on untying the shirt around his waist. She could see from his sharp intake of breath that it hurt too much to tug on it. "There might well be a lot of blood when this comes loose, and I'm going to clean the wound, stitch where I have to, and then get him bandaged up. You might need to help hold the skin together, though, because it'll be hard going using a blunt needle and regular cotton."

She set to work, and soon found herself surprised by Elise, at how strong and capable she was. They continued on in silence, Cate holding her hand out and asking for supplies as she needed them, and Elise passing them to her, placing her hand for pressure when she needed it and cutting the end of the thread when Cate had finished the painstaking job of pressing the needle back and forth through Jack's skin. It had been almost unbearable, the feel of the too-blunt needle, fighting for each thread, as if she were pressing through fabric that was too thick to be stitched. Harry had held him down by the shoulders, trying to keep him still as she'd worked, and now, under the light of a lamp and with the fire still flickering beside them, she was finally done. And thankfully, Jack's groans of agony had abated, too.

She'd bathed the needle in alcohol, as well as the incision line, in an attempt to stave off infection, and Cate knew that the only thing she could do now was to keep the wound clean and replace the bandages regularly. The rest was out of her hands, and she had no medical supplies to turn to if anything went wrong.

"You're finished?" Adelaide asked, coming in to the room with a tray.

Cate flopped back, leaning against the closest chair, her legs feeling like jelly and certainly not capable of rising yet. She could see that Adelaide had made a hot drink for them, and there was food, too.

"Yes," she finally replied. "Now we just have to pray that I've done a good-enough job of patching him up."

She sat, gathering her thoughts and steadying her breath, as she stared over at Jack. He was still stretched out in front of the fire, eyes shut and his chest rising and falling heavily. It was a blessing that he was asleep, that he'd finally succumbed to the pull of slumber as she'd finished her work, because the pain was going to be immense when he woke.

"We don't have a lot, but I have some bread here," Adelaide said, setting the tray down on a small table beside the chairs. "There's some jam too, although it's a little tart as we didn't have a lot to sweeten it with."

Cate's stomach growled as she wrestled with herself and tried to move slowly instead of behaving like a starved, wild animal. But the idea of jam, however tart, on any kind of bread, sounded like heaven to her. Harry stayed back as she took a piece and spread it, before sitting down and forcing herself to slowly savor each mouthful.

When she finished, she realized that everyone in the room was looking at her.

"When did you last eat?" Elise asked.

Cate swallowed her mouthful. "I honestly don't know." Suddenly she couldn't remember, the hours, days blurring together, her fatigue so deep, her hunger, her thirst . . . It was all hitting her like a steam train. "The morning we left the hospital I suppose, so—" She wished she wasn't feeling so foggy.

"Have another piece," Adelaide said, taking a second piece of bread and spreading it for her. "You deserve it."

Cate took it, pleased when the others settled down and ate too, making her feel less self-conscious, with Adelaide pouring them all coffee. It was the strangest scene, as if they knew one another when in fact they were all strangers sitting in a room, huddled away from the terrors of outside.

"Cate, I'm loath to ask because I can see how exhausted you are," Elise said, as her sister passed a steaming cup of coffee to her, "but I'd like you to look at Harry before you turn in for the night. I did my best, but—"

"You're injured? Of course you're injured, I . . ." Cate almost choked on her bread. She set it down and stood, ignoring the fuzzy sensation in her head, so tired she could barely stand. "I'm sorry, I should have . . ."

"Because you had more important things to do," Harry said, throwing Elise a look. "It's nothing."

"It's not nothing," Elise interrupted. "I dug out a bullet from his shoulder, and I know I got all of it, but—"

"She's not a nurse," Adelaide said, softly. "And we both think that you must be a pretty good one."

Cate forgot all about her exhausted limbs and fatigue, only interested in helping Harry now.

"You can look at me later," he muttered. "Just eat your food and rest awhile. I don't want anyone to make a fuss."

"This is what I'm trained for, to look after soldiers and tend to their wounds," Cate assured him, standing before him now, arms folded across her chest, her strength coming back to her. "Please, let me look." Cate would have happily carried on sipping her drink, and her eyelids were so heavy they were ready to fall shut of their own accord, but she would never turn her back on her duty.

Harry eventually sighed and set his coffee down, and she didn't miss the small scowl as he raised his arm. He unbuttoned his shirt and dropped one shoulder out, and she took in the bulky bandaging, realizing why Elise had been so keen for her to help him. It was up to Cate now to make sure this man had a fighting chance, too.

"How badly does it hurt?" Cate asked.

"Bad enough that I couldn't hold a rifle steady," he said.

Cate gently unfixed then unwound the bandage, careful as she examined the wound. It needed stitches, that much was clear, but if Elise had been the one to clean it, she'd done a great job.

"Well, it's not red, which is to be expected at this early stage if it's only just happened, but I'll need to stitch it properly and then we'll make a sling after bandaging it. It'll help it to heal if we keep it still."

Harry hadn't said anything, and she studied his face, not sure if she'd done or said something wrong for his expression to change so deeply.

"Harry? Is that all right with you?" she asked.

When he didn't answer, she glanced up and caught Elise's eye. She supposed they didn't know him well enough to know what was going on in his head, but something about what she'd said had affected him.

"Harry?" she asked, searching his eyes. "I know you've been through a lot, honestly I know more than most how a man feels and acts when he's been injured in the field. I've been tending soldiers for months now, and every single one struggles at some point. Plenty of men have been where you are."

"I should have died out there with all the others," he suddenly ground out. "It's not fair that I'm here and they're not, that I was the one to survive. I don't deserve any medical attention."

She was grateful when Elise came over and sat beside him, quietly taking his other hand and holding it as Cate continued to inspect his wound. She didn't know what he was talking about, but in a way she didn't need to; many of the men she'd treated since being in France suffered from a kind of survivor's guilt. "They would have wanted you to survive, trust me," she said. "No soldier wishes any of his own dead, and that means that you need to stay alive for them, to fight for them. Don't let their loss of life be for nothing, Harry. What's it all been for if you let that happen?"

Harry finally looked up at her then, and she saw that somehow she'd managed to get through to him, even if there was still a wariness to his gaze. But he was listening to her, and that was what mattered.

"There's something that feels shameful about living when others don't, once the reality of surviving sets in," he said, his voice so low she had to listen carefully to catch each word, not sure whether he was talking to her, Elise, or both of them. "It starts with a desperate need to survive, I suppose it's human nature to fight to live, but no one tells you what it feels like afterwards."

She breathed deep, his words resonating with her, washing over her as if she'd thought them herself. Hadn't she done the exact same thing? She'd fled with barely a second thought to save her own life, leaving the others behind in a split-second decision.

"I know," she whispered as tears filled her eyes. "Trust me, I saw everyone else from my hospital taken, so I know how that feels, to be the only one."

She nodded and quickly wiped away her tears, snuffling them back as she fought against the first big wave of emotion she'd felt since leaving. She'd felt scared and worried and outright terrified, but until now, she'd kept the deep, choking emotion inside her at bay.

"Patch me up then," Harry said, clearing his throat, "but drink your coffee first. You need it."

Cate smiled at him, relieved to hear him accepting her help. She was starting to realize that she was much better when she had busy hands and no time to wallow in what was already done. "Deal. And while I patch you up, we can talk about how unlikely it is that we both sought refuge in the same house."

Elise looked relieved when she glanced at her, and Cate checked Jack before going back to her coffee and finishing her bread, licking the last of the sticky jam from her fingers. And it was then, like a ton of bricks hitting her, she realized what a useful commodity she was.

Her fate wasn't sealed; wherever she ended up, whether it was inside a friendly home like this or in the belly of a German prisoner camp, she was useful. She could stitch men up and tend to wounds; she could help anyone with an injury or medical need. She didn't want to think beyond the warm house she was already stationed in, but for the first time since she'd fled the hospital, she felt oddly calm.

So long as nurses were needed, she could stay alive. Maybe she'd be stuck in France for months, maybe years, but if she kept tending to the sick and injured, she could stay alive long enough to go home one day. Or at least that was what she was going to keep telling herself. But it did help with the tremble of fear she'd been feeling at being discovered.

"Do you really need to stitch it?" Harry asked after she'd washed her hands in the kitchen and boiled up more thread along with the needle. "Can't it just heal on its own?"

"I really do need to stitch it," she replied. "The last thing I want is to see an infection there in a week's time because I was lazy and left it open."

"Anything I can do?" Adelaide asked.

"Bring a stick or something else hard for him to bite down on," Cate said, whispering "Sorry" to Harry as his eyes widened in alarm. She patted his good shoulder as she peered at the open wound winking back at her. "Unfortunately, this is going to hurt."

CHAPTER TWELVE

ELISE

"What are we going to do with all these people in our house?"

Elise sat next to her sister. They hadn't even changed into their nightclothes yet, still sitting on the bed with a blanket draped between them, fretting over the situation downstairs. They'd made up the spare bed in the attic for Jack, but it had been impossible to carry him up the narrow staircase while he was still drifting in and out of consciousness, so they'd ended up leaving him downstairs. They'd given their parents' larger bed to Cate, and Harry had insisted he was fine on the floor of the attic with an old mattress that had been propped against the wall. The attic had been her brother's space; hot and stuffy as could be in summer, with barely enough air to breathe, but it had been his and he'd loved it ever since he'd moved up there as a teenager. It had been strange seeing another man in there, and stranger still making up the room that still smelt of her mother for Cate. They'd left it exactly as it had been when she'd died; perfume on the dresser, lipstick discarded beside it, and her purse and favorite shoes on the chair that faced the bed. It had seemed like an impossible job to move anything, although Elise often walked by the room and paused to drop some of the perfume to her wrist, so it would waft up to her and make her feel as if her mother were walking a step behind her all day.

Elise sighed, finally answering her sister's question. "I don't know. Honestly, for the first time in my life, I don't know what to say."

"What will happen if we're caught? If our home is searched?" Addy asked. "What would they do to us? And do they even have the right to do that? It's still our country, isn't it?"

Elise took her hand, holding it gently as she listened to the rising hysteria in her sister's voice. It was always this way; by the time Addy started to worry about something, Elise had already done her fair share of fretting and had come out the other side of it. Her sister acted impulsively and worried later, making them polar opposites in that respect, although she knew that it had been harder for Addy. Elise and Louis had had a different experience at her age; they'd been able to have fun and meet people, whereas Adelaide had been forced to stay largely at home with only her family for company.

"If anyone comes here, we keep them in the attic," she said calmly. "We're going to be absolutely fine, so long as we can find enough food for us all and keep Jack alive." She cringed, wishing she hadn't said that last part as Adelaide's eyes widened.

"You think he might die? Did Cate say something to you?"

Elise felt like she was talking to someone much more than a few years younger than her. "No, she didn't, but the color of his skin, the way his wound looked, it seemed obvious that it might be touch and go with him." She had heard Cate talk about possible infection, and she didn't need to be a nurse to know that that could kill him without access to the right medicine.

"What did you see out there? When you went looking for him?" Addy asked, her fingers worrying the frayed edge of the

143

blanket. "How bad is it? Do you think there are any French soldiers fighting still? Did you come across any?"

Elise resisted the urge to tell her sister that she might be best asking her new admirer, and that there certainly weren't any French soldiers around, but she knew she had to be more careful if she wanted to get Addy to talk. Her sister might be naïve sometimes, but she knew how to bottle things up and keep them inside if she needed to.

"I didn't see anything, but we heard a lot," Elise told her. She knew better than to shield her too much; she needed her to be afraid, to be on guard. "And from the sounds of it, the tides of war have very much turned against us, so I don't think we'll be seeing any friendly soldiers in the near future."

Addy looked up at her. "Why do I have a feeling you're keeping something from me?"

Elise stood and crossed the room, standing by the window and parting the curtains a little. She stared into the dark, unable to see anything, and at the same time seeing everything. She doubted she'd ever unsee the massacre they'd witnessed.

"How did that Nazi soldier know you by name?" Elise finally asked, not turning, trying to sound unfazed by what she was asking, not wanting to push too hard. She knew her sister, and it would only make her hold all her cards closer to her chest.

"I wouldn't say he knows me as such," Addy replied, but when Elise finally faced her, she could see the too-hot flush of her sister's cheeks.

"I heard your exchange with him, that's all. He clearly said your name and you used his Christian name in reply," Elise continued, struggling to keep her voice on an even keel. "In fact, I believe he said it was good to see you again?" She sat, keeping more distance this time, the bed between them.

"He's the one I handed Peter over to that day," Addy finally said, raising her eyes.

Elise breathed deep. So her sister had managed to catch the eye of a high-ranking German soldier the *one day* she'd let her go out unchaperoned. Her voice defied her and she cleared her throat, trying not to stumble over her words. "I see."

Addy started to cry then, and Elise forced herself to be kind, to be patient, when in fact all she wanted was to shake her sister's shoulders and force some sense into her. Ever since she'd left her with Peter, ever since she'd chosen to help him surrender, Elise had known she needed to be more careful to keep a closer eye on her.

"Tell me, did it ever cross your mind that he might have been involved in the massacre we witnessed?" Elise asked.

"Of course it did," Addy cried. "But if you'd seen how nice he was, I just don't think he's—"

"Of course he's capable, Adelaide, he's a *Nazi*. He's capable of every terrible thing you or I could imagine, so don't pretend for a moment that he's not."

"You're acting as if I did something wrong, but I only talked to him! That's all." Addy was wiping at her cheeks now, but Elise wasn't going to comfort her. She couldn't. There was a time and place for being sympathetic, and this was not it, even though it went against every fiber in her body not to care for her sister; but what she'd done in taking Peter was wrong.

"He's going to want more from you than you might want to give, Addy. We need, *you need*, to be prepared." Elise sighed. "Men like him take what they want, they don't ask for it or sit around waiting. If he decides *you're* something he wants, then I don't know how I can protect you."

They sat, staring at one another a moment longer, silence heavy between them, Addy sniffing back tears of naivety.

"But Nazi soldier aside, we have two British men and a woman hiding in our house," Elise said brusquely, not wanting to wallow in fear with her sister any longer. "We need a plan quickly, otherwise we could find ourselves on a fast-sinking ship."

A soft knock at the door startled Elise and made Addy physically jump. Elise shot out a hand to steady her, feeling her pulse thumping at her wrist.

"It's just me," came a small voice.

Cate. "Come in," Elise called back.

The door slowly opened and Cate walked into the room, dark circles under her eyes like the blackest of shadows on the gloomiest winter night. The girl needed sleep, and she needed it yesterday.

"I couldn't help but overhear you," Cate said, her slender arms wrapped around herself. She'd been so confident and capable earlier, doing what needed to be done despite whatever horrors she'd been witness to, not to mention the fact that she'd walked through war and fought to survive in the bravest of ways. But now she looked childlike as she peeked out from beneath her fringe, holding herself, perhaps broken in a way that hadn't been obvious before.

Elise patted the bed, inviting her to sit with them. "Please don't think you're not welcome, because that's not the case."

Cate slowly untangled her arms as she sat on the very edge of the bed.

"I just . . ." She let out a loud breath, eyes shut for a beat, as if she were trying to find her words. "I know the burden I've put on you, that we've all put on you."

Elise glanced at her sister, watching as Addy leant forward and grasped Cate's hand. She'd almost done it herself, been so close to catching Cate as she trembled, but something had stopped her. The same something that had made her hesitate before opening the door to Harry and his friend; and the same something again that had made her pause before agreeing to help them or Cate.

"We'll keep you safe here for as long as we can, Cate," Elise said. "I want you to know that we'll do everything we can to hide you."

"But for how long?" Cate asked, her voice hollow. "We could be stuck here indefinitely, and that's not fair on you. If they find out what you've done, if they—"

"Shhh," Elise said, shuffling forward and placing a hand on Cate's shoulder. "We're all going to be fine, there's no point fretting about something we don't even know the answer to."

"If there's anything I can do, if there's some way of making this easier on you or somewhere else we can go . . ."

Cate's eyes were filled with tears, but not one fell, and Elise found herself wondering how this British woman had managed to survive her ordeal, let alone be standing to tell the story. She wished she knew more about what was happening around them; she'd earlier relied on an old friend of her father's for news, but she hadn't been brave enough to make the trip to visit him for some time now. All she knew was what Harry had told her; that soon their entire region would be surrounded by Germans, that the ground would be crawling with them, and that France would surely fall. He seemed certain they were only days away from the French surrendering completely, which meant things would only get harder, not easier, for them all.

"There's nowhere else," Elise told her gently. "We'll find a way through this that keeps us all safe."

"But that's the problem, I just can't see a way through it," Cate said. "I can't believe we've been left behind, that so many troops might not have made it home."

"Worrying isn't going to make you feel better," Elise said. "What you need is a nice long sleep. Everything will seem better in the morning."

It was an outright lie, a fib mothers told their children to get them to bed, although she supposed that if the problem were small, it usually did feel better when the sun rose the next day. But the truth was, she had no idea how to keep them safe. Cate was one thing; they could get away with one lie, for a woman, for someone who wouldn't be so hated by the enemy. But two British soldiers? She wasn't even going to think about what would happen to them, to all of them, if that secret were uncovered when they were in the midst of enemy territory.

"Come on, let's get you settled," Addy said, her arm around Cate as she helped her up. "My mother's bed is the comfiest in the house."

Cate stopped moving then, turning back to Elise. "What happened to her? To your mother?"

"She died of a broken heart, I suspect," Elise said.

Cate didn't ask any more questions, and for that Elise was grateful. She waited for them to leave the room and then sank down into the pillows, knowing that she was about as far from sleep as possible. Her mind was racing, trying to figure it all out, trying to think what Louis would have done, or what her father would have said.

Just take it one day at a time. She listened to her brother's words in her mind, knowing that he would have been so calm, refusing to listen to her worries. She'd always been the worrier and he'd been the free spirit, the one who'd say yes to anything just because he loved living so much.

Elise refused to cry, pushing up to her feet and going downstairs. Sleep was for the dead; Louis would have said that, too.

A sliver of moonlight fell through the smallest of gaps in the curtain as Elise walked into the kitchen. She looked around, remembering the way her father had often sat alone in the dark, hot drink in hand, lost in his own thoughts. She'd sometimes sat with him; other times she'd slipped back up the stairs, not wanting to disturb him. At the time, she'd wondered why he hadn't just gone up to bed to sleep, but she knew now that he'd felt as if the weight of the world had been on his shoulders, because that's exactly how she felt now. And she'd also seen the heavy load of guilt resting upon him too, at so vocally encouraging his son to fight for their country, only to have him slaughtered within weeks of departure.

In truth, her father hadn't been the one to make the choice; Louis had been a young man, expected to fight. But his guilt had been at how quickly he'd pushed him, how robustly he'd announced him as a hero to their homeland.

Elise filled the kettle with water to boil, and then placed her palms on the cool kitchen bench, eyes shut as she folded forward.

"Anything I can do?"

She leapt up, hand to her heart as she spun around. "Harry! You almost gave me a heart attack!"

He moved out of the darkness and closer toward her, facing her from the other side of the kitchen.

"Sorry, I didn't mean to startle you," he said, his voice soft and low. "I just didn't want you to think you were alone. In here, I mean."

She smiled as he turned on the light, running her eyes over his face, at the stubble brushing his cheeks, at the easy way he looked back at her even though they barely knew one another. She'd seen a different side to him earlier in the way he'd spoken to Cate, the way he'd almost shunned her nursing skills out of guilt for being alive. But now he looked at ease, with her at least, although maybe he was just too tired to be any other way with her in the middle of the night, standing in her kitchen. They'd clashed the night that he'd arrived, and the following day, but she was starting to think that perhaps she'd been a little too hard on him after everything he'd been through.

"You couldn't sleep either?" she asked.

His smile made his lips tilt upwards just a little. "If I'm honest, I don't know when I'll ever be able to sleep again."

She turned her attention to the water starting to boil and took two mugs down from the shelf. It was nice to have someone to talk to, even if she was still a little unsure around him.

"Coffee?"

He grunted. "I'd prefer a strong, sweet tea, but coffee will do."

She smiled to herself, surprised at how different her mood was all of a sudden at having a light conversation with someone who wasn't her sister. "I've heard English people drink tea by the gallon."

"You wouldn't be wrong."

She had no sugar to offer him, and the coffee was a strange yellow color and didn't taste like it had pre-war, but she passed him the steaming mug anyway and was pleased when he followed her to the kitchen table. Jack was snoring lightly from the floor nearby, the last dying flames of the fire dancing light across his body, and she found comfort in the regular inhale and exhale of his breath.

Elise tucked her fingers around the mug, warming them even though she wasn't cold.

"Do you keep thinking about it? What happened that day?" she asked, feeling tentative even though she'd just come out and asked him what she'd been wondering herself.

"Every time I close my eyes, I can see them, all around me," he said. "You know, we did it for the greater good, all of us full of the belief that we could actually hold the bastards off, give other men a real chance at evacuating."

She took a sip of her drink, wincing when it burnt the inside of her mouth. Harry had his hands wrapped around his mug too, only his overlapped, making the china appear small and insignificant in his palms.

She knew most of what had happened, from what she'd seen and what he'd already told her, but she sensed he wanted to talk, and she found herself wanting to know more.

"What happened in there, Harry?" she eventually asked.

"When we started to run out of ammunition, everything changed. Suddenly those men, brave men who I'd fought beside for so long, started to crumble. Some were crying, others were swearing, and some were deadly silent. It was a nightmare."

Elise waited, seeing how far away he was, his eyes fixed straight past her, as if he could see something she couldn't, and she almost turned to look for herself. But of course he was lost in his own memories; nothing was there.

"And then we thought that the worst had happened, when we had to surrender," he said, clearing his throat and taking a slug of coffee. She should have glanced away, pretended she couldn't see his tears and hear the catch of his emotion, but she couldn't, because it was too raw and there was no way she could ignore it. "We thought the worst that could happen was being marched away as prisoners of war. Not one of us could have guessed what they were going to do, that they'd just gun us down, unarmed and with a damn white flag held high."

She wanted to reach out to him, to hold his hand as she had earlier that day, but her fingers remained locked together around her mug. Harry's shoulders shuddered, his breath heaving out of his lungs, before he righted himself and cleared his throat again.

"Sorry, I just, I can't stop thinking what I could have done, what we could have done differently, if we could have all made it, if we hadn't tried to be heroes."

"You are all heroes in my eyes," she whispered, finally finding the courage to reach for him, just a touch, her fingers brushing over his and settling there, his knuckles beneath the pads of her fingertips. "And you deserved to survive, Harry. Don't for a second think that you didn't deserve to live."

"And Peter?" he asked. "I should have fought harder, I should have—"

"You did everything you could for him, Harry. There's nothing more you could have done," she said, thinking of her sister meeting the Nazi commander and what that one decision might have done to change all their fates, Addy's included. "You know, in a way, though, I do understand the guilt you feel at surviving." The words were hard to say, but she forced herself to continue. "Losing my brother, knowing there was nothing I could do to help him, it's all-consuming sometimes. I still ask myself why, why he was the one taken, and then I start to push everyone away from me, even my sister sometimes."

Harry's brown eyes pulled her in so hard that her breath caught in her throat, but she stayed put, resisting the urge to flee.

"I'm sorry," he said. "I know me saying that won't help and it sure as hell won't bring him back, but for what it's worth, I'm sorry."

She forced a small smile. "It actually means a lot to hear you say that. And I'm sorry too, for what you've been through. I'm sorry my sister let you down, that she did something like that without talking to us first."

A warm silence hung between them for a moment as they sipped and sat, eyes settling more easily on one another across the table this time.

He never moved his fingers, but he did look back up at her, and she saw the softness within him, a kindness there that pulled her all the way in.

"I can't stop thinking about him, that's all. I don't blame her, Peter knew what he wanted and I've seen how kindhearted she is, I know she did what she thought was right," Harry whispered. "But what if I'm the only survivor? What if no one ever believes what happened to us?"

Elise didn't know what to say. "Then at least there will be one of you to tell the story," she said. "It doesn't make you somehow less of a man, less of a soldier, just because you fought to save yourself, or because you're the only one left standing."

He stared back at her with such truth in his gaze, such an openness, that she knew she had to keep talking, keep telling him what she was thinking.

"I'm one of the only other people alive, other than the Germans, who knows what truly happened that day. Me, you, Addy and Peter. You were part of it, and we witnessed it. So when I tell you that I understand, that I know you deserve to live, you can believe that I mean it. From the bottom of my heart."

She watched as he swallowed, pressing the heel of his hand to his forehead, between his eyebrows, as he shuddered for a long moment, before looking back up at her and placing his hand where it had been before. Her fingers found their way straight back to him, like they'd never left.

"I want you to know that I'll turn myself in, if it ever comes to that," he finally said. "I will never let any harm come to you and your sister. If we're found, I'll say that I forced you, that you had no choice. I couldn't live with myself if I didn't."

She smiled, about to tell him he didn't have to do that, but she saw in his eyes that he needed to. He was a man desperate to right a wrong, and in the end, she knew that she'd do whatever she had to in order to save herself and her sister, too.

"Thank you."

Elise knew it was long past the point where she should have withdrawn her hand from his, but it was nice touching him. After a long moment, she forced herself to sit back and take her hand away.

"Tell me, if you were at home, who would you be with and what would you be doing?"

Elise was pleased she'd asked, because his face changed then, his smile making his eyes crinkle at the corners.

"I'd be sitting with my mother, probably. She'd have fed me up on a hearty rabbit stew because she'd tell me I looked too skinny, and we would have had pudding."

"*Pudding?*" Elise asked.

Harry laughed. "Dessert. Most likely a warm bread and butter pudding."

She could see it in her mind; him curled up in a comfy chair while his mother fussed over him and brought him as much food as she could. "What about the rest of your family?"

His eyebrows dropped a little then, dragging together as he started to speak. "My father was a miner, a coal miner, just like his father before that, and both of them died down there," he said. "It left my mother with three daughters and a son to raise on her own."

"How did she get by?" Elise asked, nursing her warm mug as she watched him, fascinated to hear more.

"I should have left school and started mining when I was fourteen, but my mother, well, she's one heck of a lady. She made me stay until I was sixteen, wanted me to get an education, and she worked herself to the bone to make sure we didn't want for anything."

"Fourteen? That's so young to start doing hard labor like that," Elise mused. "Is that normal?"

"Boys I went to school with, they all started at fourteen," he said. "Two of them were dead before the end of their first year."

"Dead?" Elise gasped. "How? Why?"

"They send you down to collect tubs of coal with a pony all harnessed up for the job. And you just keep taking the full tubs up, and taking the old tubs down. But it's nasty down there," he said.

"Accidents happen all the time, and not just to the boys, to the older men, too. I think my poor ma spent most of her life scrubbing her husband's skin and his clothes clean, and then eventually she was doing the same for me."

"She sounds like a good woman," Elise said. "It must have been hard for her to keep food on the table."

Harry's eyes were shut, as if he were lost in the memory of home. "War seemed like an easy option to me. Being a soldier sounded far better than coal."

She didn't need to ask if he'd been right. After what he'd been through, seeing nearly everyone in his regiment killed, she bet he'd have rather faced coal-mining for the rest of his life.

"Do you have a sweetheart waiting for you back home?" she asked.

His eyes opened then, slowly. "No. Well, there was someone, but I didn't love her enough to ask her to wait." She went to say something but he laughed and stopped her. "Sorry, that makes me sound terribly heartless. What I meant was that I didn't want her waiting for me, because I thought she deserved better than me, someone who loved her. We had a lot of fun, but when it came down to it, I didn't want to ask her to marry me."

"I understand," she said. "Truly, I do."

"You've had the same thing happen to you?"

She smiled. "No, not the same. But I never wanted to marry for marriage's sake, if that makes sense? I would rather be alone than promised to someone I didn't love."

It was strange how easy the silence between them was as they sat sipping their coffee, lost in thought, until Harry finally spoke again.

"And you? Tell me, what would be different for you if we weren't at war?"

Elise lifted her gaze, studying him and trying to find the right words to reply. "If the war had never begun, my house would be full of family. My brother would be here, although he wouldn't actually be here because he'd no doubt have snuck into a pretty woman's bedroom, knowing him." She laughed, remembering him and for once not feeling so sad. "And my mother would still be alive, but maybe not my father."

"They were good parents?" Harry asked.

"They were. I had a beautiful childhood filled with laughter, love and great food. I couldn't have asked for more."

They both sat quietly again, only the silence wasn't so easy this time.

"You know, Cate and Jack, they should have made for the beach at Dunkirk," Harry said, as he slowly rose. "Instead, they ran straight into the lion's den."

Elise gulped. "Should I have evacuated my sister, too? Should we have made for Belgium, or—"

"You would have only been heading into enemy lines there, too, and you'd have been turned straight back," Harry said. "Nowhere is safe, not unless you're on a boat traveling far from here, but we have this saying at home—better the devil you know than the devil you don't."

Elise met his stare. "You're saying I'm safer staying with this devil? Being at home here?"

He nodded. "I'm saying that two beautiful young women aren't safe anywhere right now, but at least here you know the lay of the land, and the Germans have no reason not to like you."

"But they have every reason to dislike you," she said. "And Cate and Jack."

It hung between them, that knowledge that two of the people hiding in her home had actually had a chance to get away. But instead, they'd managed to somehow survive the worst decision possible.

"You have to wonder how they ever made it here," said Elise. "How they managed to keep walking with Nazis at every turn."

"Maybe they've got luck on their side," he said. "A guardian angel looking out for them."

Any other time she'd have wondered if he was teasing her, but there was nothing amusing about two people surviving against all the odds.

"Are you going to tell them they made a huge mistake, or am I?" Elise asked.

"Neither of us are," he said firmly. "Because if Jack wakes up and finds that out, he'll never forgive himself."

Elise didn't say anything else. It was abundantly obvious that Harry knew all about not being able to forgive oneself, which made him the expert on the matter, not her.

"Goodnight, Elise."

She dragged her eyes slowly over his face in the low light of the lamp, at the way his shirt fell with one arm tucked up high in the sling Cate had made for him. Even one-armed and with a bruise circling his eye, he was still the most handsome man she'd ever clapped eyes on.

"Goodnight, Harry."

And as he quietly disappeared, she laid her cheek flat to the table, closing her eyes and feeling the night's silence surround her.

What have I done?

CHAPTER THIRTEEN

CATE

It had been two days since they'd arrived in Le Paradis, and Cate was starting to understand the meaning of claustrophobia. She supposed she could go outside briefly if she wanted to; she was supposed to be the cousin of Elise and Adelaide, after all, but she was terrified now of being found out. Those first hours after they'd arrived, she'd kept her head, focusing on her job and doing what she knew so well. But once she'd finally gone to bed that night and slept, fitfully despite the comfortable surroundings, all she'd been able to see in her head were the people she'd left behind. They were coming to her in her dreams, calling for her, asking her why she'd left them. She kept seeing patients bleeding, crying in pain, and her feet wouldn't move, like she was stuck in quicksand.

That's what you get for abandoning everyone.

The attic was dark with the blinds pulled, and although she longed to let the light in and breathe fresh air, she wanted to keep it comfortable for Jack. They'd managed to carry him up the night before, terrified he'd be discovered downstairs if they had a surprise visitor. He'd slept fitfully in the beginning, too, but then he'd eased into a much more settled slumber. At times she'd wondered whether he would ever wake, but he'd stirred twice now, long enough for her to spoon some water into his mouth and wipe his brow before he fell asleep again.

Cate sat beside him, peering at his face and seeing there was no longer a wet line beading across his forehead. Her hope was that any fever he'd had had broken; a quick look under his bandages would tell her if there was an infection, but she didn't want to rouse him, not when he was sleeping so peacefully. Instead she reached inside the shirt she was wearing for her ring, tugging gently at the chain that kept it around her neck. She closed her fingers around it and thought of Charlie, but her hand fell away like it had been burnt when Jack's face swam in her gaze.

It's because I'm looking after him, tending to him so often, she told herself. *I need more to eat and I need to sleep properly. Charlie will come back to me then.*

As if to placate the voice in her head, she lifted her legs up on to the bed and lay her head down on the pillow. She'd been reluctant to sleep again because she didn't want to leave Jack, and she reasoned with herself that there would be no hardship in sharing the bed with him. They were both fully clothed, she didn't need to pull the blanket on to herself, and the door was open. Not that anyone downstairs probably could have cared less what she did with Jack in the privacy of a room, but still, it meant something to her.

She lay on her back for a moment before wrestling with the notion of how cold she was, and how warm Jack would be to curl up beside. Cate moved slowly, inching across the bed until she was touching him, and finally placing her arm slightly across his chest, her body curled into his like a spoon nestling against him. And she hadn't been wrong; the heat from him warmed her almost instantly, and even though he made her heart race for another reason entirely, it did stop the panicked thud of fear inside of her.

"Cate?"

She wriggled back, embarrassed at hearing Jack say her name when she was so close to him. His voice was gravelly, dry from not being used.

"You're awake," she said, struggling upright so she could peer down at him.

"I feel like death," he groaned, trying to sit up and then falling straight back down again. "How long have we been here?"

"Two days," she said. "But after everything your body went through, you ended up sleeping for most of it."

His hand lifted slowly and landed on his abdomen. "You stitched me up again?" he asked. "I remember something about you bent over me and a man, a *soldier*, holding my shoulders to keep me still?" His eyes squinted, his face screwed up with the effort of trying to piece everything together.

Cate rose and went to get the glass of water she'd brought up earlier for him in case he woke. "Harry," she told him. "The soldier's name is Harry, and he's downstairs right now. There's three of us Brits hiding here."

She could see that Jack was starting to remember when he pushed up on to his elbows, his eyes clearer as she held the glass for him and he took a few gulps.

"Are we safe?" he asked.

Cate shrugged. "Honestly, I don't know. But there's nowhere safer we could be."

He stared straight into her eyes and it took all her resolve not to look away, scared of the way he looked at her now that they were alone. It was so much deeper than innocent flirting in a hospital full of people.

"We should have made for the beach, shouldn't we?" he asked. "I think I led us the wrong way."

Cate just smiled, not wanting him to worry. The truth was, if the evacuation had been successful then they should have made for the beach, but she hadn't known what to do, and without Jack, she'd probably have been captured or killed.

"We're here and we're safe," she said. "And you're alive. There's no point wondering *what if*."

She set the glass down and sat back on the bed, propping pillows up behind Jack's head to make him comfortable and then drawing her knees up to her chin once she'd shuffled down to the other end.

Jack was looking around the room, seeing it properly for the first time, and she only wished it were daytime so she could let some light in. They both needed fresh air and sunshine; she was starting to go mad without it.

"What are they like?" he asked. "The people who own this house?"

That was at least something she didn't have to lie to him about. "They're lovely," she replied. "Elise and Adelaide live here alone, their brother and parents have both passed away, and Harry seems to be a good man, too. I like them all."

"You trust them?" he asked, his face drawn, as if he didn't believe her.

"I do," she said. "They took us in when they didn't have to, lied for us, and came back to help me bring you to safety. If we can't trust them, we can't trust anyone."

He was silent for a bit, his breathing more labored, before he spoke again. "Where are the Germans? Are we in the middle of it all?"

She sighed. There was no point hiding it from him. "They're all around us. It's a miracle we even made it here from the clearance hospital, and from what Elise has told me, there are Nazis everywhere. They've taken over some houses nearby, and she's heard they've taken nearby St. Venant, too. Nowhere is safe, not this part of France and certainly not Belgium either."

"So we're stuck here?" he asked.

"I'm afraid so."

Cate's hands started to shake then, and a lump rose in her throat that was impossible to swallow away. She turned, angling her body away from Jack, but there was no fooling him.

"Hey," he said, reaching out his hand. "Cate, it's all right, everything's going to be all right."

His fingertips brushed hers, clasping around her knuckles, but it only made it worse. A guttural, embarrassing sob escaped from her lips, and her shoulders started to tremble more violently than her hands.

"Come here," he said, his voice cracking as he sat up. She knew the pain he was in, how much it must have hurt him, but he didn't let go of her fingers, holding on tight as she tried to steady her breath and fight the overwhelming emotion rising inside her.

"I just want to go home," she whispered. "I want this all to be over, I just want to be home."

"You might want to be home, but I'd much rather be here, in this room with you," he said, his low voice making her slowly look up at him, tears caught in her lashes and blurring her vision. "You're the strongest woman I've ever met, Cate. You want to cry, you cry. You've dealt with blood and wounds and broken men, I've seen the way you've taken everything in your stride and made everyone around you always feel better, but you're allowed to be the broken one now."

His words washed over her, only making her cry more, because he was right. He was so right. She'd spent every waking moment in France tending to others; there hadn't been time for her to be upset or worry about herself, until now.

"I'm sorry, I don't know what's come over me," she apologized, brushing her eyes with the back of her fingers and taking a big, shuddering breath.

"Come here," he repeated, leaning back down a little, one elbow propping him up as he beckoned her to lie beside him.

162

She'd been doing it only moments earlier, but that had been different. Jack had been asleep then, she'd pressed against him for warmth and comfort without it meaning anything, but lying with him now . . . She looked down, not sure what to say.

"I don't expect anything from you, Cate. I just thought we could lie here for a bit until we fall asleep. You look like you could do with the rest."

Her body was exhausted, her shoulders slumping forward, eyes even heavier from the crying. A little voice in her head told her not to, that she shouldn't trust any man like that, but this was Jack. *I can trust Jack.*

"You do realize we've already slept together in a ditch, in the pouring rain," he teased, his smile warming her. "So it's not like it's the first time."

Cate gave in then. To hell with what her mother had told her about never trusting boys. She'd been to hell and back with Jack already, and the crook of an arm had never looked so inviting.

"Men tell you things so you'll fall for them, and then before you know it, you're married with children and you can't get away even if you want to."

Cate hugged her mother tight, not wanting to let her go. "They're not all like that, Ma."

She'd seen what good men looked like; her brothers would never raise a hand to their sweethearts and they would protect her with their lives if they had to. Charlie had been the same, so like her brothers, right from when they were kids. So no matter what her mother said, she wasn't going to tar all men with the same brush just because her daddy had been a mean drunk.

Cate leaned back and looked at her mother's face, at the ugly purple bruise that curled around her right eye. He might be dead, but he'd still managed to leave his mark on one of them.

"You deserved better than him, Ma," she said. "I'll never feel sorry that he's gone."

Cate could see that day in her mind like it was only yesterday, the policemen coming to the door with news that they thought would bring a mother and daughter to their knees. And she was sure that's what it looked like to the policemen, seeing them hug and cry as the news sank in. But it was because he'd never come home drunk and beat her mother again; he'd never come home looking like murder, waiting like a snake coiled to take his anger out on one of his children. Never her, because her mother and brothers made sure of it, but it hadn't stopped her from being terrified of him.

She slowly moved toward Jack, shuffling in against him, refusing to be scared of him just because he was a man. He'd given her no reason to be frightened, and she wasn't going to let old memories of her bastard father ruin every close experience she had with a man.

"You looked scared of me just before," Jack whispered, his arm warm around her as she pressed her cheek into him.

"I was," she whispered back.

"I've got plenty more reasons to be scared of you than you have of me," he said gruffly.

She smiled into him. "Like what?"

Silence swam between them for a beat, but he didn't answer her. "You know, my daddy used to beat the crap out of me when I was younger. I can still feel the sting of his belt on the back of my legs, and his knuckles colliding with my cheeks, even though I was barely ten when he did it to me."

She swallowed, forcing a breath in and then out before answering. "How did you know?"

He stroked her hair, just one slow, long stroke before his hand settled on her arm. "Because that frightened look you gave me before is one I used to know well, so I'm guessing a man sometime, some-where, has hurt you. And before you ask, I'm not my father's son."

She listened to her own breath as memories tried to tug her back.

"Was it your fiancé?" he asked. She felt his gaze rest on the ring around her neck, and she instinctively touched it and slipped it back under her dress.

"No, he was, *is*, a good man, a kind man," she said, not want-ing to think about Charlie, not now, not when she was lying in the arms of another man, innocent or not. "I've known him since I was a kid, he was friends with my brothers. Honestly, he was almost too scared to hold hands with me for so long, let alone hit me." Charlie *was* a good man. He might not have swept her off her feet with romance and excitement, but he was steady, loyal. *Safe.* The complete opposite of her daddy, and so different to Jack, too. Jack made her heart race, made her want to press herself against him and lose herself in his kisses. Jack scared her because she'd never felt that kind of excitement about a man before.

But Jack didn't push her; he let her take her time, not moving beside her.

"It was my father, same as you," she murmured. "Only he pre-ferred hurting my mother, not me."

"He still around?"

She placed an arm over his chest, careful not to touch his ban-dages. "No. He was raging drunk one night and killed himself. Shot his own brains out in our car."

"That must have been quite the mess to clean up before you could drive it again."

Cate choked on her laugh as Jack's chest began to rumble with laughter of his own.

"I'm so sorry, that was terribly insensitive," he apologized. "I have a very warped sense of humor sometimes."

"Not at all. It's probably the best darn thing anyone's ever said to me." Cate wiped her tears away, still smiling as she shut her eyes and promised herself that it was finally time to sleep.

"Wake up!"

The hiss of words was so loud, so sudden, that Cate felt as if someone had jolted her with electricity. She sat bolt upright, hand on her head, which was pounding from being woken up so unexpectedly.

She looked around, horrified that she'd fallen asleep with Jack in his bed. But Harry clearly had other things on his mind. He closed the attic door behind him and came to sit beside her, raking his hands frantically through his hair.

"What's going on?" she asked, rubbing her eyes.

Jack moved beside her, and she turned to offer him a hand to pull himself up, his wince giving away just how painful it still was for him to move.

"Elise said it's a Nazi commander, the one who brought you to the door the night you arrived," Harry whispered. "He's come calling on Adelaide."

"Don't they have a war to finish?" Jack muttered.

Harry grunted. "I think they've already finished what they started in this neck of the woods."

Cate stood and padded silently to the door, pressing her ear to it and trying to listen. All she could detect were muffled voices, a woman's and then a man's deeper rumble, but she couldn't tell what they were saying.

"Shhh," she hissed to the men behind her, opening the door just a crack, holding her breath as she eased the doorknob back.

"I promise I'll have her back soon."

The words sent chills through her. Was Adelaide actually going with him?

"Are you certain it's safe out there?" It was Elise speaking this time. "We've been too scared to venture out at all."

"She'll be perfectly safe with me, I'll make certain of it."

His clipped, perfect French, the deep, commanding tone of his voice, sent a fresh wave of shivers through Cate, and she carefully shut the door. When she turned, the cool timber to her back, she found Jack and Harry staring at her, their eyes wide.

"Well?" Harry asked.

"He's definitely here for Adelaide," she said, starting to laugh nervously. "He doesn't know about us, he just wants to see her."

Harry was looking at her like she was delirious, and Jack's mouth had dropped open, his face pale.

"He's interested in one of the sisters?" Jack asked, looking confused.

But Harry was shaking his head. "It could be a trap. He could be seeking her out because he's suspicious."

Cate lifted her head as she heard footfalls, holding her finger to her lips. "Shhh." She backed away from the door to stand closer to Harry, and he straightened beside her, his hand finding hers, their fingers tightly clenched together. She barely knew him, but she didn't care.

Is it a trick? Have we been discovered already?

A door shut, the bang echoing up to them, and Cate held her breath. Had the commander gone?

And then a shuffle outside the door to the attic set her heart racing again.

"It's me," came a soft voice.

Cate jumped forward and thrust it open, finding Elise standing there looking as forlorn as a child who'd lost her favorite toy.

"She's with him?" Cate asked, immediately reaching for Elise and drawing her close.

Elise was like a statue in her arms, unmoving, silent.

"Do you think he knows anything?" Harry asked.

Cate took a step away from Elise, wishing she could say something to give her comfort. But it was their fault, all of them collectively, that Elise was even in this position.

"He doesn't know," Elise said. "He's just smitten with my sister from the look of it."

"It could all be part of an elaborate ruse," Harry said. He started to pace the small room, then edged closer to the window.

"It's not a ruse," Elise snapped. "If he thought there was even a possibility we had British soldiers in our home, he'd have stormed the place and dragged you out. It's her he wants, it's as simple as that."

Silence hung between them. Elise's chest was heaving, and Cate could almost feel the fear radiating off her.

"I'm sorry, Elise," she finally said. "I'm so, so sorry."

"There's no point being sorry," Elise said, shutting the door and slowly sliding down it until she was sitting on the floor. "What's done is done."

"It's him."

"Who's him?" Cate asked.

"It's the commander, the one who gave the order," Harry yelped. "Your sister is leaving with the man who massacred my entire regiment!"

Cate looked at Harry as he sank on to the bed, head in his hands.

"You're certain?" Elise's throat sounded raw.

As Harry looked up, his eyes searching out Elise's, Cate knew there was no way he was wrong.

"I'll remember that bastard till my last breath, Elise. It's him."

Cate went to Elise and sat beside her on the floor, reaching for her hand. There was nothing left to say; they just had to wait now for Adelaide to return home.

Cate squeezed her fingers, and Elise squeezed back. "I'm so sorry," she whispered.

"It's not your fault," Elise replied, her eyes shut as her head dropped back against the door.

Only it was, and they both knew it. She'd brought him to their front door that night; she was the one who'd as good as told Wolfgang where Adelaide lived.

CHAPTER FOURTEEN

ELISE

Elise's feet felt like lead as she walked down the stairs. She'd left Oscar downstairs earlier, knowing that he'd bark as soon as Addy returned, and like clockwork he'd alerted her. She kept her composure as she walked into the kitchen, prepared to give her sister a firm but kind talking to.

No.

No, no, no!

There, sitting in her kitchen, his big frame filling one of her kitchen chairs, was Commander Wolfgang Schmidt. In *her* kitchen! Sitting there like it was the most natural thing in the world.

"You're back," she managed, as he gave her a smile full of white teeth that reminded her of a wolf. A handsome, smart wolf who'd managed to make it all the way to the chicken coop. And he had no idea she knew what he'd done.

"I didn't want you to worry," he said, the glint in his eyes sending a shiver through her. "And your delightful sister offered to make me coffee."

"Did she now," Elise said, joining her sister at the kitchen counter and giving her a sharp stare.

"I don't want you to worry about having me in your home," he continued, as if he could smell the fear radiating off her. "We'll be stationed here for some time, and it won't be long before all of France is under German control. The sooner everyone becomes used to our presence, the better."

At this, all Elise really wanted was to fall to her knees and sob. Either that or scream profanities at him and all the other Nazis within shouting distance.

But Elise was known for her composure. For always reacting calmly and sensibly, for being reliable, and she wasn't going to waver from that now.

"We're just doing our best to get by and keep our heads down here," Elise said, keeping her voice even as she turned, her smile fixed. "We've heard a lot of fighting nearby, and we can only hope that things settle down soon, isn't that right, Addy?" She put her arm around her sister, dreading the news she had to tell her, not knowing how she would react.

"Rations must be very hard for you," he said, smiling when Adelaide pulled away from Elise to take him his coffee. "I can't imagine how careful you must have to be with food these days."

"It's been very hard for everyone," Elise confessed, making herself a cup of coffee and joining her sister at the table. "We're just lucky we have space to grow some of our own vegetables."

His eyes were back on Addy, and it made her sick to see the way he watched her. She only hoped her sister wasn't feeling the same toward him.

"I'll make sure you get some extra, then," he said. "For making me feel so welcome."

"Really?" Addy asked, giggling when he smiled at her. "You can do that for us?"

He laughed. "There are some perks to being in my position, and good food is one of them."

Elise kept forcing her smile, drinking her too-hot coffee just to give her mouth a break, even though she was almost certain she'd have blisters as a result. She probably looked as happy as a wet cat sitting across from him, and she needed to get better at her game face. She had a feeling she was going to be needing it a lot over the coming weeks and months, but even seeing her sister behave like a giggling teenager was grating every nerve in her body.

"Will your cousin be joining us?" Wolfgang asked, setting his cup down. "I didn't catch her name the other night, in all the commotion of worrying about the dog." His smile settled over her sister and she hated it. She knew exactly why he didn't know Cate's name; he'd been too busy fixing his gaze on Adelaide.

Elise bristled as Adelaide smiled sweetly back at him. It was like being part of a terrible game of cat and mouse, knowing she was being baited but unable to do anything about it.

"Cate," Addy said before she could. "Her name's Cate."

"And she's unfortunately not feeling so well today," Elise quickly added. "I think she caught a cold after being out in the rain the other night for so long. Silly girl was soaked right through."

As if on cue, Oscar jumped up then, pawing at Wolfgang, and Elise watched in horror as Addy playfully scolded the dog while Wolfgang leant forward, his hand on her sister's arm.

"He's fine, he's very friendly," Wolfgang said, and Elise froze until his hand fell away from Adelaide. "I can see why she was out in the cold looking for him."

Finally he finished his coffee and rose, and Elise wished the dog had more sense and knew to bite him around the ankles. Weren't animals supposed to sense these things?

"Well, thank you for a lovely hour," Wolfgang said, taking Addy's hand and pressing a kiss there. "I think France might be my second favorite country already—the women here seem to be very beautiful."

Adelaide blushed and thanked him as Elise watched on, dismayed, wishing she could hurl something at him and tell him that she knew exactly what kind of monster he was. And still, she kept her stupid smile plastered on her face.

But instead of reacting she stood and watched her sister see him out, smiling and laughing, until she finally shut the door behind him. The way he looked at her, the way he touched her so openly, made her sick. She knew that many Germans were probably no different from their French soldiers; young men who hadn't had a choice about joining the war and were just doing their duty. But this man, this Wolfgang? He'd already shown his cruelty, which in her eyes made him no better than Hitler himself. She had no reason to doubt Harry; if he said Wolfgang had been the one to give the order, then she believed him.

"Bastard," Elise whispered, wishing she had had the courage to say it to his face.

"What was that?" Addy spun around, looking as giddy as if she'd been on a date with her sweetheart.

"I have something I need to tell you, Addy," Elise said, reaching for her sister's hand. "Adelaide, I'm so sorry, but Harry, well, he recognized Wolfgang today."

"Recognized him? From where?"

"From what happened the other day." Elise swallowed, seeing the confusion in Addy's eyes. "He was the one who gave the order to shoot. It was him we watched that day from the bedroom. He's responsible for killing Harry and Peter's entire regiment."

Adelaide pulled her hand away and pushed past her, but Elise saw the shock on her face, and when she collected their empty cups, the china audibly shook in her hands.

"Perhaps Harry got it wrong? I mean, after everything he's been through, after . . ."

As her words trailed, Elise moved in front of her, searching her gaze.

"Harry's not wrong," she said, seeing that she needed to be firmer with her. "Adelaide, he's a murderer, that man you just swanned off with and made eyes over the table at. He's the reason those poor men upstairs are—"

Her sister pushed past her again, but Elise wasn't standing for it.

"Adelaide!" she scolded. "You do not walk away from me like that!"

"Why not?" Addy asked, spinning around, her hands on her hips now. "Why can't I choose to ignore you? And why are you choosing to believe Harry over me? You're not my mother, and it wasn't like I had a choice in the matter when he came calling for me!"

Her words stung, but Elise refused to acknowledge the hurt. "Well, if you don't want me to be your mother, then you'd better start behaving like an adult, Adelaide."

"Has it even occurred to you, even once, that maybe I'm acting the part?" she asked. "That maybe I decided that it would be more helpful to play along, to be the fun, flirty French girl with him?"

Elise's breath was shuddering out of her. "No, Addy. I didn't think that, because I know you too well, and that was not acting." She moved around her sister, not letting her turn away, not giving her anywhere to go. "You're starting to like him, I can see it. It's written all over your face, and I need you to understand the truth before you get too close to him."

"I'm not a child, Elise. I can handle this myself."

"Well, just remember that it's not just your life you're playing with. We have three other people in this house who need us, who need this to be a safe place." She didn't remind Adelaide that it was *her* who'd invited them in in the first place.

"I'm well aware of what's at stake here," Addy said, and Elise let her turn away this time. What was the point in fighting with her own sister? They'd only had one another for so long, and they'd barely ever raised their voices in anger, let alone argued.

"Just be careful," Elise said. "He's a very powerful, very dangerous man, and I don't want you ending up as collateral damage."

Addy shot her a sideways look, and Elise knew then that her sister was scared, even though she was going to great lengths not to admit it.

"It was him, Adelaide. I need you to see that."

"You don't know that!" Addy cried. "There are so many reasons why Harry could be wrong, I mean he might not have seen him properly, he's traumatized about what happened and looking for someone to blame, he might have . . ."

"That's enough." Elise shook her head. "Grow up, Addy. The fact that a man can be charming to a pretty girl doesn't mean he isn't capable of something terrible. Harry saw his face and he knows it was him. You can ask him yourself if you like."

"I just . . ." Addy whispered, staring out of the small kitchen window. "I just can't believe that it could have been him. He told me that Peter is safe, that he came to no harm."

Elise came to stand beside her then, sighing as Addy dropped her head to her shoulder. She slipped an arm around her waist, her sister's naivety reminding her of how different they were.

"I'm telling you the truth, Addy. Harry has no reason to lie to us, and if you'd seen the way he reacted when he saw Wolfgang . . ."

Addy shivered beside her.

"I don't like the game you're playing," Elise whispered. "I can't lose you, Addy. I can't lose anyone else I love."

Addy moved even closer to her. "Me neither."

"Then promise me you'll be careful, that you won't ever stop remembering what he's capable of, no matter how charming he is."

The creak of floorboards on the stairs told Elise they weren't alone any longer, and she dropped a quick kiss into her sister's hair.

"I promise," Addy murmured.

Elise only hoped it was a promise she could keep.

Elise stared at the mash that Adelaide put on the table, the bowl more attractive than the food inside. Once the war was over, she would make a solemn vow to never, ever eat another Jerusalem artichoke in her life again. But for now, they were better than nothing.

"Sorry, I've salted the mash to make it bearable, but we don't have a lot to go around."

"It'll be fine," Cate said brightly, as the four of them sat down to eat. The curtains were drawn, the doors were locked, and so Harry had decided to join them downstairs. Jack was still in bed upstairs, but he'd demanded that Cate eat with them before bringing a meal up to him.

Elise could almost pretend that they had friends over, the chairs around their table almost full again for once, but it was impossible to look at Harry and not remember what danger he was in. Or what he'd lived through to be sitting across from her.

"We used to think Jerusalem artichokes were animal food, or just for poor people," Elise told Cate and Harry. "But now they're one of the only things we can supplement our rations with."

"Other than the black market," Addy said as she served the mash for everyone. "Just don't eat too much or it'll give you a sore stomach."

Cate nodded solemnly, which made Addy laugh.

"As in it'll make you very gassy," Addy whispered, to which Cate finally erupted into laughter, although Elise noticed Harry never so much as cracked a smile.

"I think we all understood," Elise said. "But this stew will brighten up the plates a little."

She ladled a couple of small spoonfuls each into their bowls, tiny bits of meat and mostly carrot swimming in the dark liquid. They always had a pot of soup bubbling away; they kept it on the stove and added to it all the time, and although she'd have preferred big chunks of meat, with a fresh baguette to mop up the leftovers, it was still tasty.

"Is someone going to explain to me what the hell happened today?" Harry asked.

Adelaide shot Elise a quick glance, but Elise didn't say anything, deciding her sister could take the lead. She'd made it clear she wasn't a child and wanted to make her own decisions, so for once she was going to let her.

"I, ah, I went for a walk," Adelaide said as she sat down and picked up her spoon. "He doesn't suspect anything, if that's what you're worried about."

Harry's spoon was hovering over his bowl, shaking, but he still hadn't taken a mouthful yet. "You went for a walk with the man responsible for killing my entire regiment," he said. "You make it sound like the most innocent thing in the world."

"I didn't know," Adelaide stammered. "I—"

"Don't for a moment try to tell me that it wasn't him, or that I've got the wrong man, because I'll never, ever forget his face, Adelaide. Never."

"He doesn't know about you," Adelaide mumbled. "And you have to believe me—if I'd known, I mean, I don't even know what to say."

Elise swallowed her mouthful and set down her spoon, tempted to let Harry give Adelaide a stern talking-to, but thinking better of it. There was nothing she could do now to deflect the Nazi's interest in her. "I think what my sister's trying to say is that the commander fancies her, and that seems to be the only thing of interest here to him. And it's not like she can politely say no to him, because there would be consequences to turning him down now, I'm certain of it."

Adelaide's cheeks had turned a burning shade of red, and Elise couldn't help but feel satisfied. She deserved to be embarrassed, acting as if this Nazi were no different to any other man coming calling on her.

"How did you meet him?" Cate asked. "I was surprised he knew who you were the other night."

As spoons started to clink against china, and Harry glowered at his bowl, Adelaide spoke up, surprising her. "I took Harry's friend to surrender, and I met him at the house they'd commandeered."

"A man who we'd all agreed was to be kept in this house and cared for, instead of being handed over to the enemy," Harry muttered.

Elise raised her brows at him. She understood his anger, but it wasn't helpful, not now.

"And he took a liking to you there?" Cate asked, ignoring Harry.

"I didn't realize so at the time, but yes, I suppose he must have."

"And then I brought him right to your door that night," Cate muttered. "Yet another thing that's happened because of me."

"Nonsense," Elise interrupted. "He'd clearly taken a fancy to her that first day he saw her. Don't blame yourself for this. If anything, it's Adelaide's own fault, so please don't start thinking you're the one who brought him, because he was already coming, with or without you."

"We could use him," Harry suddenly said, his stew already long gone. His face still told of anger and frustration, but there was a light in his eyes that hadn't been there before. "I hate him as much as I hate that bastard Hitler, but to have someone on the inside, to have that connection—"

"Absolutely not!" Elise surprised herself as much as she did Harry with her outburst, slamming her hand against the table. But Harry leaned back in his chair and continued, clearly not prepared to back down.

"We need to think this through with clear heads," he counseled. "You've said yourself that there's nothing you can do to send him away, that he's already in Adelaide's life, so why not use it to our advantage? Surely she owes me that much."

"This is my sister you're talking about! We can't play her like a puppet and hope for the best with someone who's more than capable of killing anyone who betrays him," Elise retorted. "And don't you ever let me hear you say that my sister owes you, because she doesn't owe you a thing. She's the only reason you're safe in this house and not six feet under."

"Well, he's not going to kill me, is he?" Addy said beside her, her voice so soft in comparison to Elise's outburst. "He's asked if he can call on me again, and I've already said yes. I agree with Harry. I do owe him."

"No," Elise said, her appetite long gone as she pushed her bowl away. "We're not playing with my sister's life. This is not up for discussion."

"You're right, it's not," Addy said, tucking into her dinner. "Because I'm not going to sit around to wait for Harry or Cate or Jack to get caught, not when there's something I can do about it. And stop talking about me like I'm not sitting at this table right beside you!"

"How about we let the situation with the commander evolve organically?" Cate said diplomatically. "And at the same time, we try to get an understanding of what's happening beyond this village. Knowledge is power, after all."

Elise breathed more easily as she digested Cate's considered words. "I agree. We need to hear it from our own people, not from a Nazi. What do you propose, then?"

"You and Cate could leave the house when it's safe, and Adelaide can hold the fort here. If this Wolfgang comes while you're gone, then she can do whatever she feels comfortable with, but I agree that we have to step carefully."

"He must have been acting on orders, like all soldiers do," Addy said. "There's no other explanation for it."

Harry's words were as chilled as ice. "No, Adelaide, that's not right. Acting on orders would have been allowing my men to surrender and taking us prisoners of war. He gave the order, *he* chose to shoot us like ducks in a barrel and in doing so, violated the Geneva Convention."

Adelaide had tears shining in her eyes, but Elise didn't jump in to her defense. It was a fair point, and one that her sister needed to understand. She needed her to realize what this man was capable of.

"I have no intention of falling in love with the man, honestly!" Addy muttered.

"Good," Harry replied. "So long as you keep your head straight, perhaps your little stunt with him could prove useful."

"I'm not going to warn you again, Harry. My sister is not, and will never be, a pawn to be used for anyone's advantage."

"I think your sister has already pointed out that she'll be the one deciding what she will and won't be doing," he replied curtly.

Elise glared at him, wondering how she could have felt so warmly toward him just evenings ago, and so frosty now. It was like he was ready to throw Addy to the wolves if he needed to. "Cate and I will travel to Lille as soon as the fighting ceases and things settle down," she finally said. "We have little knowledge of what's going on outside our own village, but there is a friend of my father's there who I can call on. I would trust him with my life, so I know we'd be safe visiting him and asking questions."

"Shouldn't I go with you?" Adelaide asked.

Elise didn't even turn to look at her, keeping her gaze on Harry. "I thought I'd already made it clear that I don't want you in any danger?" She stuck her fork into the artichoke mash and forced it down, hating every bite but knowing she needed to eat.

"Elise," Cate said quietly, picking up her bowl and cutlery. "Would you help me to clear the table?"

Elise scooped up the last of the mash, swallowing it down and then lifting her bowl from the table. "Of course."

She followed Cate out of the room, both of them placing their bowls and cutlery in the sink. It was funny, because she'd always felt closer to her siblings than to anyone else in the world, but she found herself drawn toward Cate now. It was nice, in a way, to have another woman to talk to.

"I think you're right to be cautious," Cate said, her voice low as they stood facing the window, shoulder to shoulder at the sink. "That night I came here, honestly, it was like that commander didn't even see me, he only had eyes for your sister. And the way he was staring at her made me feel uncomfortable."

"So you agree with me?" Elise asked. "You don't think I'm being overprotective?"

"Overprotective? We're talking about your sister getting involved with a Nazi! A Nazi who gave the order to massacre almost a hundred men who were trying to surrender," Cate whispered. "You have every right to be upset."

Elise squeezed her eyes shut. She'd promised her mother that she'd look after Adelaide, that she wouldn't let any harm come to her, and she'd barely managed a year of keeping her safe. "So what do we do, then?" she eventually asked.

"Honestly? I don't have the answer to that, but if you're thinking of forbidding her from seeing him, I wouldn't. Imagine how quickly his affections could change if she turned him down?"

Elise groaned. "I should never have let her go today, should I?"

"Maybe not, but what's done is done. And I don't see that you really had a choice in the matter." Cate sighed. "It doesn't exactly make it easy with Harry encouraging her, either."

"I just don't like being this person, telling her what she can and can't do, being the one in charge when—"

"You feel like you don't even know what you're doing, and yet you have to figure out how to manage someone else as well."

Elise stared at her. "That's exactly how I feel. Like I'm suddenly the head of the family, even though I never wanted to be and I don't have any training for the job."

Cate nodded. "It's how I felt when I started nursing. There were so many expectations, so much I was responsible for even though I had no idea what I was doing in the beginning."

"So how did you get through it?"

"I think we all just do the best we can, the only way we know how," Cate said wistfully. "Somehow, in the end, we figure it out along the way. And I can tell you'll be just fine, you're already the head of this family whether you want to be or not."

"I suppose I feel sorry for Addy in a way, it's like she's been robbed of those fun years, meeting boys and having fun with friends her own age. So much has been going on and my parents became very protective of her as soon as there was even a whisper of war."

"What are you two gossiping about in here?" Adelaide's warm, sweet voice put an end to their conversation, and Elise turned and took the dishes her sister was carrying. That was one thing she had to give her sister credit for; she never held grudges, and was always perfectly happy to move on and forget any harsh words that had been said.

"Nothing important," Elise replied, wishing she could bundle Addy in a big hug and keep her safe from the world forever.

"I wanted to know if Elise had any spare sanitary items. I didn't want to ask in front of Harry, and I've had some bad cramping,"

Cate said, smiling at Elise as she turned. "And then we got carried away whispering about how handsome Harry is. I think your sister likes him."

Elise went to open her mouth and scold Cate, but then promptly shut it as Adelaide laughed and grabbed hold of her arm.

"So that's why you were so prickly at the table," Addy teased. "You should have told me you were sweet on him."

Cate grinned and mouthed "Sorry" from behind Adelaide, and Elise raised her eyebrows in response and swatted at her sister, wondering if it would have been better to tell her the truth about their discussion than have to put up with the endless teasing.

CHAPTER FIFTEEN

ADELAIDE

Adelaide stared up at the ceiling, listening to her sister breathing in bed beside her. They'd taken to sleeping together ever since the others had arrived, and she liked it. It reminded her of when she'd been younger, and Elise had always tiptoed down to her room, knowing she hated being alone in the dark. The past few days had made everything feel so different and uncertain, and even though they'd argued for the first time since their guests had joined them, she still wanted Elise close by.

Wolfgang. She turned his name over in her mind, over and over again, trying to figure out what she actually felt for him. Was he the monster her sister kept insisting he was? *Was* he the man who'd given the order that day? It had been impossible for them to see; all the soldiers had had their backs to them, but why would Harry lie? After walking with Wolfgang, being in his company, everything had started to feel blurred and she didn't know what she felt or even what she should believe. It was as if she couldn't reconcile the allegations with the person she'd spent time with.

She was scared of him, excited by him, attracted to him and horrified by what he stood for. His uniform alone marked him as being so different from her and the values she'd grown up with. Her father had had time for everyone, and would invite anyone to the dinner table; he didn't care what religion they followed or where they came from, he just liked anyone with a story to tell over wine and good food.

Papa would be so angry with me. She squeezed her eyes shut, not wanting to hear his voice in her head, trying to push him away. Because the Nazis only wanted one sort of person in this world, which was the opposite of what her father had wanted.

She'd been honest yesterday when she'd told Elise that she wanted to use Wolfgang, to distract him from what was really going on. But there was also a part of her that wanted to see him again—that was kind of thrilled to be seeing him again, to feel that unfamiliar flutter in her stomach as she walked beside one of the most handsome men she'd ever met, in his immaculately tailored uniform, basking in the way he looked at her.

It was so wrong, she knew that, but she actually liked the cat-and-mouse game. For the past year, everything had been sad. First Louis, then her parents, and now . . . Her eyes flew open again. Now they had people hiding in their home and she'd caught the eye of a Nazi soldier. It was exhilarating, and she couldn't pretend that she didn't like his interest in her. Suddenly she was feeling excited about being alive again, about the people she was spending time with.

She rose and got dressed, going into the bathroom and fixing her hair and splashing some water on her face before heading downstairs. No one else was up yet, and she moved quietly around the kitchen, deciding to make bread and humming to herself as she worked. Oscar came padding in and yawned at her before lying near her feet, and she smiled down at the little dog, pleased to have him for company.

"You're up early."

185

Adelaide got such a fright she almost jumped out of her skin, and found Cate standing behind her.

"Sorry, I didn't mean to frighten you," Cate apologized.

"It's fine, I was just lost in my thoughts, that's all."

Cate sat down at the table, and Addy washed her hands and lifted the big kettle to fill it with water.

"Coffee?"

"Please."

Addy busied herself with making it before finally taking both steaming mugs to the table and sitting across from Cate. She was a beautiful woman, with a wide mouth and warm brown eyes, and the way her fringe brushed almost all the way to her eyelashes gave her a shy look that made her seem more vulnerable than she probably was. She'd seen with her own eyes how capable Cate was when she needed to be.

"How's Jack?" Addy asked.

"He's fine. There's no infection, and he seems good within himself, but we're not out of the woods yet. I'm just pleased he has somewhere safe to recuperate."

"I'm glad to hear it." She'd secretly wondered if Cate and Jack's relationship went further than simply nurse and patient, but she wasn't about to ask.

"Elise told me that you're seeing the commander again today," Cate said. "How are you feeling about that?"

She didn't say it with any malice, but Adelaide still felt defensive. "I'm feeling just fine about it."

Cate frowned. "I'm not judging you, Adelaide. Please don't think that I asked for any reason other than I'm curious. I actually admire you for being so brave."

Addy's eyebrows shot up. "You do?" Cate had walked in the dark, with only a wounded soldier for protection, in a desperate bid to save her and Jack's life. Adelaide certainly hadn't expected to be the one called brave.

"Elise is worried about you, and to be honest I'd feel the same if you were my little sister. You're all she's got left."

Addy nodded. "I know. Honestly, I do. She's just, well, she's used to telling me what to do, that's all."

"And this time you want to be the one making your own decisions?"

Addy smiled into her coffee. "Something like that."

Cate leaned forward then, and Addy looked up at her. "Just be careful. He might be just a man falling for a beautiful girl, or he might want more than you're prepared to give. In fact, he might suspect more than you realize, so be vigilant. You might not know if he's playing a terrible game with you until it's too late."

Her words sank in and Adelaide realized her coffee mug was trembling in her hand. "I'll be careful. I promise I will." She hadn't really thought about the fact that he could be playing with her, rather than the other way around.

"Good, then can we check how that bread's looking? Because I could honestly eat a horse, I'm so hungry."

If Cate was trying to win her over, she'd definitely succeeded.

"Cate, how is it that you're so level-headed?" Addy asked once they were both standing by the oven. "I mean, you've risked everything to stay alive, you're hiding in my house and . . ." She took the bread out and turned to face her. "You're amazing. I'd be a nervous wreck, is what I'm trying to say."

Cate's quiet sob took her by surprise; a shudder shook the other woman's shoulders but lasted barely a few seconds before Cate seemed to compose herself.

"Cate, oh Cate, I'm so sorry!" Addy discarded her oven mitt and threw her arms around her. "I didn't mean to upset you."

Cate hugged her tightly, and Addy stroked her back in big circles.

"I'm fine, you just caught me off guard, and I've been holding it all in for so long," Cate said, stepping away at last. "I'm not who you think I am, Addy."

"So you're not a brave, strong, capable woman then?"

Cate's smile seemed bittersweet. "Put it this way," she said. "My insides feel like a freight train is chugging through them, and my hands shake so often that I've started to almost permanently fist them. So hearing you call me brave? It makes me feel like a fraud."

"You're not serious?" Addy asked, barely believing what she was hearing.

"As God is my witness," Cate replied. "But I've had to believe in myself all these months, Addy. There was no one there to hold my hand, and the men I nursed, well, some of them had a fate worse than death, and my job was to make them feel like everything would be fine." She took a big breath. "And some of them didn't make even a day in hospital before their bodies gave out on them, some of them were so badly burned their howls and whimpers will haunt my nightmares forever. It takes everything I have to keep those memories at bay."

"That must have been unbearable, for you I mean," Addy murmured. "I'm so sorry."

"I lost my fiancé, too," Cate said, staring at the bread as if it might hold all the answers. "He was a good man, and he didn't even last a month, and part of me will always wonder if someone kind was nursing him at the end. If he's not alive somewhere, that is, because he was classified as presumed dead, so there's always that question in my mind."

Addy cleared her throat, because it had suddenly turned dry and raspy. "Just like my brother Louis. We lost him right at the beginning as well. He was so strong and full of life, we didn't for a moment think that when we waved him goodbye he'd never come back."

"We're not so different after all then, are we?" Cate's smile was kind. "We all learn to cope as best we can. So whenever you look at me and think I'm holding everything together so well, just remember I've had more practice than you at faking it."

Addy touched Cate's hand. "Thank you for opening up to me," she whispered.

Cate smiled. "Thank *you* for making bread."

And they both laughed so hard, despite it all, that when Harry walked into the kitchen, he looked at the pair of them as if they'd gone stark raving mad.

It was time. Adelaide took a final look at herself in the mirror, running her hands down her pretty lavender-colored dress, her favorite, and staring into her own eyes for a moment. *Can I actually go through with this?* She was about to go on a picnic with Wolfgang, just the two of them, and all her earlier confidence had drained away. Her hair was softly curling over her shoulders, longer than usual, but she'd kept it that way during the war because she'd decided she liked it. She'd used a little rouge on her cheeks and pink lipstick, but she felt too young as she stared at her reflection, not grown-up enough to go on a proper date, even if she did turn twenty in a few days' time.

Elise tapped on the door then and she quickly looked away, not wanting to be seen mooning at herself in the mirror.

"I thought maybe you could wait for him near the door, so he doesn't have to come in," Elise said softly, her head against the door jamb as she considered her. "You look absolutely beautiful, Addy.

As gorgeous as Mama when they used to leave us and go out for dinner when we were little."

Adelaide did a little twirl and they both laughed. "You really think so?"

"I do." Elise came in and lifted the perfume bottle from the dresser, taking Addy's arm and dropping a little to her wrist. "And now you can smell like her, too."

Adelaide watched as Elise dabbed a little to her own wrist before setting the bottle back down.

"Addy, I know I said that I didn't approve, but I do believe in you, and I know I can't tell you what you can and can't do. If it were my choice, you wouldn't be seeing him, but . . ."

Adelaide picked up her jacket and slung it over her arm, nervous all over again as she waited for Elise to finish her sentence.

"Well, perhaps you could try to find out more about the current situation, what happened at Dunkirk and so on?" Elise suggested. "Don't make a fuss about it, just act interested if he starts to talk about the war. Make out like you know very little, just play along and get as much out of him as you can without being obvious."

"You really think I can manage it?" she asked. "I know you don't think I owe Harry, but I still feel like it's all my fault, what happened, so—"

"Hey, Harry's hurt, that's all. And you don't ever have to feel like you're obligated to do something for him. He's in our home, and that's the greatest kindness of all."

Elise had tears in her eyes, and Addy wished she hadn't been so angry with her. She'd been right to worry.

"You know I'd be lost without you, don't you?" Adelaide said.

"Maybe. Or maybe you'd be absolutely fine."

Adelaide took a deep breath and marched for the door, as ready as she would ever be. "Elise?"

"If you can't do this, then—"

Addy shook her head. "It's not that. I just want you to give Harry another chance. He wasn't trying to upset you the other night, he was only voicing his opinion."

Elise groaned. "I know. He was only trying to help, but he doesn't know us and I don't want him thinking he can take charge. We're not part of his unit."

His unit. Addy gulped. He wasn't with his unit because apparently Wolfgang had made sure there were none of his unit left. Surely it couldn't be true?

"You're certain you want to do this?" Elise asked.

A tremor ran through her, but she kept her head high, refused to give in to the fear. "This is something I can do, Elise. It's the one thing I can do for this war, for all of us, and I'm not going to back down now."

What she didn't say was how conflicted she felt. That day she'd met Wolfgang, standing there before him about to hand over a man who had a blind faith in the rules of warfare, she'd known she should be scared of him. And she had been. He'd made her want to run in the opposite direction, but at the same time, something about him had pulled her in. The way he'd looked at her, the command he held, the piercing blue eyes that were impossible not to stare into.

She touched her sister's hand, still resting on her shoulder, before moving away.

"I'm going to be fine. Try not to worry about me."

And for the first time in her life, she walked away feeling like the older sister instead of the younger one, knowing that Elise wouldn't be one step behind her if she needed her.

"I'll keep Harry and Jack hidden in the attic," Elise called after her. "Just in case you need to ask him in afterwards. I won't let them out until after you've returned."

Addy held her hand in a wave and descended the stairs, knowing she had to keep moving. If she didn't, she'd only lose her nerve. She bent to give Oscar a scratch behind the ears before edging toward the front door, flashing Cate a quick smile. She barely had time to compose herself before there was a brisk knock, and she reached for the door handle and opened it.

"Adelaide, you look beautiful." Wolfgang was standing with a small parcel, his hat under his arm as he passed the gift to her. "I would have preferred to give you flowers, but given the circumstances I thought you might be more grateful for eggs and cheese."

She smiled, her nerves slowly fluttering away. "Thank you, it's very kind. We've been saving eggs and sugar to make a cake, so this is very much appreciated."

When she took the parcel, his fingers brushed hers and she looked up into eyes as bright as the sky on a cloudless day. If he hadn't been a Nazi, he was the type of man she'd have declared her love for and vowed to marry one day, talked long into the night about with her sister. But she needed to keep reminding herself that he *was* a Nazi. He was the enemy.

Addy thought of Harry and Jack cooped up in the attic. And that he'd kill those men up there without a second thought.

"Let me put these in the kitchen," she said, leaving him standing at the door momentarily.

"What's this?" Cate whispered.

"A gift from my date," Addy replied, hastily returning to him and taking his proffered arm as the door swung shut behind her.

"Where are we going?" she asked, shyly glancing up at him.

"Like I said, on a picnic," he said, leaning in and speaking into her ear. "With some of my men close by to make sure we're safe. I don't want us dodging gunfire."

It was easy to forget that a war was still raging around them, that a stray bullet could end her life as quickly as anyone else's, and she found that she wanted to know more instead of being kept in the dark about what was happening.

"Wolfgang," she said, her fingers curling around his arm as they walked. "Can I ask you something?"

"Of course."

"Can I trust you?"

He paused, looking down at her, a slight frown changing his features. "Is there something you need to tell me?"

Addy considered her next words more carefully, trying not to show her fear. "No, I mean, can I trust being with you? We're on opposite sides of this war, and I don't want to feel afraid of you, that you could do something to hurt me or my family because of that. I don't want to feel nervous or scared when I'm with you."

Addy knew how easily she could fall for him when he stepped in front of her and clasped her hands, smiling down at her in a way that made her feel seen, made her feel like a woman, for the first time in her life. She'd asked him truthfully, but if Cate or Elise were listening, they'd probably have applauded; she'd already managed to draw him into the palm of her hand.

"Adelaide, the French people are going to have to get used to German soldiers living in France. Soon, your country will be controlled by Germany. We're here to stay," he said. "But here, right now, I am just a man taking a beautiful woman on a picnic. There are no sides here, and I don't want to talk about war. With you, I just want to be a man."

Adelaide stared into his eyes, looking for any hint that he might be lying, that he could be using her for information as she was about to use him, but found nothing.

"Thank you," she said, because she couldn't come up with anything else.

"Now come on, I don't have long and I want to spend as much time with you as possible."

Addy let herself be drawn into his web, knowing that she needed to tread lightly, but still taken with the fact that a man, any man, had gone to such lengths to steal a couple of hours with her in the middle of a war.

"You were very brave coming to our quarters that day," Wolfgang said as he stretched his long legs out on the grass. Despite all the rain they'd had earlier in the week, the ground was dry now, and Adelaide sat beside him, her legs curled to one side. She found herself staring at the dark fabric of his trousers, wondering how he could look so immaculate despite the months he must have been away from home.

"Brave or stupid?" she finally replied.

He chuckled. "Perhaps a little of both. I certainly wouldn't recommend doing it again, though, unless you're coming to visit me of course. No one would touch you now, but the other day . . ." His gaze was steady. "Let's say I'm happy I was there to intervene."

"I don't know a lot about rank," she admitted, plucking at the grass and watching her own fingers instead of looking up at him. Perhaps he was waiting for a thank you, but she didn't give him one. "But I saw the way the other soldiers looked at you when you walked out that day. They were frightened of you, weren't they?" Maybe that alone should have been a sign that she should have been frightened, too.

"Not frightened," he corrected. "I'm their superior and they respect my rank. It's the way it has to be in any army."

He opened his bag, and her stomach gave a growl of approval. She'd never known hunger before the war had begun, not true, gnawing hunger.

"Next time I'll bring wine. The chateau we've commandeered has an impressive cellar," he said, grinning as he produced cheese wrapped in a soft cloth. "But this, well, this promises to be just as good."

Addy's mouth watered as she stared at the cheese, knowing she should refuse it on principle—he'd stolen it from the home he'd strolled into and taken over. It didn't belong to him, and that meant she shouldn't be consuming it, but . . . she was so, so hungry all of a sudden, and if she didn't eat some of it, he'd only have it all. She vaguely knew the family who owned the chateau, and she told herself they'd prefer a French woman to be consuming it than a Nazi.

"You like cheese?" he asked.

Adelaide laughed. "I'm French! Of course I like cheese."

He produced what appeared to be a quince jelly, and some cold boiled eggs, and for all her good intentions, she couldn't turn the food down; even knowing that she was eating and her sister wasn't, she just couldn't say no.

"Maybe one day I can take you on a proper French picnic with a fresh baguette and cold meats too, but for now this will have to do."

Adelaide looked at him, really looked at him, and saw a glimpse of the man he might have been if he were French. Or if Hitler hadn't risen to power and turned his people into Nazis. Because right now, Wolfgang *was* just a man trying to impress a woman; it was as simple as that. She doubted German people used to be all that different from French ones.

"Do you truly think you'll stay here?" she asked. "Your German army, I mean?"

He nodded, but she didn't know how to read him, how to tell whether he was being that man she'd seen before, or the commander version of himself. Maybe she was kidding herself that they weren't one and the same.

"I'm sorry to be the bearer of bad news, Adelaide, but the French army stand no chance. The British troops have all evacuated—for some reason I'll never understand, an order was made to halt the land assault on British soldiers at Dunkirk beach—and the rest of the Allies have run, too. There is no one left to save the French, so you need to hope that your government does the right thing and makes way for our Führer, because if not, the consequences will be dire."

She swallowed, trying not to show any emotion, not wanting him to see how much his words had rattled her. Surely Hitler couldn't end up controlling France?

"Your government is expected to announce their defeat within days, so when I said that you should get used to seeing my fellow countrymen here . . ."

Adelaide forced a smile, deliberately thinking about the food he'd brought again, knowing she needed to steer the conversation in another direction. "Let's not talk war or politics," she said as sweetly as she could. "I'd far rather hear all about your family back home while we devour that round of cheese."

His laugh was hearty, and she took the small knife he'd had wrapped with the cheese and started to cut it. She stared for a moment at the tiny, curved blade in her fingers, wondering how hard she'd have to drive it into his skin to do any damage. But the thought passed as quickly as it had arrived, and she offered him the first piece. There was no way she could attack a German commander and get away with it, let alone be successful enough to kill or seriously wound him.

"I should have said ladies first," he said.

Her shyness slipped away, as if she were acting a part in a play. She suddenly realized she could actually do this, behave as if she were someone else, someone so much more confident and worldly than she really was.

"I want to see the look on your face when you taste it," she teased, pushing her dark thoughts away. "I dare say it's aged to perfection, so it should be delicious."

He shut his eyes as he placed it in his mouth and she waited, watching for his smile. It only took a few seconds before he was grinning at her, and in that moment she knew then that being involved with a high-ranking German wasn't the worst move for a woman. If they were to stay? If he was right about the German army not leaving? She would have better rations and be kept safe from other soldiers who might otherwise lurk around two women living on their own. Many of her neighbors might hate her when they returned for accepting the enemy, but if Wolfgang was right and their government was going to announce defeat? What option would any single woman have other than to accept the presence of German troops? Than to take up with a German soldier?

"Adelaide?" Wolfgang asked.

She raised her chin, a piece of cheese touching her lips as she took a small bite, coyly looking up at him. He reached out and stroked her cheek, his calloused fingers brushing roughly against her skin, before one of his fingers crooked and he gently swept a stray strand of hair behind her ear.

"May I kiss you?"

She swallowed, glancing at his lips and then nervously back to his eyes again. There was a hunger there that scared her, knowing what he wanted from her, even though he hadn't been anything other than a gentleman to her so far. She wasn't exactly experienced with men, no matter how much she'd tried to convince her sister and the others at the house that she was.

He seemed to take her silence as an invitation, because his hand cupped the back of her head then, tilting her face up ever so slightly as his lips slowly moved to hers. It was a warm, quiet kiss, just a simple, fleeting press of his lips over hers, before he pulled away.

She heard a series of pops, and Wolfgang's hand covered hers protectively. He looked over his shoulder and she wondered if he had soldiers stationed right behind them, or whether he was looking to see if anyone was approaching. The meadow they were sitting in was pretty, with flowers dotted through the grass, although where he'd chosen for them was safely tucked away from sight by a cluster of trees.

"Was that fighting nearby?" she asked.

"Not close enough to worry about," he said, but the moment he spoke there was a deep drone from the sky, and soon an enormous German Luftwaffe aircraft passed overhead, and Addy's heart started to race with fear.

"How about we finish this food and then we pack up and get you home?" he suggested. "I don't want your sister worrying for your safety, and perhaps it wasn't the best day for a picnic. There are still small groups of insurgents we're finding, hence the gunfire."

Adelaide had suddenly lost her appetite, although she made herself graciously take the boiled egg he passed her, forcing little mouthfuls down. She'd learnt never to waste food, not now.

"Can I call on you again?" Wolfgang asked, touching her fingers.

Adelaide didn't hide from his gaze this time, knowing she needed to draw on every ounce of confidence she had. "I would like that very much."

He might have been capable of terrible things, but as she sat beside him, in that moment, she couldn't help but wonder how many dreadful things Allied soldiers were capable of too, and if Wolfgang was really so different to the man her brother might have become if he were still alive.

Adelaide walked inside and shut the door behind her, leaning against it for a moment, eyes shut, remembering the kiss. *He kissed*

me. And she'd liked it. More than liked it; her skin had tingled and she'd wanted to lean straight back in to feel those warm, full lips of his against hers.

"I take it the date went well?"

Her eyes flew open. Elise was sitting, a book in her lap, feet up on the little footstool that had been her father's favorite.

"It was fine," she stammered, righting herself and going straight past Elise and into the kitchen. But her sister followed her, and she knew there was no way she was going to avoid talking about Wolfgang. It was silly—for some reason she wanted to keep her time with him secret, to have something that was just for her. But he'd told her things that needed to be shared.

"Your cheeks are very flushed," Elise said. "He didn't do anything to—"

"He didn't do anything," Addy interrupted, embarrassed and wishing her face wasn't so easy to read. "But I am seeing him again this week."

"So soon?" Elise echoed. "You've already made plans with him again?"

"Well, it seemed like a better idea than waiting for him to turn up unannounced, given the circumstances."

They stared at one another until someone whistled from upstairs, and Elise called back. Clearly they'd organized a signal while she was gone.

"All clear, come down!" Elise called.

Addy poured herself a glass of water for something to do, slowly drinking it and trying to clear her head. Being rude to her sister for no reason wasn't acceptable, she knew that, but she just wanted time to relive what it had felt like to be kissed by a man. She'd had bumpy-teethed kisses with boys her own age when she'd been younger, but having a man like Wolfgang take charge and actually kiss her, knowing exactly what he was doing, had been something else entirely.

"How did it go?" Harry asked. "Anything worth sharing?"

Addy set her water down and turned, finding Harry standing staring at her, running his fingers through his hair. But Cate was absent, and so was Jack, who'd barely left the attic bedroom since he'd arrived.

"I think we should go upstairs, so I can tell everyone," she said, not looking at Elise.

"He told you something important?" Elise asked.

Addy nodded. "I know you hate him, Harry, but I'm just not so sure it could have been him. I mean, he's told me twice now that Peter has received treatment for his wounds. Would he do that for him if he was capable of such things?"

Harry glared at her with such anger, such coldness, that she wrapped her arms around herself.

"I know you think he did something dreadful to your men, Harry, but today, being with him, it made me realize that we're all the same. We're just people who end up fighting for our country and the people we love. He's a brother and a son, and his mother and sister want him back as much as we want our loved ones home."

"Only *we* don't murder in cold blood," Harry muttered. "They're barbarians, Adelaide. I don't think they're like us at all. And what's to say he's not stringing you along about Peter?"

Maybe he was right and she was being naïve, but it was hard for her to make sense of it all. Tears swam in her vision then, but she didn't want to acknowledge them in case Elise saw.

"Tell us what he said." Elise was looking worried.

Adelaide noticed that her sister was angled away from Harry, not looking at him and certainly not appearing overly friendly.

"He said that the British soldiers are gone, evacuated from the beach at Dunkirk in their thousands," she said. "And he also told me . . ." Addy took a deep breath as Elise and Harry seemed to hang on her every word. "He also said that the German army is here to stay, that they're expecting to occupy our country, and that our government will turn France over to Hitler within days." Adelaide couldn't hold her tears back then; they fell rapidly down her cheeks. "The French army has as good as surrendered, and there's no other country coming to save us, which means our alliance with Wolfgang could mean everything to us. He might be able to keep us safe."

"He told you he'd keep us safe?" Elise asked.

"Yes," she whispered.

Harry went quiet before turning and walking straight back upstairs. "I'll go and tell Jack the news. But Adelaide?"

She waited for him to speak, saw the anger in him as he balled his fists at his side.

"Using this Nazi is one thing, but don't forget who he is. Every single man in my regiment had a family, too. They were all sons, husbands, brothers and sweethearts. They were men who deserved better than to be slaughtered while their own captain held a white goddamn flag." Tears were glistening in Harry's eyes now, his pain so real and raw that Adelaide felt a fool. "That man you're flirting with? One day he'll be called to answer for what he did, because as long as I survive, I will never forget. Never."

As he left, Elise opened her arms and hugged her, holding her tight as Addy cried into her hair, her body shaking. Was she being naïve to think Wolfgang wasn't capable of murdering Harry's friends in cold blood? Or was she right, and Harry just wanted to blame him because he wore the same uniform as the man who'd given the order that day?

"We're going to be fine, Addy, I promise you," Elise whispered in her ear. "I'm sorry I've been so short-tempered with you, I just hate sitting at home, worried about whether you're safe or not.

Whether you'll even make it back home. But I trust you. There's no way someone as sweet as you would ever fall for a monster like Wolfgang."

Addy clung to her sister, hating that they'd been pulling apart the last few days, and hoping desperately that Elise would never find out how butterflies danced in her stomach whenever she was with the man they all hated. "When I'm with him, it's hard to see that he's a monster. I know he is, of course I do, but . . ." But what? She liked the attention? She liked the way he looked? She liked the way she felt special when she was with him? It all sounded pathetic, even to her own ears, now. "It's hard to remember that when he's so different with me."

"Men can be like chameleons sometimes," Elise murmured. "He's probably well versed at being charming when he has to be, and maybe you'll never see the other side of him, but you need to remember how quickly things could escalate if he ever finds out what we've done. He could go from sweetheart to monster before you have so much as a whisper of warning."

Addy breathed in the scent of her sister and stole her warmth, still folded into her arms. And not for the first time, she wished their mother were still alive, so Elise could just be her sister instead of having to be the one in charge.

CHAPTER SIXTEEN

CATE

"I can see her coming along the path."

Cate was waiting for Elise to return, anxiously packing some supplies they might need along the way for their little trip. She wasn't sure yet where they were going, but she'd wrapped some dried fruit and a slice of bread, and filled a container with water. Then she'd added in a flashlight in case they didn't make it home before dark.

"You're all jittery," Jack said, sitting up in bed. "You've been making me dizzy with all that pacing."

Cate laughed. "Sorry. I just had this strange feeling that she wasn't going to come back."

"It's not unusual to feel that way, Cate," Jack said somberly. "There are enemy soldiers stationed everywhere around here, and fighting could break out anywhere. There could still be pockets of British soldiers waiting to take a stand."

Cate didn't tell him that she firmly believed any of those pockets would have been found and killed by now.

"Promise me you'll be careful?" he asked.

"If you promise me to keep resting while I'm gone," she replied.

"What, did you think I might leave the house for a stroll or take Adelaide to a dance, perhaps?"

She rolled her eyes. "I'm serious, Jack. It's a miracle you've survived all this, so please just be careful. The longer you stay in bed—"

"I know, I know," he said, throwing his hands in the air. "I promise I'll follow orders."

Cate heard Elise downstairs, but she decided to sit with Jack a moment longer before going down. Since the morning she'd woken lying in bed with him, she'd barely touched him, other than to routinely check his wounds, and she found herself aching to connect with him.

Her heart was still brimming for Charlie, the pain of losing him, losing the life they'd planned together; still raw. She'd kept up with the pretense that he might be alive for Lilly's sake more than anything, knowing in her heart there was little chance he'd survived, and now that she was alone without Lilly, she felt more than ever that he was truly gone. Jack made her feel something that Charlie never had, and she couldn't pretend it wasn't true. She only wished she'd known what had happened to Charlie, to have that closure, to know for sure. He'd been such a good man; even walking by his side had made her feel safe, the total opposite of her father, which was why she'd always been drawn to him. Why she'd said yes to marrying him when he'd asked, even though she'd wondered if it were enough to be fond of someone rather than in love.

And then there was Jack. Jack who made her feel things she'd never felt before, but who scared her more than anything. Because with Jack, she felt everything: every brush of his skin to hers, every look, every moment. There was nothing safe about her feelings for Jack. She sat just far enough away from him that they weren't touching, her palm on the bed, fingers waiting to sneak over to his.

"I don't know how we're ever going to get out of here, Jack," she said, keeping her voice low.

"I should have taken us to the beach that day," he said, shutting his eyes as if he were in pain. "I should never have brought us here. Knowing all those soldiers were evacuated . . ."

"Stop." She did let her fingers dance toward his then, holding on to him. "We don't know if we would have got there in time. I just keep thinking about Lilly and hoping she made it, that somehow she got there and made it on to a boat."

Jack didn't try to reassure her; and he couldn't have even if he wanted to. There was no way of knowing whether she'd gotten there or not.

Jack moved his hand out from beneath hers, palm closing over the back of it as he lifted it and pressed a slow, warm kiss to her skin. Her heart started to beat erratically as her breath caught in her throat, and she summoned all her courage to do something she'd never thought she'd be brave enough to do.

He seemed to sense it, but he stayed still and let her come to him, her mouth parting and slowly touching his, her lips moving slowly, hesitantly. It was clumsy at first, he not moving and she not sure, not having kissed anyone but Charlie before, but the moment his arms reached for her, everything changed. One minute she was sitting beside him, the next she was rising and moving closer to him, sitting on his thighs as his hands buried themselves in her hair, as his lips started to dance more knowingly against hers.

"Cate!"

The call was so close she leapt up, bumping her head on the low ceiling above his bed, making them both laugh even as she winced in pain. But before she could move too far away, Jack caught her hand, kissing the inside of her wrist this time and sending fireflies into her belly as his eyes stayed locked on hers.

"I've been wanting to do that since the first day I saw you," he whispered. "You walked past my hospital bed, and you were the most beautiful woman I'd ever seen."

"You were delirious on morphine," she murmured back.

"I wasn't then, and I'm sure as hell not now."

Cate bent, slowly, bravely, pressing one final kiss to his lips. "I'll see you soon."

"Be careful," he said.

"You know I will be."

"Take this," he said, taking a small blade from beneath his pillow, something she hadn't even known he possessed. "Just flick it like this," he said, demonstrating a fast flick of his wrist, "and don't think, just act."

Cate took it, not asking questions, not wanting to think about what situation she might be in to need to use it. "I will."

Walking away from Jack was one of the hardest things she'd ever done, but once she started moving, she didn't look back.

"There you are," Elise said, standing at the top of the stairs. "Everything all right?"

Cate blinked away her tears and cleared her throat. "I'm fine. Or at least I will be. What did you find out?"

"St. Venant has definitely fallen—it must have been where I heard all the fighting the day before you arrived," Elise said, frowning. "There were hundreds of British soldiers there before the Germans took control, maybe close to a thousand, and only a few got away."

"The rest were killed?" Gooseflesh punctuated Cate's skin.

Elise lowered her voice. "Rumor has it that some were executed instead of being taken prisoner of war."

"You think it was Wolfgang there too, don't you?"

Elise's expression said it all. "I think he's dangerous and I don't want my sister anywhere near him, but it could easily have been another commander. Perhaps they're all the same?"

"So where are we heading to? Are we still going?" Cate asked.

"Yes, we need to travel to Lille. It's under German occupation, but there's no reason we can't try to make it there. My friend's father might be able to help us."

"He might know how to get us out of France?" Cate asked.

"Apparently there's an underground network of sorts, and from what I learnt today, my father was loosely part of it."

Cate's eyebrows shot up. "What do you mean?"

"We'll find out more in Lille, but all I know for certain is that they've been secretly moving Jews to safety, so if they can find a way to move them—"

"They might have a way to move us."

"Exactly."

Cate followed Elise downstairs, filled with hope that one day, maybe, she and Jack might just make it home after all.

"It's a strange thing, living in a house with somebody and feeling like you know so little about them," Elise said later, as they walked.

Cate smiled. "I know. I feel so close to you and Adelaide in some ways, but I know next to nothing about you both, really."

"She told me that your fiancé was listed as presumed dead?"

"He was. It seems like a lifetime ago now."

"Is that your engagement ring you wear around your neck?"

She'd barely spoken about Charlie to anyone, almost wanting to keep her memories just for herself so she didn't have to admit she'd never see him again, which seemed stupid given the kiss she'd just shared with Jack.

"I put it there on the ship sailing from England to France," she told Elise, trying her best to chat normally, but feeling jittery about being so exposed along the side of the road. "I never in a million years thought he'd be gone so quickly, though."

"Had you known him for long?"

"He was friends with my brothers when I was growing up, and I am, *was*, best friends with his sister. We actually worked together as nurses, right up until . . ." She swallowed, wondering as she did every day whether Lilly was still alive. "She fled for the beach to be evacuated and I ended up here. The last time I saw her she'd taken an ambulance to try to save more injured troops, and she was driving away from the chateau we were stationed at."

Elise's smile warmed her. "She sounds like a great best friend."

"She is."

They walked in silence for a long while, listening for danger, braced for gunfire or the yell of a German officer telling them to halt. But surprisingly, they were over halfway to Lille before they encountered a patrol, and they just stood to the side, arms linked, eyes downcast.

"Don't look," Elise whispered. "They've no reason to bother us. We're not doing anything wrong."

But as hard as she tried to keep her eyes averted, Cate found herself looking up, which garnered a whistle and call from the passing German soldiers. She forced a smile and a little wave, and the soldiers must have had somewhere to be, because they didn't stop. Even so, she slipped her hand into her pocket and felt the weight of the small knife, feeling better just for knowing it was there.

When they eventually reached Lille, Cate could sense Elise's horror at what confronted them. She'd been there before herself, and recalled it as a pretty city full of beautiful architecture, and now some of those houses had walls missing or crumbling down. She supposed the only consolation was that the town center was largely untouched.

It was hard to take in.

"I can't believe it," Elise murmured beside her, her footsteps slowing. "It used to be so beautiful, so . . ."

Cate linked her arm back through Elise's, drawing her close. "And it will be beautiful again one day." She didn't know why she said it when she had no way of knowing, but something within her told her that it was true. There was no way Europe could be overtaken by Hitler, not forever, and she couldn't imagine for a second that Britain would fall to his rule either.

"They're everywhere here, so we have to be careful," Elise said as they started to walk more purposefully again. "And if anyone asks us what we're doing here, we've come to visit our uncle who's unwell."

The streets were deserted, other than a stray cat lying in a puddle of sunshine, and Cate's heartbeat elevated again; she was certain they were going to be shot at or that something terrible was about to happen. Her ears were straining for every possible noise, and she jumped when a door slammed nearby.

"Calm down," Elise whispered. "We have every right to be here, we're not doing anything wrong."

Maybe not, but Cate was still plagued with nerves.

"Here, his house is still intact, so that's a good sign." They hurried along and knocked, and even Elise fidgeted on the spot. Cate half-expected enemy troops to answer, having commandeered the place, but there was a shuffle followed by the door opening barely a crack.

"Mr. Bernard?" Elise asked, leaning toward the opening.

"Who's asking?"

"Elise DuPont. Claude's eldest daughter."

The door flew open then, and an old man propped up by a walking stick beamed at Elise as if his long-lost daughter had just shown up.

"Elise! What are you doing out here? It's not safe for you to be leaving home and traveling so far."

"I'm fine, honestly I'm fine. *We're* fine," Elise said, gesturing back to Cate. "This is my cousin, Cate. May we come in?"

He beckoned them inside and Cate gratefully followed Elise, glancing over her shoulder to see if anyone was watching them, but seeing no one.

"Come down to my cellar," he said. "Away from prying ears and eyes."

They went down, and Cate was surprised to find a table and four chairs in there, surrounded by bottles of wine and boxes stacked haphazardly.

"I'm so sorry to hear about your father, Elise. He was a good man."

"We miss him terribly," Elise replied. "It's been such an awful year for us, for so many of us."

"And this *cousin* of yours?" he said, chuckling to himself.

"She's a nurse, with the British army," Elise said, as he opened a bottle of wine without even asking them if they wanted any and pouring more than a splash into three glasses.

"A nurse, huh? And how did you end up with a British nurse for a pretend cousin?"

They all sat down together and Cate spoke, nervous about sharing her secret but seeing that Elise was prepared to put full trust in him. "When the Nazis came I escaped from the clearance hospital I was stationed at," she said. "I found myself on Elise's doorstep and she was kind enough to take me in."

"The story doesn't end there, though," Elise said, lowering her voice. "I have two British soldiers in my home, too."

The old man looked like he was about to fall off his chair and he slapped his palm on the table. "Soldiers?" He made a loud tutting noise and then drained his glass of wine. "You are too kind-hearted, just like Claude."

Cate could see the pain on Elise's face at the reference to her father.

"You think he would have done the same?"

"I know so." He sighed. "And now you need my help to get them home, I suppose?"

A noise upstairs startled them, but the old man shook his head, smiling. "You have your hidden secrets, I have my own," he said. "Your father and I weren't so different, but I'm an old man and don't have as much to lose as you do."

Cate couldn't believe it; he had someone, or more than just someone, hidden in his home, too.

"Elise mentioned there was a network of sorts, an underground collection of people?" Cate asked. She lifted her glass and took a hesitant sip of the wine, hoping it would calm her nerves.

"You heard right. There is a network that is expanding all over France, and we're only going to get stronger if those bastards take hold here. We've been smuggling Jews to safety, but soon we might be joining the fighting, too." He sighed again. "The German presence here is too great for us to fight it physically, but that doesn't mean we're helpless. We got rid of them during the Great War, and we'll get rid of them again."

"So can you help us?" Elise asked.

"The first day of the new moon, when it's not visible in the sky, we have an evacuation planned," he murmured, his ruddy elbows propped on the table between them. "You get your three to the beach at Calais then, and a rowboat will be waiting to take them to a larger ship. We have three downed British airmen who've been recuperating for some time, and they'll be on that boat too."

Cate reached for Elise's hand and gripped it. "You really think we could make it back to England?"

His smile lit his eyes. "If the Luftwaffe don't catch sight of you, then yes, I do. There are always risks, and if you can't make it this time we plan on doing it with every new moon, when the night is bathed in true darkness. There are more formal evacuations taking place from Brest, but it's a long trek by foot to get there, and I think this is your best option."

"We'll be there," Cate said, nodding at Elise. "Unless something unforeseen happens, we'll be there."

Elise was silent, and Cate wondered what she was thinking. "Elise?"

"Can you make the evacuation for four people?" Elise finally asked.

Four? Why four?

"Who is the fourth?" the old man asked.

"Adelaide," Elise said. "She's caught the eye of a Nazi commander, and I want her taken to safety."

He seemed to study Elise before acquiescing. "If we agree to this, can we count on you to assist our underground network around the coast?"

Elise had her arms folded across her chest now. "Yes. You get my sister to a place on that boat and I will fill any role to assist your resistance."

His nod was curt. "Let me check with a friend tonight," he said. "We have more Allied men in hiding than you'd ever imagine, so places are limited, but I need someone else I can trust. You can both stay the night, and we'll have an answer by morning."

When he left them to get some food, Cate turned to Elise, not able to believe what she'd heard. "How do you even know Adelaide will go if you organize her passage?" she asked. "And you're willing to sacrifice yourself for her?"

"Joining this network is the right thing to do, and I can't do that if my sister is mooning about with a Nazi, can I? No one would trust me for a second."

Cate wasn't about to question her. She owed Elise her life, and Adelaide was her sister, so it wasn't anything to do with Cate. But she did know that if it were *her* sister, she'd probably enter the same kind of bargain in order to keep her safe.

"So long as you know what you're doing," Cate said.

Elise didn't reply. She just sipped her wine, and Cate decided to do the same.

The next day, once Elise's friend had confirmed that there would be space for all four of them, Cate and Elise left and headed back home. The air was a little cooler now, and Cate lifted her long hair off her neck to let the breeze brush her skin. She wished they'd set out earlier, because it would be late by the time they got home.

"I know this sounds crazy, when I've only known you for such a short time, but I'm going to miss you," Cate said.

Elise opened her mouth to answer, but Cate quickly spoke up again. "Sorry, that does sound ridiculous, I just mean—"

"It's not ridiculous at all," Elise said. "I feel the same. I mean, I still feel guilty about the way I spoke to you that first night. I was so close to telling you to walk out the door, and if you hadn't said you were our cousin, I might have done exactly that."

"I don't think you would have," Cate said. "I could see the compassion in your eyes, it was just blurred a little with worry."

"I could have turned Harry away, too," Elise admitted. "I saw him on my doorstep with his friend, covered in blood and so desperately needing help, and my first instinct was to slam the door shut and hide."

"To keep you and your sister safe," Cate said gently. "No one would judge you for putting her first, not when you've already lost all your other family members in the course of a year."

For the first time since Cate had arrived in Le Paradis, she saw Elise's eyes sparkling with tears, and she instinctively slung an arm around her shoulder.

"Don't hug me, I'll only start crying," Elise murmured.

Cate ignored her, keeping her arm around her and pretending she didn't see the silent tears that rained down Elise's cheeks. She had her own demons inside, her own pain at losing someone she loved and then so easily developing feelings for another man. Jack had her all twisted up in knots, and that kiss . . . She shook her head slightly, as if it might help her dispel the memories. But it did nothing of the sort.

"Tell me more about Harry," she eventually said, when Elise had stopped crying. "I can tell there's maybe something between you?"

Elise looked surprised. "You mean romantically?"

Cate laughed. "Sorry, I've obviously got it all wrong. I just thought there was something, a spark I suppose, between you. I presumed you liked him."

Elise seemed to think on that for a long moment. "Well, I suppose I was drawn to him in the beginning, but there's nothing going on between us. Besides, he'll be leaving soon."

"Are you still angry with him for wanting to use Addy to get information?"

Elise sighed. "Maybe I overreacted. I'm just so used to being the one in charge. I didn't like how quick he was to suggest using her as a pawn."

"I have a feeling he regrets what he said, because it's obvious how he feels about you, if you know what I mean," Cate teased. "I've seen the way he looks at you."

"Stop!" Elise hissed. "You're completely wrong, he doesn't look at me like that at all!"

Cate just laughed, although their mood sobered when they finally reached the outskirts of Le Paradis and came face to face with a German patrol. Elise's fingers caught hers then, and they walked closely together, eyes down. They had nowhere else to go, other than to make a run for it back toward more German troops in Lille or into the trees, and she doubted either of them were capable of outrunning guns and soldiers.

"Halt!"

The booming, deep voice made them both freeze, and they didn't take another step as two soldiers came closer.

"Don't you know it's too dangerous to be out here?" one of them asked.

"Of course," Elise said, and Cate squeezed her hand when she heard the tremble in her tone. "But we were visiting our sick uncle in Lille. We haven't heard much fighting and thought it would safe enough to go."

"Open your bag."

Cate dropped the bag and stepped back, not liking the soldiers being so close to her. And secretly she was terrified to talk or even look up, in case they realized she wasn't French.

"I don't think Commander Wolfgang Schmidt would be very happy about this," Elise said, her voice louder, clearer than it had been before.

That made the soldiers both look up. The one looking in her bag put it down, not finding anything of interest, and Cate was just grateful she'd kept the knife in her pocket instead of pulling it out.

"You know the commander?"

Elise's chin was jutted defiantly now, and Cate admired her for her sudden show of strength. "He's courting my sister, Adelaide.

I'm returning home to her now, and I suspect he may even be waiting at our house."

"Let her pass!" one of the soldiers urged the other.

Cate bent and picked up her bag before they hurried off.

"Slow down," Elise whispered. "We need to look relaxed, like it's the most natural thing in the world for us to be out here."

Cate forced her breath and her feet to slow, allowing Elise to steady her until they were out of earshot.

"Cate, can I ask you something?"

"Of course, anything."

"Is it wrong of me to want Adelaide to get on that boat? Should I be letting her make her own mistakes, or am I right in deciding this for her?"

Cate thought for a while, seeing the house come into view and knowing they didn't have long. "I think you're right. If she were my sister or my daughter, I'd know that no matter how strong she thinks she is, she's powerless against a Nazi commander. He might fall in love with her, but he could also kill her without a second thought if he ever finds out who you are hiding in your attic. I'd want her gone, too."

"Thank you. I needed to hear that."

"Can I be completely honest with you, though? Without offending you?" Cate asked, stopping at the steps of the house as darkness started to fall around them.

"Please. I feel like we're closer already than most of the friends I've known in my entire life, so whatever you have to say, I want to hear it."

Cate glanced up to make sure Adelaide hadn't come to the front door, but there was no one there. "I'm worried she could end up falling for him, and forgetting who he truly is. He's charming her and making her feel special, and sometimes it's hard to turn away from that kind of attention."

Elise looked uncomfortable, but she nodded. "Go on."

"You need to find a way to talk to her without offending her, to explain that men are like peacocks, strutting around and doing anything and everything to attract the female they want. She needs to see the situation for what it is, otherwise she'll never agree to leave."

"I know what you're saying, and you're right," Elise said. "I just don't know how to make her listen to me."

"Let me then," Cate said. "Sometimes it's easier to take coming from someone other than family, and there are some things I can tell her that I've never spoken about before. I know she'll listen."

Elise gave her a quick hug, and Cate willingly returned it.

"You have my blessing to say whatever you need to her," Elise said. "I'll never forget you when you go, Cate."

Cate smiled. "Trust me when I say that I'll never, ever forget you, either."

CHAPTER SEVENTEEN

Elise

Elise shut the door behind them once they were inside, surprised to smell something cooking. She and Adelaide always took turns preparing meals, but she'd expected the others to have eaten long ago and simply to have saved something for them to eat cold when they returned.

"Addy, what smells so good?" she asked, following her nose into the kitchen.

"Soup," Harry replied, spinning around and making her laugh out loud at the girly apron tied around his middle. "I wanted to have something nice for you when you got home."

Elise couldn't believe it. "Thank you, that's very thoughtful of you."

"It might taste dreadful, but Adelaide gave me some pointers, and if I'm honest all I've done is the chopping of vegetables and the stirring. We saved some bread from lunch, so you've got that to dunk into it as well, but Adelaide had a terrible headache and she couldn't stay up and wait any longer."

"I'm going to head straight upstairs to bed," Cate said, backing away. "I'm exhausted after that walk."

But Harry was quick to stop her. "At least take a bowl with you," he said. "I did this for both of you."

Cate grinned at Elise, but she just glared back at her, not liking what her smile indicated, and soon it was just Elise and Harry alone in the kitchen together. It felt too intimate, which was silly because he was standing at the stove and she was sitting at the table now as he fussed over her, so they weren't even close.

"Did you cook at home, before the war?" she asked.

"Not even once," he admitted. "My mother would never believe you if you told her."

Elise's first instinct was to insist Harry sit down, then take over herself, but she refused to give in to it. She was always the one taking care of everyone, and the way Harry was fussing over her made her think that this was the very reason he was doing it. From that first night they'd sat up late in the kitchen together talking, he'd somehow managed to actually see her for who she was.

"So what made you cook for me tonight then?"

"Someone needs to look after you," he said, setting the steaming bowl in front of her, along with a piece of loaf on a side plate. Harry lingered at her side, and she wasn't sure where to look or what to do, so she picked up her spoon and dipped it straight into the soup.

She blew on her spoonful and eventually took a sip, surprised at how nice it tasted. He was sitting across from her now, and she knew there was only so long she could avoid his gaze.

Cate was right. There is something between us.

"Thank you," she eventually said. "I don't know when I last sat down with nothing to do and had someone take care of me."

He shrugged. "You deserve it."

"Harry, there's something I need to tell you," she murmured, setting her spoon down.

His eyebrows were raised expectantly, but he didn't say a word.

219

I don't want him to leave. I want to keep him hidden here. I self-ishly want him all to myself.

She took a deep breath. "I've arranged to smuggle you out of France, at the next new moon."

Harry couldn't have looked more surprised if he'd tried. "I'm leaving? I expected you to come home and say there was nothing you could do, that it was impossible."

She toyed with her soup, needing to do something, *anything*, to stop herself seeing the crestfallen look on Harry's face, because it so closely mirrored her own feelings.

"Honestly? So did I. But if we can get you all to the beach at Calais, at midnight on the new moon, there will be a boat waiting. It's dangerous, but it's something, and I think it might be your only chance to leave."

"Calais?" he asked. "I thought that place was blown apart?"

"It is, but that won't stop a rowboat from coming in under the cover of night."

Elise ate then, wolfing down her soup and mopping up the last of it with the dry piece of bread. And when she finished, she could feel Harry's eyes on her.

"Is it wrong that I'd rather stay here with you?"

She pushed her bowl away, heat rising in her body and flooding her cheeks. "It's not," she said. "If I'm honest, I've gone from being so worried about having you all here to feeling heartbroken at the idea of you leaving."

"All of us, or just me?" he asked, his voice gruff now.

"I've grown very close to Cate so I'll certainly miss her, but you, well, you're different, I suppose." *Different?* Why had she even said that word to describe him?

"Elise, it's not easy for me being here," he admitted, clasping his palms together and leaning forward. "I'm in here hiding while your beautiful country is being overtaken by Nazis. Everything I

220

fought for, everything my friends gave their lives for, it seems like it was for nothing. And there's nothing I can do about it." His voice dropped. "I've never felt like a coward before, but the way I encouraged your sister to see that commander while I hide in here myself—"

"It's forgiven," Elise interjected, realizing in that moment that she was no longer angry with him, not now that she understood how he was feeling. "I'm not angry with you, Harry, because my sister made her own mind up. Whatever I felt toward you at the time was because it was easier to blame you than her." She swallowed. "Or myself."

She watched the heavy rise and fall of his chest.

"Truth be told, I think she fell a little bit in love with him that day she took Peter, and that's on her. That was *her* decision, not yours."

"But if I hadn't come here in the first place, if I hadn't put this burden on you—"

Elise shook her head. "They're stationed here, Harry. Don't you see? He would have crossed paths with her sometime, seen her long blonde hair and beautiful blue eyes, fallen for those full lips of hers that curve into a smile. This is not on you, or me or Cate or Peter."

She could see now that Adelaide was going to tread her own path, and all she could do was try to guide her as best she could.

"I'm used to leading men into battle, taking charge, being in control of my destiny," Harry said, his head falling into his hands. "And today, instead of doing that, I stayed at home and made soup and sent you to war on my behalf."

Elise laughed, her hand flying to cover her mouth, embarrassed that she was laughing when Harry looked so broken.

"It wasn't supposed to be amusing, seeing a man at breaking point," he said dryly.

"I'm sorry, Harry, I'm so sorry, it's just—" She stifled a laugh again. "Well, it was *particularly* good soup, so I was only wondering if you'd found your true calling in the kitchen!"

His lips kicked up into a smile. "Oh, that's funny, is it? A man pours his heart out, and you tell him that he may as well give up and just make soup? Is that how you see me?"

They both started to laugh then, Elise wiping at her eyes as Harry pushed to his feet, his arm no longer held in the sling.

"It's not funny," he said.

Elise was still smiling. "Oh, but it was. I haven't laughed, truly laughed, for such a long time. I can barely remember the version of me that even laughed so freely."

"You look beautiful when you laugh," he said, his eyes suddenly serious. "I'll have to find some more recipes so I can see this side of you more often."

He moved slowly, deliberately, to sit close to her on the edge of the table. In an instant, everything seemed to have changed between them.

"Come to me," he said, his arm at his side, his smile warm. He wasn't pulling her, pressuring her, reaching for her, just sitting and inviting her to come to him.

Elise's legs moved of their own accord. She should have shaken her head and brushed off his advances, but she was being drawn to him like a bee to pollen. She wanted this. She wanted to have something just for her, something to feel good about. Something to make her forget everything else.

Her steps were hesitant, her eyes avoiding his as if somehow she'd lose all her confidence if she looked at him, truly looked at him.

But suddenly she was there, in front of him, breathing heavily, as he opened his legs slightly, giving her room to walk into him. Harry slowly lifted a hand, palm open, fingers outstretched, and her own palm fitted against his like a glove, skin alive to his touch, craving more.

He was everything she'd ever wanted and nothing like she'd imagined all at once. He wasn't a French man from a nice family within a day's travel of her home, not someone she'd been able to swoon over and whisper about to her mama and sister. But he was a good man, a brave man, a soldier who'd seen so much and could still be so gentle to her, a soldier who might be from another country but who seemed to understand her like no other man had before.

"I don't want to leave here, on that boat," he whispered as he slowly pulled her closer, his breath warm against her cheek. "I know it's crazy, but I want to stay. *With you.*"

She shut her eyes, breathing in the scent of him. "It is crazy. You can't."

"But what if I did?"

She answered his question the only way she knew how: with a kiss. Her lips seemed to know what they were doing, parting and pressing against his, moving slowly at first and then faster, hungrily, as her arms lifted and looped around his neck.

Harry's fingers were in her hair, stroking, as he kissed her back.

"Should we go upstairs?" he asked, huskily, against her skin, as his mouth left hers and pressed against her neck, all the way down to her collarbone until a hiss of pleasure escaped her lips.

Elise came crashing back to reality then, realizing how easily she'd fallen into his arms, how willingly she'd kissed him with so little encouragement. But staring at Harry, at those eyes that seemed to see her for who she was, she knew her answer was yes.

She glanced at the dishes on the table and, for the first time in her life, thought *to hell with it.*

One night I get to do something for me, something reckless, something forbidden.

"Yes," she whispered, taking his hand again and tugging gently.

But when he stood, he didn't move, instead pulling her against him and wrapping his arms around her. She was careful of his shoulder, pressing her face to his chest and embracing his waist.

"I meant what I said before, Elise, about not leaving you," he whispered into her hair. "I'll see the others to safety with you, but I won't leave you behind. I can handle a gun well, unlike Jack, if we need one."

She didn't tell him that he didn't have a choice, because maybe he did. Maybe he could help the underground resistance; maybe there was a place for him here? Or maybe she was getting carried away with a fairy tale that simply couldn't happen.

His hands stroked her hair, her back, all the way to her waist, then beyond, and she shuddered against him. They could debate logistics in the morning.

"Take me to my room," she murmured, standing on tiptoe as she spoke into his ear.

"If you tell me I can stay," he whispered back.

Elise shut her eyes, knowing in her heart that she could never force him to go.

"You can stay," she whispered back, as his hand slipped into hers and she led him toward the stairs.

―――― ❧ ❧ ――――

In the morning light, Elise pulled the covers around her bare skin as she stared at Harry in the bed beside her. The night before came flooding back, and she shut her eyes, partly embarrassed and partly proud of herself for being so bold. Harry's eyes were shut, his lashes thick and dark against his cheeks as he slept peacefully.

Not for the first time, she wondered how she'd live if he were discovered in her home. She'd lost so much already to the war, but to see someone she cared deeply for taken, injured or . . . she swallowed, *killed*. She could almost see an SS officer marching through her home, looking for someone, looking for Harry, and shooting him dead right in her attic.

She refused to listen to her thoughts and instead rose, finding her clothes and dressing. She'd never had the chance to see Adelaide when they'd arrived home, and suddenly all she wanted to do was wrap her sister in her arms and hold her.

Elise tiptoed from the room, not wanting to wake Harry, and went to look for Addy. The sun was already up but she had no idea what time it was, and she expected to find her either in bed or downstairs fixing breakfast.

"Addy?" she called softly, knocking on her bedroom door and nudging it open. She wasn't there, although her bed was already made.

The bathroom was vacant, so Elise padded downstairs.

"Addy?" she called again.

But downstairs she found Cate sitting at the table, coffee cup in hand. Alone.

"Have you seen Adelaide?" Elise asked.

Cate shook her head. "I presumed she was still in bed. I've been up for an hour or so."

Panic rose within Elise as she ran back up the stairs. "Addy!" she called, louder now, not caring who woke. Where was her sister?

Elise ran from room to room, pushing doors open, and then hurried up to the attic, startling Jack who was sitting on the edge of his bed.

"Has my sister been up here this morning?" she asked.

Jack frowned. "I haven't seen her since yesterday."

Elise looked out of the window, scanning for her, but not catching so much as a glimpse of her sister's blonde head.

She walked slowly back down from the attic and found Harry standing in the door to her bedroom, his shirt buttons undone and his hair all mussed.

"What's happened?" he asked.

"Adelaide isn't here. She's gone," she said, hardly able to believe what she was saying. "When did you last see her? Was she even here when we got home last night?" Was there a chance that she'd been gone all this time? That while she was wrapped in Harry's arms, she'd been completely oblivious to the fact that her sister was missing?

"She was here, Elise. I promise you, she was here."

Cate was behind her then, her hand warm on her shoulder. "Don't be too hard on her, Elise. If she went willingly to him . . ."

Elise groaned and stepped into Harry's arms, not caring that Cate was watching or that Jack had come down the stairs from the attic.

Harry held her as she cried. Her first thought was that something terrible had happened to Adelaide, but Cate's words had held the truth. Her sister had gone to her Nazi boyfriend, and instead of climbing into bed with Addy and being with her, she'd chosen to be with Harry instead.

She only hoped it wasn't a decision that she'd live to regret. Because if Adelaide didn't come home . . . Elise pressed herself even closer to Harry's chest.

"What if she's told him about us?" Jack asked.

Elise forced herself to turn in Harry's arms, and saw the worry etched on Jack's and Cate's faces. "Even if she's in love with him, I know my sister, and she would never, ever give any of you up." She trembled, fear thrumming through every fiber in her body. She only hoped she was right.

CHAPTER EIGHTEEN

ADELAIDE

Adelaide found Elise, Cate, Harry, and Jack sitting upstairs in the attic, eating dinner. They'd spread out a picnic blanket, one that brought back vivid memories of lunches with her siblings when they were children, outside on the grass. But this wasn't a fun picnic like the ones she remembered, but a necessity to ensure their houseguests remained undiscovered.

She guiltily wondered if they would have been at the table downstairs had she not been out with Wolfgang; Addy could only imagine their fear at the prospect of her arriving home with him.

"Hi," she said, raising her hand as she stood in the doorway. Every pair of eyes turned to watch her.

"Hi." It was Cate who spoke first, gesturing to the meager quantity of food laid out on the blanket. "You must be hungry, come and join us."

Addy smiled and walked silently over to Elise, her head down as she sat beside her, wriggling closer even though her sister hadn't said anything to her. They'd been so close all their lives, Elise always only one step away, always there for her, and she suddenly needed to be with her, no matter how angry she was.

But as she lay her head on Elise's shoulder, her sister still didn't say a thing; she just took her hand and held it as she resumed a conversation that must have started long before Addy had arrived home. She'd been expecting an interrogation about where she'd been, anger followed by a stern telling-off, but Elise acted like she'd been there all along, and she certainly didn't seem angry. It was like a silent truce of sorts, and as she held her sister's hand, she realized there was nothing in the world she cared more about than Elise.

"So we have maybe ten days, give or take, until the new moon," Harry said, putting down his plate of mashed artichokes. "We had a full moon a few nights ago. I couldn't sleep and I just stared out at it for hours, it was so high and round in the sky."

Addy looked away guiltily, thinking of the food that Wolfgang had given her, which was so much more palatable than the tasteless slush Harry was eating.

"Why are you concerned about the moon?" Addy asked, lifting her head slightly from Elise's shoulder.

"Because that's the night they're leaving," Elise said, as Jack and Harry turned their attention back to their dinner. "We made contact with Papa's old friend Mr. Bernard, and he's arranged passage for us, so long as we can all make it to the beach and stay hidden until the boat comes for them."

A shiver ran through Adelaide. "Will it be safe?"

Harry's eyes were hard. "As safe as sneaking into a boat on a beach potentially surrounded by enemy troops could ever be."

Cate's expression was kinder, softer than Harry's, and Addy wondered why he was being so short with her. Had something else happened while she was gone, or was he just worried about leaving?

"An underground movement has started, a resistance of sorts, and they're helping to liaise with the British army," Cate told her.

Addy sat back, her thigh pressed against Elise's as she took the plate of food Cate offered, not wanting anything to eat but not liking to be rude. Or perhaps she should have simply refused so there was more to go around.

"Adelaide, where were you last night and today?" Elise whispered, turning to her as they talked about the new resistance movement. "I've been worried sick."

Addy rolled the mash around in her mouth, not wanting to tell Elise the truth but knowing she had to. "I didn't think you'd approve, so I didn't wake you. I went to meet him early this morning."

"This morning or late last night?" Elise asked.

Adelaide raised a brow, staring straight back at her sister. "You were the only one tucked up in bed with a man all night, Elise." Her sister's cheeks flushed a deep pink, and Adelaide wished she could take back her words. "I'm sorry, I shouldn't have said that."

"There's a big difference between Harry and Wolfgang, so please don't compare them," Elise snapped. "But you're right, I was with Harry, and I should have been keeping an eye on you instead."

Adelaide shook her head. "No, you shouldn't. Because I'm capable of making decisions for myself."

Elise seemed to chew her words over, silently reaching for her and putting an arm around her. "I'm sorry. You're right, I was just worried. I promised myself I wasn't going to be angry with you when you got home, but I wasn't sure if you *were* coming back. I didn't know what had happened to you and I started jumping to all sorts of conclusions."

Adelaide grimaced, the weight of what she'd done hitting her as her sister spoke. "I'm so sorry, I should have left a note." She'd been so fixated on seeing Wolfgang, she hadn't thought for a second about how worried her sister might be.

"Addy, we have something for you when you've finished eating," Cate said, interrupting them as she stood.

In the corner of the room, on the bedside table, was a cake, with a single candle placed in the center. Adelaide gasped, looking from Cate to Elise. She hadn't had cake in almost a year!

"Who did this for me?" she asked, pushing up to her knees as Cate brought it over and put it in front of her.

"Your sister," Cate said. "She's been saving the ingredients for weeks, from what I can gather."

"Oh, Elise, thank you so much."

"Happy birthday, little sister," Elise said, her smile appearing strained. "The eggs from your commander meant I could make Mama's recipe, so I hope I've done her proud."

Addy hadn't expected Elise to do anything special for her birthday, not with everything going on, but to know that she'd been planning it for weeks and saving precious flour and sugar? Tears pricked her eyes as Cate leant forward and struck a match, and all four of them sang for her, their voices low and husky.

Adelaide looked at Harry, then Jack, and finally Cate, before blowing out her candle and shutting her eyes. She saw the attic as it used to be, saw her brother lying on the bed, throwing a pillow at her as she crept in to annoy him, saw her sister sitting at the top of the stairs, calling to their mother below. She could see Mama with her apron on, singing in the kitchen, and her father sleeping on the sofa, Oscar curled on his over-sized belly.

"Make a wish, Addy," Elise whispered beside her.

Adelaide shut her eyes even tighter, her head spinning. *I wish we could go back to normal, that this war was over for good.* It was a stupid wish, one a child might make and expect to come true, but it was the only thing she could think to ask for.

"To many more birthdays to come," Elise murmured, kissing her head as Cate cut the cake and put it on to plates.

Adelaide took the first plate, her fingers closing over the dainty little fork. It had been a long time since they'd indulged in cake or used their mama's best china and cutlery. Once, cakes had been as commonplace as cheese and beautiful baguettes, but now they were as rare as hens' teeth and she savored every bite.

When she finally looked up, licking every last morsel from her fork and seeing all the others do the same, she noticed the way that Harry was looking at her sister. The animosity was long gone, and had been replaced by an almost-protective gaze that was impossible to miss. Maybe that was why he'd been so curt with her before—he was cross with her on Elise's behalf.

"So let's run through this again," Jack said. "The more we go through it, the more likely we are to be successful."

"Even making it to the beach is going to be difficult," Harry said, setting his plate down, her birthday celebration well and truly over as the discussion turned more serious. "Can you pass me the map?"

Jack grunted as he leant forward, clearly in some degree of pain still.

"So by my calculations, we need to walk all night, find somewhere to hide during the day, then resume our walk again the next night," Harry said. "Elise?"

"Yes, but I think we need to allow some time for anything unexpected. What happens if we have to hide from a patrol or we have to change course?"

"Well, we can't leave too early, because we've nowhere to hide, but I agree. We work in an hour in case something unforeseen happens."

"What happens if you miss this boat?" Addy asked.

It was Cate who answered her. "We have to somehow make it back here safely again without anyone seeing two British soldiers, and then wait another month for the next new moon."

"And even then, they might not take you," Elise added. "Imagine the volume of people they're trying to smuggle in all directions! I don't think you'll have the luxury of another shot, unless we make it to more formal evacuations planned for much further down the coast."

"Will you leave in the dark?" Addy asked, her pulse starting to race as she realized what she was going to have to do.

"Dusk," Harry said, still studying the map. "Although it's hard to say where we'll end up staying after the first full night of walking. I want us to cover as much ground as possible in the first eight hours, so I'm suggesting we leave before nightfall. Which means getting out of this house and Le Paradis under Nazi noses."

Adelaide looked at her sister. "I'll distract Wolfgang," she said. "I'll find a way to keep them away from the house to give you all time to leave."

"Absolutely not!" Elise cried.

"It's the only way," Addy said. "You can go with them to lead them there, and I'll come up with a ruse."

"What kind of ruse?" Cate asked.

"*No* kind of ruse," Elise countered. "Adelaide is not risking her neck for this. I forbid it."

"You *forbid* me?" Addy asked. "Elise, you need to think this through, pretend I'm not your sister. I'm in the unique position of having influence here, an influence that no one else has."

"And what if he finds out what you've done?" Elise asked, her voice quiet, low, full of so much emotion that all Adelaide's anger disappeared.

"He'll never find out," she murmured back. If she were careful, if she made him think she was more loyal to him than anyone else . . .

"Please tell me you haven't fallen in love with him?" Elise whispered, tears swimming in her eyes.

"Of course I haven't," Addy answered quickly, shaking her head. "But I have him wrapped around my little finger, so it won't be a problem to keep him busy, away from the house." Her lies had become too easy, falling from her tongue with barely a second thought. She might have him wrapped around her finger, but the question of love wasn't so easy to answer.

"I don't want to speak against you, Elise, but I think Addy could be right," Cate said. "How else can we be sure of getting Harry and Jack out of the house?"

"She's right." Jack spoke up then. "Having the boat organized is one thing, but getting us out of here?"

Elise didn't answer. Instead, she rocked back and forth for a moment, then collected some of the plates and left the room.

Addy hurried after her. "Elise, wait!"

But Elise only held up her hand without turning. "Just give me a minute, Addy. I need time to think."

Adelaide didn't return to the attic, instead going to her parents' room and standing at the dresser to look over her mother's things.

I miss you so much, Mama, she thought as she lifted her bottle of perfume and inhaled deeply, feeling traitorous that she'd dabbed a drop to her wrist before going to meet Wolfgang. She lifted her mother's pearls then, holding them, needing something, anything to connect to her again, guilt washing over her as the day's events unfolded in her mind. She should have put an end to Wolfgang's advances, should have kept him at arm's length instead of letting him get so close. But Elise had been right. Her sister was *always* right, and this time was no different. Only this time, Adelaide had lied instead of admitting the truth.

Because the truth was, she *was* falling in love with him, no matter how much she tried to remind herself of who he was or what he was capable of. Because when she was in his arms, with his whispers in her ear and his eyes dancing over hers, it was impossible to believe he was a monster. He made her feel alive; he was like no man she'd ever met before, and she couldn't stop thinking about the last time she'd seen him.

"You came."

The surprise on his face was genuine as she skipped across the grass and ran into his open arms. The cool buttons of his jacket crushed against her chest as she lifted her face to him, no longer thinking about what she was doing. In the beginning, she'd been careful; but now she was following her heart and little else. It had started out as a dangerous game, and she'd just made it even more dangerous.

"Did you think I'd leave you waiting here for me?"

Wolfgang laughed. There was a vulnerability about him that hadn't been there before. Every other time she'd been with him, he'd been almost impossible to read, slightly guarded perhaps, but today she sensed something almost boyish behind his smile. Maybe for once they'd both dropped their guards to show their true selves.

"My men are going to stop respecting me if they find out I'm sneaking off to see you so often," he grumbled, but he was anything other than grumpy when he bent down and brushed a kiss over her lips.

Everything about him made Adelaide's heart race. The pistol he kept on him made her nervous, the way he looked at her made her feel beautiful, the way he held her made her shiver with anticipation.

"I think my sisters would like you," Wolfgang said as he sat down on the grass and pulled her down with him.

"I doubt that very much," she replied, landing beside him and not bothering to make a show of resisting when his arm went around her. "Why would they like a French girl?"

His laughter was soft. "Look at you," he murmured. "You're perfect. Soft blonde hair, blue eyes, and skin as creamy-pale as butter. You're the most beautiful girl I've ever set eyes on."

"You're just saying that so I'll keep kissing you," she teased, embarrassed by his compliments.

"Not true," he said. "I've thought that from the moment I first saw you. I think I ended up in Le Paradis for a reason."

She froze then, an image flashing through her head, feeling like she was back in her bedroom looking out, watching all those men falling to their death. Only she still couldn't see Wolfgang, still couldn't believe it had been him, even though she knew deep down that it must have been.

Adelaide scrambled to her feet and walked a few steps, catching her breath.

"What's wrong? Was it something I said?" Wolfgang came after her, as attentive as ever, his hand warm on her arm, his voice low.

How could a man have such different sides to him? How was it possible for him to be so cruel, and also so kind?

"Nothing, I just—"

He smiled and stood in front of her, opening his arms. "Come here. We can just stand here a moment."

She clung to him, her fingers clenching his jacket and her cheek to his chest, listening to the steady thump of his heart. Addy didn't believe for a second that he'd hurt her, but she couldn't shake the memory of those British soldiers, falling one by one.

"Is something on your mind?" he asked.

She forced the thoughts away, knowing she had to say something, anything, other than the truth. "Talking about your family before, it only reminds me that you could be gone soon."

His chuckle was loud against her ear. "I'm not going anywhere anytime soon, certainly not back to Germany," he said. "Perhaps closer to Paris, but I won't be leaving France."

She swallowed. "You sound so sure."

"Adelaide, your prime minister resigned today, and he's been replaced by Marshal Henri Pétain," Wolfgang said. "The war in France is over, they're probably signing the armistice as we speak. France has officially been conquered."

Tears welled in her eyes. Her beloved France had actually fallen.

He must have sensed her emotion because his fingers curled beneath her chin, tilting her face up to his.

"Is something upsetting you? Something you need to tell me?"

Fear arrowed through her body as if her blood was on fire with it. It was almost like he knew, that he was giving her the chance to tell him. But there was no possible way he could know they were hiding soldiers; surely he would have stormed the house already if he'd had even an inkling.

"I just, well, I suppose I keep thinking that this can't go on forever between us," she said, which wasn't a lie. She had been wondering what this was and what was going to become of it, and how long it could last.

He softened then, clearly believing her. "That's all? There's nothing more?"

She shook her head, chewing on her bottom lip, embarrassed at what a performance she was giving him. Since when had she become such a good actress?

"How about we just enjoy each day as it comes," he said, pressing a kiss to her forehead as his fingers dropped away from her chin. "Just know that I have no intention of ever forgetting about you, Adelaide, nor leaving you behind."

She laughed, despite it all. "I think my sister would have something to say about that."

"Well, maybe we'll have to find her her own German officer," he said. "Unless she's already spoken for?"

Adelaide thought of Harry, seeing her sister curled into the crook of his arm in bed when she'd looked in on them before sneaking out to see Wolfgang. "No, she's not," she lied.

Wolfgang took her by the hand again and led her back to the pretty meadow. She'd gotten herself way in over her head with the commander, and she had no idea how to get back out.

Or if she even wanted to.

"Adelaide?" Elise's voice jolted her from her thoughts and she turned, her mother's pearl necklace still in her hand. "I'm sorry about before," Elise said, sitting on the bed and patting the space beside her. "Can we sit for a bit?"

Addy joined her and traced her fingertips over the pearl necklace.

"I miss her so much," Elise said. "Her and Papa. Some days I feel like we're just biding our time, waiting for them to come home. It's as if we'll walk through the door one day and Papa will be asleep in his chair and Mama will be singing and cooking in the kitchen."

Adelaide could see them just as Elise described, only she imagined her brother walking through the door too, tossing his hat on to the table as he passed.

"I miss them too," Addy replied. "Like you wouldn't believe."

"Addy, you asked me not to treat you like a child, so I want you to know that I trust you. If you think you can help us by luring Wolfgang away, then it seems sensible."

Addy couldn't hide her surprise. "You do?"

"I do. I suppose I was so worried that you might develop feelings for him that your allegiance to Cate and the others might be compromised, but I can see that was unfair. It was you who fought to save them from the very beginning." Elise enveloped Adelaide in a big hug. "I love you so much, Addy. I'm sorry I've been so hard on you—it's only because I want the best for you."

Adelaide inhaled and slowly let her breath go. "He told me today that France has officially fallen."

Elise stood and walked back to the dresser, and Adelaide watched as she touched lightly all their mother's possessions. "Papa's friend said he was expecting it. It's almost impossible to believe, isn't it?"

"It is."

"Adelaide, the day the others go, I'm going to go with them, to help guide them."

Addy nodded. "I heard you say that earlier. It sounds like a good plan."

"But I want you to come too," Elise added, and Addy could tell there was something more, something bigger that her sister wanted to say.

"All right," she replied. "I suppose I can somehow get him away and then double back and meet you somewhere."

Elise came back toward her then, sitting and taking her hands in hers. "Addy, I want you to go to England with the others. To safety."

Adelaide laughed. "You what?" But her laughter fast died away as she saw that Elise was serious.

"It's too dangerous for you to stay, with Wolfgang here. What if he finds out you've deceived him?"

"Why? He won't even know what I've done. It'll be far more suspicious if I disappear!"

Elise squeezed her fingers. "But you'll be gone. He can wonder all he likes, but at least you'll be safe."

"And you? Are you going, too?"

Elise shook her head. "No. I'm staying, but I want to help the resistance, so I don't know what my immediate future looks like."

Adelaide pulled her hands away as they started to shake, eyes locked on her sister's as she stood. "Has this been your plan all along? To get rid of me?"

"To keep you safe!" Elise went to stand too, to reach for her, but Adelaide stepped away, wrapping her arms around herself.

"But I don't want to leave," she cried. "I don't want to leave here, I don't want to leave you, and I don't want to leave . . ."

Elise's face fell. "I was right all along, wasn't I? You are in love with him."

Her sister's words were soft, kind even, but the weight of disappointment they held was obvious, and Adelaide turned sharply on her heel.

"Addy! Don't walk away from me," Elise pleaded.

Adelaide spun around, anger pulsing inside her. "I'll do my part, Elise. I'll lure him away and I'll help to get them to the beach. I'm capable of holding up my end of the bargain, but I won't be told where I'm to live."

Elise stared at her in silence, and Adelaide walked straight out of the door and into her bedroom, crawling beneath the covers without even bothering to change into her bedclothes. She wanted to hate her sister, wanted to scream at her and slam her door, but she didn't.

Because everything Elise had said had been right, and now she had to choose between her heart and her head. Or figure out a way to choose both.

CHAPTER NINETEEN

CATE

Cate sat on the edge of the bed, systematically checking over Jack's wound. She'd avoided eye contact with him when she'd come in, telling him simply to take off his shirt, and now she was staring at his skin without really seeing him. The wound itself had healed well, despite her very basic stitching, but she could tell that he was still in pain, even though he'd gone to lengths most days to insist he was absolutely fine and didn't need to be fussed over.

She looked up when he caught her wrist, his fingers curling around her skin. "What's wrong?" he asked.

Cate pressed her palm flat to his chest, taking a breath and fighting the overwhelming urge to cry. "Nothing's wrong."

"Liar," he teased. "You can't live in such close quarters with someone for this long without knowing something's up."

Cate squeezed her eyes shut, riding the wave of emotion before opening them again. "I'm worried that it all seems too good to be true, our escape I mean. I was there with Elise, I heard the plan and I know it's our best option, but—"

"You're worried we won't even make it out of the village," he finished for her.

She groaned. "Exactly. I mean, how can we expect to even make half an hour, an hour on foot? There could be Nazis at every turn and darkness isn't going to save us."

"Because we've done it before," he said. "And we can do it again. That's why it's going to work."

She nodded. "Perhaps." The last thing she wanted was to be negative, but could they really be that lucky a second time? And what if the boat wasn't even there, and they were waiting for nothing? "I feel like we're leaving so much up to chance, and I don't like it."

"Cate, we're going to be fine. Don't worry."

"Don't worry?" she cried. "Jack, don't try and placate me like I'm a child, of course I'm going to worry! There's every chance that any of us could be shot dead a week from today."

He pushed his shirt down and sat up, and she bristled as he reached for her, pulling her hands away and settling them on her lap. But she knew that her anger was less about Jack and more about her. Ever since they'd kissed, guilt washed over her every time she so much as looked at him.

Her fiancé had been presumed dead for less than a year, and instead of continuing to mourn him and give him the respect he deserved, she'd fallen straight into Jack's arms. And she couldn't even blame being stuck in the house together, because she'd fallen for him back when he was one of her patients in hospital. She might have held back her feelings then and tried to keep her distance, but the fire had already been lit, all the same.

"Cate, what's wrong? You're usually the calm, capable one," Jack said, doing his best to catch her eye.

"I've told you, I'm worried," she snapped.

But the way he looked at her, the way he always looked at her, meant she couldn't lie to him. She was worried, but it was so much more than that. She stood and reached for his things, the clothes

241

he'd been wearing the day before, and folded them, needing to do something, liking the feel of his jacket in her hands.

And then something fell to the floor. She bent to reach for it, her fingers closing over it as Jack leapt forward, grunting as he scooped it up and tucked it into his pocket.

But he wasn't fast enough. She'd have recognized the photo anywhere.

"Where did you get that?" she gasped.

He shuffled back, his hand still covering his pocket.

"Jack, give me the photo," she demanded.

"Cate, please, I can explain." His voice was a whisper, cracked, dry.

"Give me the photo," she said, trying not to cry, as Jack slowly reached into his pocket and pulled the crumpled, lined photo out and passed it to her. He held it between his fingers, and she could see that they were trembling, but she didn't care. When he finally let it go and the photo dropped into her hand, she froze.

It was her.

It was the photograph of her, on a summer's day, before the war. A photo that only one man was supposed to have in his possession.

"How did you get this?" she asked, backing away from him.

"Please, Cate, let me explain. I can—"

"Don't come any closer to me!" she cried, looking around, feeling like a trapped animal. *How does he have this?*

But as she turned to run for the door, still clutching the photograph, Jack was too fast, loping past her and slamming into it, his back to the timber, blocking her way.

"Cate, please, just sit down and I'll tell you the truth—give me the chance to explain."

"Explain how you have the photograph I gave my fiancé before he left for war? My fiancé who's missing, presumed dead?" She was crying now, tears streaking down her face. "I don't even know you, Jack, do I? I have no idea who you really are!"

He slumped down, skidding his back down the door until he was sitting in front of it, but standing or sitting, it was still blocked. She was still trapped.

Cate backed away to the farthest corner of the attic space, sitting under the window and staring at Jack, wondering what else he'd concealed from her. And as she looked at the picture, faded but still so obviously her, a deep pain erupted in her stomach. There was no reasonable explanation for him having the photo in his possession. How long had he even had it?

"How did you get this?" she whispered. "And don't you dare lie to me."

"I haven't been honest with you, Cate," he said, shaking his head, his regret painted all over his face. "I should have been, but I haven't."

"Well that's abundantly obvious," she muttered.

"I knew your fiancé," he said. "I was with Charlie the day he died. We were in the same unit and the day we came under fire, we lost him and four other men in our regiment." Jack swallowed and wiped his eyes. "He'd talked about you, shown me your photo, and when he died . . ."

It was like an arrow had been shot straight through her. "He's dead? Charlie is actually dead?"

Jack reached for her, but she swatted him away.

"Yes, he's dead. I was with him, but everything after that is such a blur, there were so many men falling, and . . ."

She was barely holding it together, her fists balled, nails digging into her palms. "You took this photograph from his dead body? You thought you could steal it?" All this time, she'd known deep down he was gone, but to actually hear it from Jack was something else. It was like receiving the news all over again.

"No, Cate. It wasn't like that," Jack said. "He was holding it, it was the last thing he saw before he died, and when I bent down and closed his eyelids, I didn't want to just leave it. Not when it meant so much to him. It didn't seem right to leave it behind in the mud."

Emotion choked her, but eventually she managed to get her words out. "You didn't think you should have tucked it into his jacket? To leave it with him?"

Jack's head fell. "I didn't," he said. "But I took it because I wanted to find you. I wanted to show your photo around and be able to tell you how he died."

"But you didn't," she whispered. "Did you?"

"All those months I kept looking at your face—I would have recognized you anywhere, and when I woke up in hospital and saw you standing there over me, I thought I was dreaming." His voice cracked.

She swallowed, her throat like sandpaper, not bothering to wipe the tears from her cheeks.

"Cate, I wanted to tell you, but I was fighting for my life. You were the only thing keeping me going, my light amongst so much darkness, and then I just couldn't. I kept thinking that if I told you, I'd take away what little hope you had, and I couldn't do that to you. Then too much time had passed, and suddenly I just didn't know what to say—"

"So you said nothing at all," she finished for him.

He slowly stood as Cate watched, eyeing the door, ready to flee when he moved. It was like being stuck in a room with a stranger. But instead of blocking her as she'd expected, he turned the handle and then stepped aside.

"You can leave, Cate. I'm not going to force you to stay in here, I only wanted you to hear me out," he said. "The truth is, I think I fell in love with you before I met you. Your smiling face was what I held on to in my darkest days, huddled in mud. Staring at it was what kept me going. But when I met you . . ." His voice was ragged.

"Don't Jack, please don't," she begged.

"I've loved you since that first day, Cate. You must know that, you must realize that what I feel for you is so much more than this photo?"

"It wasn't yours to take, Jack," she cried.

"It wasn't, you're right," he said. "But I was the one who was with Charlie as he passed, I was a good friend, I was a good soldier. I didn't do anything more than take something he'd shown me of his own free will. I should have told you before now, I should have at least given you the closure of knowing what happened to him, and for that I'm sorry. I'm so, so sorry."

Cate crumpled forward, gasping, tears making her shoulders tremble as she let them all out.

"I'm the same man you met in that hospital, Cate," Jack whispered, close to her now, his hands reaching out. "Nothing has changed. Nothing about the way I feel about you or you feel about me has changed."

She shrugged him away, but he didn't stop, wrapping her in his arms. She fought against him, slapping at his chest, beating her fists into his shoulders, before finally slumping into him, letting him hold her, the fight within her slipping away. "You're wrong, Jack. The way I feel about you has most definitely changed."

"I'm sorry," he murmured. "I should have told you, I should have been honest, but Cate, you need to hear this. He saved the lives of our friends, we both hauled them so far to get them out of harm's way, and your Charlie, he didn't even know the bullet was coming. He was gone before he could have felt anything, and I need you to know that." He sobbed. "Please, this doesn't have to change anything."

She clung on to him, needing to be held in that moment, but knowing at the same time that she needed to leave. "It does," she cried. "It does change everything, Jack. Because you lied to me, and you had a connection to my past that you kept hidden." *You knew Charlie—how could you have known him and never, ever said?* It only made her feel more guilty about moving on, following her heart instead of her head. Her only relief was to hear he'd died a fast death.

"Cate, please," he whispered, his thumb gently wiping the tears from her cheeks.

"Leave me, Jack," she said, finding the courage to move away from him. "We have a big week ahead of us and I just want to be alone."

He stood, hands hanging at his sides, his eyes filled with tears. And she knew, for as long as she lived, she'd never forget the forlorn way he stared at her as she backed away and then ran to her room.

Cate shut the door and curled up on the bed, her knees touching her chin as she cried like she'd never cried before. She loved Jack, she'd fallen so hard and fast for him, but like her mama always said, a man will say anything to get close to a girl.

They're like peacocks, strutting around, doing anything to attract a female and lure her in.

Charlie hadn't been like that. Charlie had been kind and sweet. She'd known him her entire life.

But he never made me feel like Jack does.

She wept into the bedcovers as she remembered the day her father had passed, as she fought against the wave of memories: all the times she'd vowed not to be fooled or hurt by a man.

"He's dead, Ma," her brother said, his eyes wide with disbelief as he stood in the doorway. "Killed himself with his own gun."

Cate turned to her mother, expecting tears, about to wrap her arms around her, but her mother's face wasn't full of tears; it was stretching into a smile. They'd been braced for him to arrive home drunk, his staggering footfalls on the verandah their alert that it was time to protect Ma, for her brothers to end up with black eyes for their efforts if he was in one of his drunken rages.

"You're sure of it?" her mother asked.

"Oh, I'm sure. The police just came and said to pass on their condolences."

"He's dead," Ma whispered. "Oh my Lord, he's dead!"

She jumped up with a fervor Cate hadn't seen in years, grabbing her by the hands and twirling her around as she screamed with joy.

"He's dead! He can't hurt us any more! The old bastard is dead!"

Soon her brother was dancing with them, like crazy idiots around the room, and before long her other two brothers had joined them, all singing and laughing as if they'd received the best news of their lives.

And it was only later, when they'd collapsed around the fire, her mother's arms around Cate's shoulders, that her mother had whispered in her ear.

"Don't you repeat my mistakes, love," she said. "Men will trick you and pretend to be something they're not, just to get you to be with them. Your father pretended to be a good man, a kind man, and as soon as we were married I met his fist. He didn't care whether I had a babe in my belly or in my arms, he hit me whenever he was feeling down about the world."

Cate nodded, leaning into her, inhaling her mother's familiar scent of perfume mixed with cooking.

"I won't," she promised. "I won't ever let a man do that to me, Ma."

As she pulled a blanket over her, shivering and crying still, she refused to believe that she'd repeated her mother's mistakes. But Jack had hurt her; maybe not with his fists, but the pain was no less for that.

He'd known who she was, he'd known her fiancé, and despite everything they'd been through together, she didn't know if she'd ever be able to fully trust him again.

She imagined him upstairs, lying on his bed, staring at the ceiling maybe as he regretted what he'd done, what he'd kept from her. But as much as she would have loved to go back to him and curl in the crook of his arm, whispering her forgiveness to him, she knew she couldn't.

Ma would never forgive me.

And she would never forgive herself.

CHAPTER TWENTY

CATE

TEN DAYS LATER

Cate had barely spoken to Jack since the night she'd found the photo, and as she came face to face with him in the kitchen, she found it almost impossible to meet his gaze. She'd stuck to her guns, staying strong and listening to her mother's voice. He'd been relatively easy to avoid the past week, as both men rarely left the attic unless it was nighttime, and she'd made sure to go to bed early each night.

But they were about to be in close proximity for hours as they tramped for the beach at Calais, which meant they needed to get along.

"Any word yet from Elise?" Jack asked.

Harry was pacing the living room now, raking his fingers back and forth through his hair.

"Nothing," Cate replied.

"How long can we wait?" Jack asked.

"We're not going without her, so we wait as long as we need to wait," Harry snapped, glaring at them. "There wouldn't even be an evacuation plan if it wasn't for Elise."

Cate traded glances with Jack, knowing she'd have to tread carefully.

"I agree that we can't leave without her, she's an important part of the plan," Cate said, her voice low. "But we may not get an opportunity like this again, so—"

"We're not leaving without her, and that's final."

She looked from Harry to Jack, not sure what to say. She didn't want to leave without Elise and Adelaide either, but this was their only chance at getting home.

"Cate, can we talk a moment?" Jack said, gesturing toward Harry. "Alone?"

She glanced at Jack, about to say that there was nothing he couldn't say in front of Harry, but changed her mind. He moved into the kitchen, just out of earshot, or at least out of sight.

"About the other night . . ." he started.

"Please, Jack, can we just not talk about it?" she asked. "We have a long journey ahead of us and—"

"I'm sorry," he said. "I just want to say that I know what I did was wrong, and you're right for hating me. And I wanted to say that I'm so sorry, just one more time. I'm so, so sorry, Cate."

Cate stared into his beautiful dark brown eyes, wishing she could forget that he'd lied to her. "I don't hate you, Jack. But I don't want to talk about it. I want us to focus on our journey." She brushed away her tears and sighed. "I can't even wrap my head around it all."

He nodded. "Fair enough."

"What do you think we do about Elise and Adelaide, though?" she whispered. "We owe them everything, but if something's happened to them, if there's a chance—"

"Someone's here," Jack interrupted, grabbing her hand as he ducked down low.

"It's me." Elise's voice rang through the house. "Me and only me."

Jack slowly stood and Cate's heart stopped pounding as she walked out to see Elise, her ashen-white face sending shivers through Cate.

"What happened? Did you find her?" she asked.

Elise's eyes looked too big for her face, her cheeks hollow and the color completely drained from her skin.

"She's gone," Elise said. "Adelaide has disappeared. There's no sign of her."

Cate pulled Elise down on to the small sofa with her, forcing a smile, knowing that Elise was the one who needed help now, more than any of them. This was about family; this was about the one person in the world Elise had left.

"She's not gone," Cate said, trying to sound upbeat. "Adelaide had a job to do, and wherever she is, whatever she's done, it's because she's doing what we agreed on."

But Elise's face told another story. "She should have alerted us by now," Elise said. "She's not following the plan."

"If she'd betrayed us, we'd know it. They'd have stormed the house," Jack said.

"*Betrayed us?*" Cate almost tripped over her own tongue trying to get the words out. "Adelaide is no traitor."

"But what if she has told him? What if she went to him and something went wrong? How far did you look for her?" Harry asked. "We need to get out of here. I'm not letting that bastard slaughter anyone in this room, not on my watch, not with a boat waiting for us. We have to go."

"I agree, we leave now," Elise said, her voice too even, too static.

"Elise," Cate whispered. "We can't just leave Addy. She's your sister, and she's—"

"Harry's right, we have to leave. I've looked everywhere for her, but bar walking into the German camp and demanding if she's there, there's nothing else I can do."

"But your plan," Cate murmured. "You wanted her to be safe, you wanted her on that boat."

"Wait, Adelaide was coming back to England with us?" Jack asked.

Cate nodded. "She was. Elise made a bargain to keep her safe."

"What exactly did you bargain, Elise?" Harry asked, standing over her. "What the hell did you bargain?"

"Myself," Elise said. "I bargained myself, to the resistance, to fight for France."

"Christ," Harry swore, starting to pace again, his hand angrily tugging through his hair. "I thought . . ." His voice trailed off, and Cate wondered what he had intended to say.

As Elise stood, Cate couldn't believe how stoic she was being. "Elise, we can wait longer. The original plan was that we leave anyway and meet her an hour's walk from here. She could meet us still, perhaps she just had to change the plan at the last minute?" But she could tell from the look on Elise's face that she had already well and truly given up hope.

"No. If she were sticking to the plan, she would have waited for me, she wouldn't have left the house without seeing me first. I knew when I woke up and she was gone that everything was unraveling. And she was supposed to leave a sign. Remember? She hasn't done any of those things."

Cate wished she had answers, or something helpful to say. "You think she's fallen in love with him, don't you?"

Elise's throat bobbed, the only telltale sign that she was upset. She didn't speak for what felt like a long while but could have been only a couple of minutes. "I know she has."

Cate's own belief in Adelaide wavered then. If even her own sister thought it were possible . . . "Elise, she knows what kind of man he is. I don't believe she could have."

But she also saw the way Elise looked over at Harry before she spoke again. "I know how easy it is to fall for a foreigner, so who am I to talk?"

Cate knew as well as Elise that there was no comparison between Harry and Wolfgang, but she understood the sentiment. "You really think we should go now?"

Elise nodded. "What if I choose to believe that she hasn't gone to him, that she hasn't betrayed us, and then SS officers storm my house looking for you and shoot you where you stand? I'd never be able to live with myself."

"I'm so sorry, Elise. I know how badly you wanted to get her away from here."

"But if I leave her behind, if I'm wrong . . ." Elise shook her head. "She can always come back here. No one will suspect anything, I suppose, and I can recruit her into the resistance with me later. If he hasn't corrupted her, that is."

Elise picked up her bag and Cate quickly did the same, and soon they were all standing, staring at one another, in the center of the room. There was no arguing with Elise when her mind was set. It was the first time since the night Cate had arrived that they'd all been downstairs together, and Cate found herself standing beside Jack again.

"We leave now," Elise said. "We follow the plan, moving as fast as we can when it's safe. It's going to be dark soon, so we have no time left to spare."

"We start out as a group," Harry added. "If we need to split up, we do so, and we make our own way to the beach. Here are your maps."

Cate took the one he passed her, pulse racing as she studied the markers for where they were to go. Alone, in the dark, she doubted how successful she'd be, but she would do her best.

"If we're separated, it's each man, *or woman*, for themselves," Harry said. "No one goes back for anyone else, we don't slow down for anyone. You just get to the beach."

Cate sucked back a breath as Jack looked at her. She knew in her heart of hearts that Jack wouldn't go on without her, no matter what Harry said.

"I think we should wait a little bit longer," Cate said, the words spilling from her before she had time to stop them. "Until it's almost completely dark."

All three sets of eyes turned to her.

"That's not what we agreed," Harry said.

"I actually think she's right, I'd rather have to go much faster under the cover of complete darkness," Jack said. "But what if something has happened to Addy and she's told him about us? With that in mind, I think we have to take our chances out there in the open rather than be sitting ducks, and we already have less time than we wanted to get there. We're going to be pushed to make it at all."

Elise didn't contribute to the conversation, but she did turn and leave them for a few seconds before returning holding a pistol. She loaded it in front of them and passed it to Harry.

"Here," she said. "You can take this, keep it under your jacket. At least it might give us a fighting chance against one or two soldiers."

Cate hated the sight of the gun; after all the wounds she'd nursed, all the men she'd held who'd cried in pain from bullets that had ripped through their skin, she didn't want to see one ever again. But if Harry had it, at least he could protect them.

Jack looked perturbed, probably because he would have preferred to have one too, but his injury wasn't healed, which made Harry the logical choice.

When Elise swung open the front door, Cate's heart nearly pounded clean from her chest, but she forced herself to follow the others outside. She expected instant gunfire or shouts to erupt around them, but instead they were greeted by silence.

She quickly looked around, hoping to catch sight of Adelaide, but there was no one there. The plan had been that she would lure

Wolfgang away under false pretenses and his men with him, then meet them once he'd left. It had been an ambitious plan, and one that involved deceiving him into believing there were British soldiers holed up in the opposite direction to where they were going, and Cate hadn't liked it any more than Elise had. And their backup option, if Adelaide couldn't get away from him, was that she'd discard her red scarf on the tree by the meadow she had often disappeared to with Wolfgang. That would be Addy's signal that she wasn't coming, that she'd had to stay with him instead of coming back. It was the worst-case scenario; or at least it had been, because none of them had imagined that she could ever betray them. Not sweet, quietly spoken Adelaide, who'd been the one to save them all in the first place. But part of the plan had also been that she would tell them when she was leaving, so they could time her. Instead, she'd just slipped out without anyone knowing, and had never come back.

"Come on, let's go," Harry said.

"I'll be the one giving orders," Elise snapped, pushing past him to lead the way. "You're the one who landed on my doorstep in the first place, and you suggested Addy go to that godforsaken Nazi, so forgive me for not wanting to hear the sound of your voice just now."

Jack's fingers brushed past Cate's then, their knuckles grazing, and despite how angry she'd been with him she caught his hand and held it for a few steps, needing someone, *something*, to take hold of. She knew Elise wasn't really cross with Harry, she needed someone to blame and he was an easy target for her to be angry with.

Because if Adelaide had done the unspeakable . . . Cate shuddered. It didn't matter what anyone said, she wouldn't, *couldn't,* believe it.

"Are you all right?" she asked, not sure if she was imagining the strain on his face.

Jack said nothing, giving her only a tight smile in reply.

"Jack?"

"I'm in pain, that's all," he said. "Something isn't right inside me, hasn't been right since I started bleeding on our walk here."

She nodded. "We just need to get you to that boat. Even more reason to get moving." Cate refused to think about all the things that could be wrong with him, even as her mind started to race. But it was a flash of white that distracted her in the end.

"Elise, look! There's Oscar!"

The little dog came trotting out of the trees near the house, breaking into a run when he saw them. Elise bent low and scooped him up as he came near, his pink tongue lolling out as he licked at her face, his leash still attached to him.

"He's panting heavily," Cate said. "Do you think Adelaide could be coming back?"

They stood and listened for a moment, ears strained.

"She's not coming," Elise said, her voice flat as she held up Oscar's tattered lead. "Addy loves this dog more than anything, and she would never have let go of him. And if she did, she'd have been running and hollering after him."

Cate exchanged a long look with Elise, who kept the dog tucked under her arm.

"We need to go," Jack said. "I'm sorry, Elise, but we can't wait."

Elise had tears shining in her eyes, but she forged on ahead, and Cate noticed that she never, not once, looked back. It was as if she knew her sister wasn't coming; but Cate kept looking for her, certain that she was about to see a mane of blonde hair flying in the wind behind Adelaide as she raced to catch up with them.

CHAPTER TWENTY-ONE

ADELAIDE
ONE HOUR EARLIER

Adelaide had drifted along on her own and had then sat beneath a hefty oak tree for hours, wrestling with her thoughts. She'd become so used to being under her mother's wing, and then Elise's, and now she was all alone.

I'm not alone.

She lay her head back against the rough bark of the tree, eyes shut, lost in thought. She wasn't alone, because Elise was waiting, always waiting, with open arms; and yet right now, she'd never felt more alone in her life. And with a choice to make that was ripping her in two.

She stroked Oscar, who'd loyally and patiently followed her and then sat in her lap. His rough coat was familiar beneath her fingertips, and when she finally rose, she had his lead between her fingers. It was time to go.

When she reached the two Nazi soldiers on guard, stationed well ahead of the house where Wolfgang was living, she raised a hand and waved, making sure to smile. She received a warm wave in response.

This was why she was so lucky: she'd become untouchable. She was marked as Wolfgang's, and not a hair on her head could be harmed. It was like nothing she'd ever experienced before.

"Could you take a message to the commander for me?" she asked, speaking slowly to make sure they understood her German, which had improved since meeting Wolfgang, although they mostly spoke in English since they could both converse fluently in it.

She passed a folded piece of paper to one of the men, knowing it wouldn't be worth their lives not to pass it on to him. And then she went to wait, by the same tree she'd sat under, Oscar trotting along beside her, her constant partner in crime.

She'd asked Wolfgang to meet her, said that she had to see him. She'd toyed with whether to go through with it or not, whether her ruse would be plausible, or if she was even going to go ahead with a ruse at all.

But in the end, there had been only one decision she could make.

"I can't back down now," she whispered to Oscar, bending to pick up her little dog and bury her face in his fur as she tried her hardest not to cry. "What's done is done." She just hoped her sister would forgive her for not having said goodbye before she left the house. She'd gone about everything the wrong way, but there was nothing she could do about that now.

It's too late to change my mind, even if I want to.

"Adelaide!"

She turned at his call, and as he strode toward her it came naturally to her to open her arms to him. His eyes lit up, and he no longer seemed to hide from her, his smile wide and genuine as he held her against his chest. And just as it had felt natural to go to him, it also felt right to lift her face to his, expectantly, for the kiss she knew would follow.

"What a nice surprise. Is everything okay?"

She leant against him, fitting snugly under his arm. She still had Oscar's leash looped around one wrist, and she smiled as Wolfgang reached down to pat him.

"Everything is fine," she said. "I just hadn't seen you in a few days and . . ." Lying hadn't ever been something she was good at, and she decided to play embarrassed instead of continuing on. She held her tongue as they started to walk, heading for one of their favorite spots well away from sight.

"Adelaide, I have some news for you. We're going to be moving on soon," he told her, frowning as he met her gaze. "I know that will come as a shock, but I'll make sure to come back and see you as often as I can. Perhaps if we end up in Paris, you can eventually come and join me?"

Her stomach lurched as she stared up at him, committing him to memory. She hadn't been lying to Elise when she'd told her that she hadn't forgotten what he'd done; the trouble was simply that the longer she spent in his company, the easier it was to make excuses or pretend it wasn't even him at all.

She batted the thoughts away. No matter how she felt about him, she was going to protect her sister and her friends, and if that meant betraying Wolfgang, then so be it. Nothing ran thicker than blood, and she loved Elise more than anything or anyone in the world.

"There's actually something I wanted to talk to you about, too," she started, hesitantly.

"Go on," he said.

She looked down at how shiny his black boots were and found herself wondering if he polished them himself as he passed her on the narrow part of the track. But she quickly forgot his boots as she realized it was her chance to leave the scarf, her sign for Elise. She unlooped it then as he moved ahead, quickly letting it slip from her fingers to catch on a branch while his back was to her.

"Addy, what were you going to tell me?" Wolfgang asked, suddenly turning back around. Her heart sank when she saw him look past her and frown. "Isn't that your scarf back there? Did you drop it?"

Adelaide feigned surprise as he brushed past her to retrieve it, taking it from him, knowing she had no choice but to accept it. She could feel everything starting to unravel and a bead of sweat broke out on her top lip. "Thank you. Silly me."

He gave her a strange look but kept walking, and she took his arm, trying to stay calm.

She'd been going to tell him that there were rumors of Allied soldiers, send him in the wrong direction, anything to keep him and his men away from her home, and she knew it would be plausible if she kept her head. He had no reason not to believe her; she had his trust, and she'd also already brought a British soldier to him. All those nights worrying that Peter might have given them away had been for nothing; he'd clearly kept his mouth shut. Either that or he wasn't alive any longer.

And she had to do it soon, before it was too late. She'd already taken too long deliberating to waste another minute.

"Commander!"

The shout was loud, and two soldiers came running toward them. Adelaide jumped back from him, not sure whether he wanted to be seen with her so intimately cuddled against him, but he reached for her hand and kept her close.

"It had better be important." His voice was more growl than anything, but the two men were not deterred.

She swallowed, instinctively clutching Oscar's lead.

"Commander, there've been reports of two men on the run. They're not from around here, and we suspect they're Allied soldiers."

Wolfgang's hand pulled away from hers as he gave the soldiers his full attention, and she wished the ground would open up and swallow her. It had to be Jack and Harry.

"Where were they coming from?" Wolfgang asked.

Adelaide wanted to run. She wished she could grab Oscar and disappear, but as she eyed the pistols all three men carried, she knew she'd never be able to get away.

"Sir, a word in private," one of the soldiers said, as the other stared at her, his eyes as cold and hard as ice.

She knew then it was over, that there was no chance she was ever getting away from them unless she could somehow convince Wolfgang that his own men were lying to him.

"Just say it," Wolfgang ordered. "Where were they seen?"

The soldier coughed and then stared straight into her eyes. "It was the men hidden, keeping watch. They were seen leaving from her house," he said as he pointed at her.

No. No, no, no!

"Adelaide's house?" Wolfgang asked, sounding incredulous. "You must be mistaken."

He's had men watching our house! How could we not have known? Not have seen them?

"They were with two women too, one blonde, one brunette."

Adelaide swallowed, trying to stay calm, to not react outwardly as Wolfgang's eyes went from warm to hard and narrowed in a split second. That description had sealed her fate. It was most certainly Elise and Cate.

"Adelaide? Is this true?"

He stepped toward her and she stumbled back, frightened. The Wolfgang she'd so hesitantly fallen in love with was gone, and she knew then what a mistake she'd made in ever trusting him. Every step, every flash of anger in his eyes as she cowered away from him took her back to that day, watching him and his men in horror from their parents' bedroom window. Only this time, she was the one in his sights, like an animal being hunted with nowhere left to turn. And she knew in that moment that it *had* been him who'd given the order; she could see it now, her imagination immediately putting a face to the man who'd yelled *fire*.

He lunged at her then, grabbing her by her hair, gripping it so tight she cried out in pain.

"Wolfgang! You're hurting me!"

"Tell me, is it true? Were you hiding soldiers all this time?"

His breath was hot on her face, spittle landing on her cheek as she tried to twist out of his grip.

"Why are you even asking me?" she cried. "Of course I wasn't!"

"Is that why you asked me to meet you? To draw me away? I'm no fool, Adelaide."

She was crying now, unable to stop, sobbing as he twisted her hair around his fist even harder, so tight she thought it was going to rip clean off her scalp.

"You're certain it was her house? That it was her sister?" Wolfgang yelled.

"Yes, sir," they called back in unison.

"You bitch!" he spat, backhanding her so hard that she went flying, landing on her elbows on the hard-packed dirt.

"Wolfgang, please!" she begged, scrambling to her knees and trying to get up. "I can explain!"

"Leave us!" he roared, as his polished black boot lifted and connected with her cheek, the crack of her bone shattering so painful it sent her reeling. "And hunt those bastards down. Now!"

She clawed at the dirt, on her knees again. "Stop, *please* stop!"

This time he was reaching for Oscar, and she fought against him, trying to stop him as he lunged for the little dog.

"Tell me the truth or I'll shoot him!" Wolfgang snarled.

"No," she cried. "Oscar, run! Go!" She threw a fistful of dirt at him, letting go of his leash as she screamed at him. "Go!"

But Wolfgang had his sights set on her again, forgetting the dog, hauling her up by her long hair as she cried and pleaded for mercy, his eyes wild as he sneered.

He was going to kill her. *Oh my God, he's actually going to kill me!*

"I would have done anything for you, Adelaide." His lip curled. "And what did you do with my trust? You used it against me. You bitch."

She braced for another blow, but it never came, and she squinted up at him, her eye swelling already from the kick to her face, pulsing with pain.

"Please, Wolfgang, you know how I feel about you. Why would I lie to you?"

He ran a hand through his hair as it fell over his forehead, and he looked like a madman. "I'm going to ask you one last time. Were there other survivors that you kept hidden?"

She swallowed, defeat crushing her as she staggered in front of him, slumping to her knees.

"Sit up and answer me!" he screamed.

"I came to tell you, that's what I was about to say, when we were walking," she whispered.

"You're lying!"

She was lying. Of course she was lying, and as her vision began to swim, she knew there was nothing she could say to convince him otherwise. "I had to choose my sister," she cried. "It was protect my sister or choose you, and . . ."

Wolfgang had gone deadly quiet, and she stopped speaking as tears ran down her cheeks, as she struggled to breathe past the blood in her mouth.

"You betrayed me, Adelaide." His words were low and sinister, menacing, and she watched in horror as he took his pistol from its holster and raised it, aiming for her head.

"No, Wolfgang, please," she cried, scrambling to get away from him. But his hand was in her hair again, clutching her, not letting her move.

"You're nothing but a disloyal traitor."

Her mouth opened to plead with him as his finger curled around the trigger, but she knew it was no use.

Adelaide shut her eyes and saw her sister. She saw her family, all sitting around the table, laughing, waiting for her. *Calling for her.*

And then she heard a sob, and realized it was her own.

CHAPTER TWENTY-TWO

ELISE
FORTY-EIGHT HOURS LATER

Elise was numb. She was going through the motions of walking and keeping lookout, but her mind was a million miles away. *How did I let this happen?*

The truth was, she knew. She hadn't told Cate, probably would never tell Cate, that she'd had an argument before they left with Addy. It was the reason she'd known she wasn't coming back, and why Addy had decided to leave instead of waiting for her. And it was all she'd thought of since they'd set out.

She pressed her hand to her heart as she walked, as if somehow, miraculously, it could stem the pain. But it did nothing to ease her suffering. Or her guilt. If only Adelaide had followed the plan, and if only she hadn't tried to convince her to leave France again.

"You still expect me to get on that boat and sail for England?" Addy laughed as if it were the greatest joke she'd ever heard. "You're serious? You actually think I'm going to leave France?"

Elise stayed calm, realizing her error the moment she saw her sister's reaction. "Yes. I feel it's the only way to keep you safe."

"And what about you?" Addy asked. "Who will keep you safe? Because I can tell right now that you're still not planning on leaving with me."

"Addy, please, just hear me out," Elise pleaded. "You can take Oscar with you, no one will turn down a little dog under your arm, and it means that you can get far away from Wolfgang so you don't have to do anything you don't want—"

"What are you trying to say? That he's somehow forced himself on me?" Addy sounded hysterical now, and Elise felt as if she were dealing with a child; although when it came to her sister, that wouldn't be the first time.

"I'm only saying that he's a very powerful man, and if you ever don't want to see him again, things could become difficult," Elise carefully said. "Besides, I thought you were only seeing him still to help the cause?" It was a ruse to get her sister to admit her true feelings, and it worked.

"What if it's not a ruse anymore?" Addy asked, staring out the window. "He's been so lovely to me, he treats me well, and if our country becomes part of Germany one day . . ."

"Don't you dare say that, with such acceptance!" Elise stood, storming toward her sister and taking her arm, forcing her to turn around. "France will not be home to the Nazis, not now and not ever. Have you forgotten what they've done? Have you forgotten our brother?" Her breath seemed to hiss out of her, she was so angry. "We stood, side by side, terrified of that man you claim is so lovely. You know he gave that order, you were the one who begged me to take in Harry, and with a few dates and a handful of eggs, you suddenly think that bastard is lovely?"

Adelaide's hand was so fast that Elise didn't see the slap coming, but she certainly felt the sting across her cheek.

"You're defending him now?" Elise asked, shaking her head as she pressed her palm to her inflamed skin. "I feel like I don't even know you anymore!"

"I'm telling you that with me, he's someone else," Addy said. "I know what he's capable of, but all soldiers are capable of terrible things. I just didn't understand war before."

"Oh, and now you're suddenly an expert?" Elise's heart sank. She knew there was no point arguing. "There are rules in war, Addy. Rules that stipulate what is and isn't acceptable. A white flag means surrender, and those men aren't allowed to be killed in cold blood, they're to be taken prisoner. And likewise, hospitals are to be off-limits, the red cross signaling a safe zone."

Adelaide was staring back at her, but it was like she was already gone.

"Your commander, he did something that no soldier should ever do—he committed murder, a massacre of a large group of Allied soldiers, and I can only hope that one day his actions are revealed. Maybe one day he'll feel the terror of someone putting a bullet through his head or a bayonet through his chest."

Adelaide's face was red, her eyes full of tears, but Elise wasn't going to go easy on her, not now. If she wanted to be treated like an adult, then that was exactly what Elise would do.

"If you think you're in love with him, then go to him. See what it's like to be with a monster," Elise said. "But if you do that, you're no sister of mine."

Adelaide's eyes widened as she registered what Elise had said. Then slowly, deliberately, she turned her back.

"Get out of my room!" Addy cried, and Elise heard the painful catch in her voice, the emotion that she was struggling to keep down.

"I love you, Addy. I've done everything I can to keep you safe, to show you that I love you, but I don't know the woman you're becoming," Elise whispered. "I only hope your commander is the man you think he is, because if you let us down tomorrow and choose him, he's all you'll have left."

It shouldn't have surprised her, given that Adelaide had always tried to see the good in everyone, believed that everyone deserved redemption, but it still hurt that she could be so foolish.

Elise knew she'd always regret walking away from her sister; she wished she'd gone to her and held her, refused to take no for an answer and listened to her instead of being so hurtful. But she couldn't change the past, no matter how much she wanted to.

The sky was inky now, the landscape around them almost impossible to see even though her eyes had adjusted to the darkness. She was slightly ahead, with Harry close beside her, and Jack and Cate were silently bringing up the rear. They'd ended up staying together, but she was starting to think it was time to pair off, anxiety clutching at her throat as she kept straining to hear whether they were alone or not. Every rustle, every murmur, sent a wave of fear through her that was greater than the last, and they had to make their way around the outskirts of a village now; there was no other way.

"We're approaching another village," she whispered, stumbling a little over something in the dirt. Harry caught her arm and she straightened, grateful for his quick reactions. "I think it's best we split off into pairs and we'll see each other at the beach at Calais." She adjusted the bag on her shoulder, Oscar tucked inside it, surprised at how heavy he was to carry.

"Agreed," three voices whispered back in the dark to her.

"Tread carefully, though," Elise warned. "Calais was decimated weeks ago when the German tanks came through—they as good as flattened the place so you never know what could have been left behind."

Cate whispered a kiss to her cheek, and they embraced quickly before she and Jack started to move left, and Harry took up his position by Elise's side. But they hadn't been parted for more than minute before a sickening crack pierced the air. Was it a gun shot?

"Jack! *Jack!*" Cate's whisper was panicked as Elise ran back toward them.

They'd largely resisted the urge to use flashlights so far, but Elise fumbled with hers now and turned it on, trying to see the others. Elise and Harry saw them out to the left and started to run to catch up with them.

"What was that?" she whispered to Harry.

"I think someone's on to us." Elise put her arm around Cate when they reached her, as Jack took the flashlight from her.

And then they all heard it. Elise felt Cate stiffen. *Dogs.*

Oh my God, we're not going to make it.

"We need to find somewhere to hide," Jack said. "We're never going to outrun them if they have dogs."

Elise didn't say what she was thinking: there was no way they were going to out-hide dogs, either.

"We're so close," Cate cried. "Surely we can make a run for it, surely we can just keep going?"

"I don't know about you, but there's no way I can run for more than an hour. And that's what it would be, minute after long minute trying to keep up that pace to avoid them," Jack said.

"Harry," Elise said, reaching for him, catching his fingers as he turned away.

She grabbed the front of his jacket and pulled him in, whispering into his ear. "I love you, Harry. I'm so sorry. I blamed you because I was angry with myself, but I'm so sorry."

"You're forgiven," he whispered back, and she quickly kissed his lips. "A hundred times over, you're forgiven."

Hearing Harry's words gave Elise the strength to keep going, and she used her flashlight to quickly scan the area. "Come on, we can do this. We find somewhere to hide, and we don't stop until we do. No one is taking me down without a fight, not when we've already come this far."

Elise turned off the flashlight and started to hurry onwards. She'd never been so scared in her life, and she reached into her bag to keep her hand around Oscar's mouth in case he barked back or let out a growl.

A voice came to her on the wind then, just a whisper, but she knew the enemy was getting closer, and there was only so long before they were found.

They're coming.

The four of them moved fast, but it was Harry who found the barn, grabbing her hand and dragging her toward it. They started to run, climbing a fence then stumbling, tripping more times than she could count, but they did it. She'd half-expected fingers to curl around her neck from behind or a gun to be rammed into her skull, but there was no one behind them yet.

"Come on," Jack said as he flung the door open. "Get in."

Harry hesitated, but Elise didn't let go of his hand. She felt his pain, knew the pain of his memories as he was faced with holing up in a barn as Nazis descended again, but she needed him.

"Please, Harry, come on," she whispered.

"There are horses in here," Cate exclaimed, as a soft nicker came from the shadows. "Quickly, we can hide in their stalls."

"I think they'll find us," Elise whispered, almost too scared to talk at all in case her own voice caught on the night wind. "This is the first place they'll come!"

Harry softly shut the barn door behind him and they waited, trying to let their eyes adjust. But as she started to move, started to look for a hiding place amongst the hay, she felt Harry stiffen.

"Elise," he whispered, moving to stand in front of her, fumbling for her hands and then clutching them.

Her panic was rising, but she focused on Harry, on listening to his voice and feeling his hands in hers. This wasn't how it was supposed to happen.

"I love you, Elise. I should have told you days ago, but I love you, so much, and I wasn't lying when I told you all those weeks back that I'd give myself if I needed to, to keep you safe."

What is he talking about? Give himself?

"Harry, whatever you're about to do—"

He kissed her, his lips almost missing hers in the dark, and she pressed her mouth back against his, holding him tight.

"If I survive, I promise I'll find you again," he said, pressing the pistol into her hand. "I love you."

"Harry!" she cried.

"Jack, hold her, don't let her follow me, and get her and Cate to that damn boat."

"Harry!" she cried again.

But before she could reach for him, Jack held her back just as he'd asked, and Harry slipped out the door. And when he turned his flashlight on, too far away for her to go after him, as she peered through the grubby little barn window, she knew exactly what he'd done.

Harry had sacrificed himself to give them time to get away.

He was gone.

CHAPTER TWENTY-THREE

ELISE

The scream inside her own head was so loud, so piercing, that she almost wondered if she'd actually uttered it. But given that Cate didn't clamp a hand over her mouth as they huddled in the horse stall, she was almost certain she hadn't made a noise.

The voices were louder now, shouts and commands sluicing the air, and Cate passed her a small piece of bandage.

"Tie this around Oscar's mouth," Cate whispered. "Make sure he stays quiet."

Anyone else would probably have let the dog go, but he was too special to her. Adelaide had loved him like a child, and before that he'd been her brother's much-loved sidekick, so she wasn't about to release him and hope that he'd survive on his own.

She did as Cate asked, but her hands were trembling so much that it took three attempts to tie the knot as he struggled in her arms. When she had, she closed the bag he was in, and lay down.

Cate's arm was over her, and as the shouts turned to cruel taunts, Elise squeezed her eyes shut. She imagined they were SS officers if they had a dog, and she knew the brutal reputation they had, too.

The same as Wolfgang's.

"I surrender." They were two words that Elise had never thought she'd hear from Harry, not in a million years, and she shuddered, thinking of the first time he'd tried to do the same. She braced herself for a shot, or a scream of pain, but there was nothing other than a thud. She imagined he'd been kicked and had fallen heavily to the ground.

"I surrender," he yelled again, his voice carrying to them through the slightly ajar barn door.

"Are you alone?"

Elise held her breath and Cate stiffened beside her.

"I am alone. I've been on the run for weeks, I survived the fight at Le Paradis."

"You're sure there's no one else with you?" The flashlight the officer held passed nearby, covering the grass and moving over the window Elise had been looking out of only moments earlier.

"All my unit was killed, it's only me. I'm the only one left."

Perhaps they didn't believe him, or there was a tell in the way he spoke, because the light cast nearby again. It flashed through the door, passing so close that it made the two horses in the barn restless. She wanted to leap to her feet and run straight out the door to get as far away from the Nazis as she could, and if the soldiers hadn't had a dog with them, she would have. But the thought of trying to outrun a big German shepherd, or having the beast rip poor little Oscar to shreds if she dropped her bag, kept her flat to the ground.

"It wasn't your pretty little girlfriend back in Le Paradis, was it? The fancy blonde?"

Elise's blood ran cold then, and Cate was suddenly half on top of her, her fingers curled across Elise's mouth, pinning her down and keeping her quiet.

"Shhh," Cate murmured, barely audible, in her ear.

"I don't know what you're talking about," Harry said, followed by a loud grunt. She almost felt his pain, knew they'd likely punched or hit him with something in the stomach for simply looking at them.

"Commander Schmidt put a bullet through that pretty little head of hers for betraying him." Both officers laughed. "Ruined her golden hair, otherwise we might have all had a turn with her."

Vomit rose in Elise's throat and she pushed Cate's hand away, fighting against the desire to be sick. She stayed low, on her knees, shaking as she dug her nails into the hay. Violent spasms wracked her body, her head pounding so hard she thought it was going to explode as she fought to stay silent, to not react violently and furiously to what she'd just heard.

Adelaide is dead. Her beautiful, loving, innocent sister hadn't betrayed them; she'd been killed trying to do what she thought was best. She'd been murdered for trying to help.

The laughter from the officers filled the night air, obviously thinking they'd captured Adelaide's true lover, and not knowing that the person who would suffer the most from their news was lying hidden in the dark.

She felt for Oscar in her bag, taking comfort from the softness of his fur, knowing that she'd been right. Adelaide would never have let him go, she would have searched to the end of the earth for the little dog, and she cried silently against him, her tears leaving his fur wet and matted.

"She never betrayed us," Cate whispered, folding her arms around her. "She was loyal right to the end."

If only I hadn't let her go. If only I'd found a way to get her on the boat.

Elise was numb, her nails digging into the dirt now, and when they couldn't hear the officers any longer, Cate hauled her up, holding her until she was steady on her feet.

"I'm so sorry," Cate whispered, her embrace warm and so full of love that Elise just wanted to collapse into her.

She held her for only a few seconds before letting go.

"Elise, we have to go as soon as they move on."

Cate didn't need to tell her twice. They might not make it to the beach, but they certainly couldn't turn around and go back home, either. And she wasn't letting those bastards drag her back to Wolfgang, not until she had a way of getting revenge, of doing something to wipe that self-assured smile off his perfectly Aryan face.

But another sob erupted from deep within her then, as reality hit her hard, the truth of what had happened like a weight crushing her to the ground.

Adelaide is dead.

She shook her head as if it might help shift the thoughts, but the words just kept repeating over and over in her mind.

Harry is gone. Adelaide is dead.

They only had one chance at this now, and they had to make it count.

She stifled her sobs, each one bigger and harder to swallow than the last, and forced herself to her feet. This was it, and she wasn't going to let Adelaide's death be for nothing.

CHAPTER TWENTY-FOUR

CATE

I can do this.

Cate stopped, breathing heavily, but not nearly as heavily as Jack, and she knew that if it weren't so dark, she would have been checking his abdomen; she'd caught him groaning in pain earlier, and although he'd insisted he was fine, she hadn't believed him.

"How are you doing?" she asked him.

"Fine," he muttered, his pace increasing. "I'm doing just fine, don't you worry about me."

But when she cast her light over him, she could see that his face was wet from the exertion. Something was terribly wrong inside him, she just knew it.

"We don't have far to go," Cate said, feeling Elise shiver beside her, wishing she could comfort her friend but knowing that the best thing they could all do was focus on putting one foot in front of the other.

"Please," Jack murmured. "Go on ahead if you can go faster."

Every word sounded pained, and a piece of her heart shattered every time she looked at him. She'd wasted so much time being angry with him, when it was something that should have been forgivable, given everything else they'd been through together.

"Don't try telling me to leave you, because it's not happening," she said. "I'm not getting on that boat without you, and that's final, so we all go at this pace."

Cate turned her attention to Elise, just as worried about her ability to keep walking as Jack's.

"Elise," she whispered, as her friend fell back. "We need to keep going."

Elise hadn't just slowed, she'd stopped entirely. She had dropped down low, her arms caught around herself in a little huddle on her haunches, and Cate stopped too, to wrap her arms around her.

"All I want to do is comfort you, but—"

"We need to move," Elise said woodenly, as if she wasn't really there. "I know. I just . . . just needed to rest. I don't know if I can keep going."

Cate refused to cry, knowing she needed to stay strong. She was the trained nurse; she was the one who could lead them to safety. She was the one they were all depending on now, even though Adelaide's death and Harry being taken hurt her almost as much as Elise. She'd grown to love Addy, and Harry was a good, kind-hearted man.

Much to her relief, Elise rose and started to move slowly.

"You might need to go on ahead," Jack said, out of breath as he doubled over. "Something's not right, I can tell."

Cate didn't dare look at his wound, not wanting to know how bad it was when they were racing against a clock and there was nothing she could do. "You're walking whether you like it or not," she said. "Now come on. We've survived the unsurvivable once,

276

you and I, and we're not giving up now, not with a boat waiting to take us home."

Her words of encouragement seemed to work, because Jack suddenly made a Herculean effort to right himself and start moving again.

"I should have forgiven you, Jack," she continued, not caring that Elise was listening. If Jack didn't make it, she wanted him to know how she truly felt; she didn't need to live with any more regrets. "I don't care that you had my photo or that you didn't tell me about Charlie." She was panting from the exertion of helping him with every step and whispering at the same time. "Charlie was a good man. He was kind and sweet and so different to my daddy, and that's why I said yes to marrying him," she continued. "But when I received that telegram, it was like I'd lost one of my best friends. I didn't love him the way . . ."

She stalled, losing her nerve, not sure whether she could actually say it. But these weren't normal times; everything was heightened, the likelihood of death so much greater than it had ever been before, and everything left unsaid could end up being left unsaid forever.

"I forgive you, Jack," she murmured. "I forgive you, and I love you, so you're going to make it to this boat and hang on long enough to get to a doctor, all right?"

His grunt told her that he'd heard, and tears started to stream down her cheeks as she fought for every footstep, stumbling but refusing to give in to the physical pain. She was exhausted and emotionally wrung out, her legs were burning and her feet hurting, so she could only imagine how hard it was for Jack.

"Those days in hospital, the time I spent caring for you, they were some of the best days of my life, Jack. I'll never forget all those times you caught my eye or made me smile when everything seemed too much. I've always been so scared of truly falling in love with someone—my father scarred me for life, but you've shown me that I don't have to be afraid. So believe me when I say that we need to make it to that boat, because I want the chance for us to start over."

Jack's fingers found hers, clutching tight as they walked, and when Elise's hand touched her back, their arms looped around Jack as they helped to support him, she knew her words had touched her friend, too. Her poor, heartbroken friend who now had to face a life without her sister.

"We can do this." The words hissed out of her. "It's not so far."

In truth they had a long way to go, but compared to how far they'd already come, it was nothing.

And she'd been telling the truth before; Charlie had been more of a friend than a lover. His kisses had been warm and reassuring, his touch had been kind, but she knew in her heart that all she'd wanted was someone to trust, someone who wouldn't hurt her. But Jack made her feel alive, and that was more important than a hidden photo.

"We can do this," she whispered again, as much for herself as the others.

Hundreds or maybe even thousands of steps later, Elise directed them through some dense trees, and the ground suddenly changed beneath Cate's feet, became soft.

Sand. They were walking on sand!

Cate's mouth was dry; she would have done anything for a drink of water or to be able to sink to her knees and just breathe, but they had no idea whether they were too late, whether they could have only minutes before the boat left without them, if it was even still there at all.

"Stop," Jack grunted, collapsing between them.

"No!" Cate gasped. "No! Get up!" She yanked at Jack's arm but he was a deadweight. "Jack, get up!"

Elise dropped beside him, and Cate stared down in horror, her eyes adjusted to the dark now. She could make out both their shapes, and as much as her body ached and yearned to fall beside them, she wasn't giving in, not for a second.

"We're so close, come on," she pleaded. "Jack, you need to find the strength. Get up!"

But Jack wasn't moving, and he certainly wasn't talking. All she could hear was the labored sound of his breath.

"Jack?"

Elise turned on her flashlight, and Cate's heart dropped when she saw his face. His lips were parted and he was wheezing now, the sheen on his face giving him a strange pallor; even his eyes looked sunken, like someone close to death. He was much, much worse than she'd feared.

"Jack, you can do this," she whispered, but she knew there was no way he was moving of his own accord.

"We're going to have to carry him," she said, staring at Jack's body and wondering if it were even possible. "There's no other way."

"I know," Elise said, turning off her flashlight. "But even if we have to drag him, we have to try."

With the light off, it seemed even darker, and Cate had to fumble to take hold of Jack's legs. Every moan that escaped Jack's lips sent a sharp pain through her, but the only thing worse than his pain would be being left behind, and Cate wasn't going to let that happen.

"Down! Get down!"

Elise's command pierced her as she let go of Jack and fell to the ground, stumbling and then landing heavily on her side.

There's someone here. Cate's face was in the ground and she blinked away the sand that clung to her lashes and caked her lips. *It's over. We've come so far, and it's all over.*

She heard a whimper, before realizing it had escaped her own mouth.

"Who's there?"

The call cut straight through her, but not for the reason she'd expected. They were British. *They're British!*

Cate didn't wait. She clawed at the ground as she launched forward, tripping as she rose and lifted her hands as a light cast over her face, blinding her. She squinted, shielding her eyes with one hand as she kept the other high in the air, not wanting there to be any mistaking who she was. That she was friendly.

"My name is Cate Alexander and I'm a British nurse." She tried to speak confidently but her voice was barely there. "I'm a nurse," she whispered, before dropping to her knees, the weight of everything, the pain of everything, felling her.

"Cate, I'm Oliver," one of the men said, rushing forward and clasping her elbows, drawing her back up to her feet.

"There's more!" the other man said, and she spun around as the flashlight illuminated Elise, on her knees, hands in the air, and Jack's unconscious body lying in the sand.

"Please, help us," Cate whispered. "We need to get him on the boat. *Please.*"

The two men lifted Jack between them, far more easily than she and Elise could have done, and she hurried to his side, keeping up with them with a hand on his body as they lugged him across the sand.

"The boat's here, we thought you weren't coming," said Oliver, the familiarity of his accent taking Cate home, washing over her and making her believe she was actually going to see England again, that it wasn't just a dream. "You only just made it in time. Ten more minutes and we would have left without you."

"Elise?" Cate turned and saw that Elise was trailing behind.

"I'm here," Elise said, but it was so dark that Cate could barely see her.

The gentle wash of water told Cate they were close to the ocean now, but there were no flashlights, so it wasn't until the cold, wet sea lapped at her ankles that she knew it was real. And then lights flashed, three times in fast succession.

"That's our sign," one of the men said.

"Elise?" Cate turned and found her friend close behind her now, and she reached for her, holding her hand as they waded out. The boat was only small, just big enough for them all, and she knew they had to move fast, in case there were patrols nearby. If the Nazis saw them, if they were discovered, their shot at freedom was over.

"Lift him."

Cate put her hands under Jack's back and did her best to help, standing on tiptoe as they heaved him up into the boat. Her lower half was soaked through now, her boots sodden as she clambered up into the boat, breathing heavily as she landed like a fish being hauled on a line, scrambling to right herself.

"We need to go," someone said, but in the dark she could barely make out the faces. She bent low over Jack, ear to his mouth, her fingers frantically searching at his neck for his pulse.

He's still breathing. That's all that matters.

"Stay with me, Jack," she murmured. "We're so close, do you hear me? Just keep breathing."

She stroked his forehead, hoping he could feel how strongly she felt for him. When he lifted a hand and touched beside his eye, she wasn't sure what he was trying to tell her, until his trembling hand hovered over his chest, before pointing at her.

I love you. That's what he was trying to tell her. *I love you.*

"I love you, too," she whispered, pressing a kiss to his forehead, lips hovering as tears slid from her cheeks to his skin. "I love you too, Jack. So don't go leaving me, do you hear? You hold on."

"This all we're waiting on?"

Cate sat up, scanning the people in the boat. Where was Elise?

"Elise?" she asked, panic rising as she realized there were only men around her. "Elise!"

"I'm here."

She feared they were dangerously exposed standing there, but as she turned on her flashlight it gave her enough light to see her friend still standing in the water, her hand on the side of the wooden boat.

"Elise, quickly, get in," Cate urged, holding out her hand.

But Elise didn't take it.

"Come with us," Cate begged, as Elise finally took her hand. "I can't leave you behind, not now. Get in the boat."

In her haste to get Jack to safety and get into the boat herself, she'd forgotten that this was supposed to be goodbye to Elise. But after everything that had happened, surely she wasn't going to stay?

"Elise?"

But Elise's hand pulled away from hers the moment she said her name.

CHAPTER
TWENTY-FIVE

ELISE

"Elise!" Cate said again, as Elise tried to back away. "Elise, you have to come with us. I can't leave you."

It would have been so easy to say yes and go, but she'd already made up her mind. She'd never forgive herself if she turned her back on France now.

"I can't," she said, as the boat rocked, putting more distance between them. "I have to stay and fight for my country."

Tears ran freely down her face, the pain inside her building to an almost unbearable crescendo. She'd lost so much, and now she was saying goodbye to Cate, too. She pushed through the water then, reaching for Cate as the men on the boat pushed their oars down, the splash of their paddles the only sound other than her moving through the water.

"I'm going to miss you so much," she said as Cate reached down for her. They embraced. Elise held her tight, tried to convey in her hug how much she loved the nurse who'd come unexpectedly into her life and ended up being like a second sister to her.

"I'm going to miss you, too."

"Last call," one of the men muttered. "You coming or not?"

Elise pulled away and reached into her bag, lifting out the little dog. She pressed him to her chest, kissing his scruffy head.

"Take him," she cried to Cate. "Keep him safe and love him, for Addy. I need to know he's safe."

She thrust the whimpering little dog toward her friend, eyes straining until she could see his white fur nestled in Cate's arms, listening as Cate comforted him. Elise helped to push the boat out further, crying so hard she couldn't see anything through the blur of her eyes, resisting the urge to reach out to one of the men and beg them to pull her over the side.

"We can't take a dog with us!" a male voice objected.

"Just you try and stop me," Cate shot back.

Elise stood, the water up to her waist, as the last person in the world she loved disappeared into the night. *Thank you.* She wanted to thank Cate for taking Oscar, to call out to her one last time, but when she opened her mouth, the only thing that escaped was a cry.

Eventually she waded back to shore, soaking wet and starting to shiver as she ran low up the beach and crouched down in the dunes, wiping at her eyes as she caught her breath.

She sank her fingers into the sand then, balling them and focusing on the soft granules sticking to her skin and sliding in her grip.

Adelaide has gone, Harry has gone, Cate has gone. I'm all alone now.

But she refused to shed any more tears, refused to think about Adelaide and what it must have been like at the end, with the cold nose of a pistol pressed to her head.

The Nazis had taken everything from her.

"I stay and fight for France," she murmured to herself as she forced her body up and stood, hand on her heart, filled with the most overwhelming sense of purpose.

The war has only just begun, and I have nothing left to be afraid of. There is no one else left to lose.

Elise secured her bag over her shoulder and started to walk. She was going to join the underground movement, not just for Adelaide and Harry, but for everyone who'd lost someone to the Nazis. She wasn't going to stop until all the Wolfgangs in her beautiful country were either dead or facing the justice they deserved.

And it was a promise she was prepared to keep.

"*Vive la France*," she whispered as she looked toward the inky-black sky.

Vive la France.

CHAPTER TWENTY-SIX

CATE

Cate didn't have time to mourn for what she'd left behind. The little boat was battered by waves as they moved into deep water, and she clutched Oscar tight under one arm, the other holding the side of the boat to stop her falling in. But it was Jack who worried her. His groans grew deeper every time the boat slapped down, and she feared that he wasn't going to make it. She'd thought he was healing so well, but now she realized he'd been hiding his pain from her, knowing there was nothing else she could do for him. And after walking for so many hours without stopping, the exertion had been too much. Again.

They were so close, but Jack was almost out of time.

"Here we go. Nice and steady."

Out of nowhere, a huge ship appeared out of the darkness, and their little boat bounced beside it. She watched in amazement as the man next to her flashed his light three times, and someone on the enormous ship returned the signal.

"Watch your heads!"

She looked up, ducking as something that looked akin to a coffin was lowered over the side. The men around her scrambled to get Jack in, and she only wished she could go up with him; but it seemed the next one was for her, and she carefully got in, not releasing her grip on Oscar.

"They're not letting you take a stray on board a hospital ship."

"Just you watch anyone who tries to stop me," Cate said. Anyone who tried to get her to throw Oscar overboard was going to have to throw her with him, because she was taking the dog back to England with her, no matter what anyone said.

The box lurched and banged against the side of the ship before moving upwards into the air, and Cate buried her face in Oscar's fur, whispering to him as they moved, inch by inch, until they were suspended over the hulking boat and then guided down to the deck.

"Out you get," someone said, and she quickly sat up and climbed over, finding herself surrounded by orderlies.

Cate blinked, thinking her eyes must be betraying her.

"Welcome on board the *Dinard*," one of the orderlies said. "Are you injured?"

"No, but my friend Jack, the one who came up before me, he needs to see a surgeon. He has internal injuries and—"

"Ma'am, he's already on his way to see the doctor. I'm sure you're in shock from seeing his wound, but—"

"I'm a nurse," she said. "I was left behind during the evacuation of Dunkirk."

"Cate?"

She heard her name being called, and she spun around, not able to tell where it had come from. Was she hallucinating?

"Oh my God, *Cate*!"

Someone pushed through the gathered orderlies, and as Cate's feet gave way, as everything she'd been through suddenly caught up with her, she collapsed into warm, familiar arms.

"I'm here," a woman's voice soothed. "I knew you'd make it."

"Lilly?" she croaked. *How can it be Lilly?*

"Did you truly think I was going to leave you behind? I've been searching for you ever since we parted." Lilly kissed her cheek. "You have no idea how good it is to see you again!"

Cate started to laugh then, shutting her eyes as Lilly's warm arms embraced her. "I must be dreaming. This can't be real. You're can't really be here."

"Let's get you to a doctor for a check-over, just in case," Lilly said.

"Don't let them take my dog," she whispered. "You have to keep him safe. You can't let anyone hurt him."

Lilly didn't miss a beat, and when Cate opened her eyes, as orderlies lifted her on to a stretcher, she saw that Oscar was nestled in Lilly's arms.

"I promise, he's safe," Lilly said. "And so are you."

Cate couldn't keep her eyes open any longer, and as blackness swirled around her as she finally gave in to her exhaustion, all she could think of was home.

We're almost there, Jack. We're almost home.

"Cate, are you awake?"

Cate blinked, her eyes adjusting to the light. She moved her fingers and found they were being held, and when she looked she saw that Lilly's warm palm was pressed to hers.

"I thought it was all a dream," she said. "But you're really here, aren't you?"

Lilly smiled. "I'm really here, and so are you."

Cate looked around, sitting up as she searched the room. "Where's Oscar? Where's my dog? Lilly, I—"

"Oscar is fine," said Lilly, her hands on Cate's shoulders as she gently pressed her back down. "He's in my room tucked up in my bed, so he's perfectly fine for a while."

Cate's heartbeat started to settle, and she was grateful that Lilly kept her hands on her shoulders a while longer, the touch alone helping her to calm.

"And Jack?" she asked, trying not to sound too eager for information, despite the dull ache inside her at just thinking about what might have happened to him.

"Jack's fine too," Lilly said. "He's had surgery already, and he's expected to make a full recovery."

Cate shut her eyes again, breathing deeply as she thought about him. It was a miracle he'd survived after everything he'd endured, and she only hoped that this time, he'd be able to rest and recuperate.

"How did you make it, Lilly? How did you end up here?"

Lilly sighed and sat on the bed, and when Cate shuffled over, Lilly lay down beside her, their heads together on the pillow as Cate reached for her hand.

"I was going to say that it's a long story, but it appears we have plenty of time."

They both laughed, and Cate relaxed against her friend, so relieved to be with her, to have someone to care for her after everything she'd been through.

"The ambulance you saw me in was one I took from the beach when we all arrived," Lilly said. "It had just been left, abandoned, and when I saw the keys still in it, I knew I had to go back to get the patients who couldn't walk all that way. I couldn't just leave them behind."

"It seems like a lifetime ago, that day, doesn't it?" Cate mused.

"It certainly does."

"And what happened when you left? Did you get all those patients to the beach?"

"I did. But I have a scar to show for it." Lilly lifted her leg and pulled up her skirt, exposing a rippling red mark that ran down her thigh. "I saw a man, a British soldier, on his own, collapsed on the road. I knew I had space for one more since Jack hadn't made it onboard, so I stopped to help him in, and when I went to drive away, I was stopped by SS officers. There was one standing at my door just as I was about to close it."

Cate gulped, squeezing her friend's hand even tighter. "And then?"

Lilly sighed. "He was so close I could smell the onions on his breath, and he yelled 'Surrender' at me," she said. "And when he ordered his men to leave my patients on the road, I slapped him, clean across the cheek."

"Oh Lilly, you didn't!"

"Oh, I did," she said, laughing. "But the bastard pulled out his dagger so fast and stabbed me straight in the thigh, so I screamed and slammed my foot on the accelerator, flying past the other German soldiers and not stopping until I reached the beach!"

Cate laughed; she couldn't help it. "You took on a German SS officer and managed to win? I should say I can't believe it, but somehow I can."

"Well, I only *just* won," Lilly admitted. "I still had his dagger in my leg when I arrived at the evacuation point, and if it hadn't been for the doctors who saw me collapse then and there, I would have bled out on the sand."

"Thank God they were there," breathed Cate. But as glad as she was for Lilly, her thoughts turned to those for whom there had been no doctor, those who hadn't made it. She couldn't put off telling Lilly what she knew any longer.

"Lilly, I had some terrible news since we parted ways." Cate swallowed as tears welled in her eyes. "Charlie's dead, Lil," she murmured. "I found out that he didn't make it, I'm so sorry."

Lilly turned and put her arms around her. "I know. There was another telegram waiting when I arrived back in London. How did you find out?"

"Jack knew him. They served together. He was with him."

"So tell me, you and Jack . . ." Lilly whispered.

Cate stiffened. Lilly was her best friend, but she was also supposed to have been her sister-in-law, and they were talking about Charlie.

"Jack's a nice man, Cate. You don't have to hide the way you feel about him, not from me."

Cate stayed silent, wrestling with her words, not sure what to say.

"We don't choose who we fall in love with, so if he's the one, he's the one," Lilly said, as if it were the most simple thing in the world. "The only thing I've cared about all this time is finding you, and I have a feeling I have Jack to thank for that."

"I tried to fight the way I felt about him from the moment I saw him," Cate said. "I didn't want to be disloyal—"

"You're not being disloyal," Lilly interrupted. "Charlie always said that if he didn't make it home, he wanted you to be happy. We both heard him say that, Cate."

Lilly was right; he *had* said that, but hearing Lilly say it, hearing her acceptance, was what Cate had needed.

"Are you sure?" she asked.

"Cate, honey, you're *alive*. That's all I care about, and you forget that I was there, I saw the way Jack looked at you. You two were never fooling anyone but yourselves."

Cate managed to laugh. "Thank you," she said. "I just can't believe you're here, that we're together again."

Lilly hugged her before standing. "It's no coincidence, Cate. I volunteered for the hospital ship the moment I found out they were planning return trips, and I never stopped telling anyone who would listen that there was a British nurse left behind."

Lilly bent over her then and they just breathed, forehead to forehead, for the longest while.

"I love you, Lil. I've missed you so much."

Lilly kissed her cheek and smiled down at her. "You do realize I'm going to lose my job if anyone finds that scruffy little dog in my cabin, don't you? So it's lucky I love you, too."

"Oscar is worth it," Cate said, trying to return the smile despite the heaviness in her heart. "His owner . . ." she said, as her voice wobbled, "his owner gave her life to save mine."

Lilly's eyes filled with tears as she hugged her again. "Then I'll care for him like my life depends on it. I promise."

As Lilly held her tightly once more, Cate remembered Adelaide. She remembered her smile and her kindness that first night, when she'd pretended Oscar was her own. Without Adelaide, she would never have had a chance of making it home at all. Without Adelaide, perhaps every single one of them would be dead by now.

I'll never forget you, Addy. Not a day will go by when I won't remember your sacrifice.

And as Lilly held her, rocking her in her arms, she finally succumbed to sleep.

EPILOGUE

It was the birds taking flight from the low-hanging branches of the fruit trees that made Elise look up, and she startled when she saw a man coming up the path. His beard was scraggly and his clothes old, and her heart skipped a panicked beat as she stood and looked for her son, scanning the garden.

"Louis!" she called, holding up her skirts as she ran to him.

Louis waved to her from the tree he was climbing, and she gestured for him to come down, glancing over her shoulder at the man, who'd stopped now, but was on her path still.

She cursed her gun being so far away. Since France had been liberated, she hadn't carried her weapon, but she was wishing she had it with her now.

"Louis, get down!" she demanded, reaching for him and catching his hand. He landed in her arms with a thump, almost knocking her off her feet, and she held him tight against her chest.

"Mama!" he protested, but she ignored him, setting him down but keeping a firm grip on his hand.

She looked at the man and then at her front door, knowing that if she had to, she could run the distance and protect them both. If there was one thing that war had taught her, it was that she was more than capable of looking after herself. And she wouldn't hesitate to shoot this man if he tried to hurt them.

"Stay where you are!" she called, moving Louis slightly behind her. "This is private property."

"Elise," the man called back, holding his hands in the air as if to surrender, showing her that he had no weapons. "It's me."

Me?

She squinted, lifting her free hand to shield her eyes from the sun.

It can't be.

She studied his stature, the clothes hanging off his skinny frame, his long, unkempt hair. But as he walked slowly closer, his hands still raised, and she kept staring, something about his eyes stopped her from running for the house.

"Elise?" he said again.

His voice was hoarse, as if he hadn't spoken in a long while, but the way his warm brown eyes shone, she just knew.

It's Harry.

"Harry?" she whispered, no longer used to his name on her lips.

It was his smile that told her it was truly him, even disguised by a beard, even attached to a face so thin she could barely comprehend it was the man she'd once known and loved.

"Oh my God, Harry!" She let go of Louis's warm little hand, running the last few yards between them and opening her arms. "Harry!"

When his arms closed around her, lips to her hair as she pressed her face to his chest and listened to the still-familiar beat of his heart, for a moment it was like he'd never left. Elise cried happy tears into his shirt, not caring that he was skin and bones, or that his tattered shirt smelt like it hadn't been washed in years. It was Harry, and she'd take him any way he came.

"I can't believe you're alive." She leaned back in his arms and stared up at him. "I can't believe it. I just—" Elise blinked through her tears. "I just can't believe you're actually here, standing in front of me."

"Let me look at you," he said, stroking her face. "You're the only thing that's kept me going all this time, and I had this terrible feeling that I'd finally make it back to you and you'd be gone."

She didn't tell him about the bullet that had skimmed her thigh and almost killed her, or the knife wounds to her stomach; she could so easily have perished, but somehow, miraculously, she'd lived to see the end of the war that had claimed the lives of everyone she loved. Everyone, except Harry.

A shiver ran through her as she remembered her son behind her. "There's someone I'd very much like you to meet, Harry," she told him, smiling up at him as she turned, keeping one arm looped around his waist.

Before she could tell Louis to come closer, Harry cleared his throat and pulled away from her, dropping to one knee. She saw his mind working as he perhaps tried to figure out who the boy might be.

"Elise," he started, and she laughed as Louis blinked back at them. "I have a son?"

"You do. His name is Louis, for my brother."

Harry's arms were open and he dropped to both knees as Louis slowly, tentatively, walked forward.

"Louis, this is your papa," Elise said, switching to French as she waved him over. "Come and say hello. Your papa has come home!"

Louis took a few more steps, glancing at his mother before the biggest grin she'd ever seen spread across his face as he sprinted and then launched into his father's arms. Her usually shy little boy almost knocked Harry clean off his haunches, but he righted himself and managed to stand with Louis in his arms. Arms that were bone-thin, but still had enough strength to hold his son.

"I never thought I'd see this day. I never thought for a moment that you could have survived, that you'd make it," she said, crying now as she embraced Harry, wrapping her arms around the man she'd mourned for and yet still loved for so many years, and the little boy she'd fought so ferociously to protect from the minute she'd discovered she was pregnant. She'd never, ever let herself believe that Harry could be alive, not after all the loss she'd suffered, not after Adelaide.

"Well I'm here now, and I never intend on leaving you again," Harry whispered, his lips pressed to their son's head now. "And to think I had this little man waiting for me, too. I only wish I'd known."

Elise slipped her hand into his then and led him inside, her heart fuller than it had been in as long as she could remember.

An hour later, when Harry had eaten a small meal and Louis was contentedly playing with his toy truck in the living room, Elise sat beside the bath on a stool as Harry lowered himself into the warm water. She'd clipped his beard with scissors before he'd undressed, and now that he was lying, head back and eyes closed, she soaped his cheeks and used a blade to shave him. At first she was hesitant, not wanting to cut him, but the more she slid it across his skin, the more confident she became and slowly, before her eyes, her Harry started to appear.

They never said a word as she soaped his back and washed his hair, carefully trailing her sponge across deep scars that hadn't been there when she'd last touched him, his bones protruding as if he'd been starved for months, if not years. When she was finally done, and steam had long since stopped rising from the water, she stood and reached for a towel, holding it out to him as he stepped from the bath.

She should have been embarrassed at seeing him naked after so long, but nothing about seeing Harry again was as awkward as she'd imagined.

"Sit here," she said, pulling the stool in front of the mirror on the wall. "I'll cut your hair while it's wet."

Harry wrapped the towel around his waist and sat, and she took the chance to wrap her arms around him, leaning down from behind and pressing her cheek to his. A cry escaped her lips then, a cry she'd tried so hard to swallow down, and tears started to flow down Harry's freshly razored cheeks too. They both cried, quietly, arms around one another, until Elise finally found the strength to rise.

"I'm sorry," she said, laughing as she wiped her eyes. "I just—"

"Can't believe it?" he asked.

She smiled down at him, wishing she didn't feel so sad, but unable to stop it. "No, I can't. I don't think I'll believe it for days, maybe even weeks. It's too good to be true after all the pain."

Harry's eyes found hers in the mirror as she stood behind him, her hands in his hair. "I had terrible thoughts of you with someone else. I thought if I found you, if I actually made it all the way back here, there was a chance you'd have a husband, that you'd have long since forgotten about me."

"Never," she whispered, bending down and pressing a slow, warm kiss to his lips when he turned his head. "I've been too busy looking after our son and telling him all about his brave papa who sacrificed everything to make sure I could live."

She ran a comb through his hair then, standing behind him and staring at his reflection in the mirror, hating how hollow his cheeks seemed. But he was still as handsome as ever, even without enough meat on his bones.

"Tell me what happened that night, Cate. Did Jack make it?"

"I hope so. He made it to the boat, and Cate with him." Elise's bottom lip started to tremble and she bit down on it, trying to

297

stop the sudden, sharp wave of emotion building within her. She never let herself think of that night; she never went there in her memories, because there had never been anyone to look after her, to pick up the pieces if she let herself fall.

"And what of you?" he asked. "What happened to you, Elise?"

"I stayed to fight," she said simply. "I was transient until I was due to give birth, and then I helped in any way I could in the background. The resistance became a powerful force, and I was with them every step of the way."

She started to cut his hair then, blinking through her tears as that time, the time she'd lost Harry and her sister, came back to her. *Don't go there, don't go there.*

"And you? How is it that you're even alive?" she asked, not wanting to talk about herself.

"I only just survived," he murmured, tears glinting in his eyes, reflecting back at her in the mirror as he bravely kept his chin lifted. "I survived almost five years as a prisoner of the Germans, and the only thing that kept me going was you. It was a hell like I could never have imagined, something I will never speak of for as long as I live, and the fact that any of us walked out of there alive . . ."

She placed her hands on his shoulders, wanting to give him strength, to silently tell him that she was there for him, that she understood in a way that only those who'd lost and suffered could.

"It's a miracle," he finally said, the words choking out of him. "How a human can live like that, can even *exist*—"

A haunted look etched his features as he trailed off, and she vowed then and there never to ask him what he'd been through. She knew what it felt like to want to leave the past where it belonged.

"Harry, I . . ."

The sob that erupted from deep inside him hit her like a punch to the stomach, the noise strangled, tortured as he crumpled forward. She dropped the scissors and wrapped her arms around him, cradling his head, her lips pressed to his forehead as she cried over him, tears drowning her kisses as he cried and cried with her.

Elise curled like a child on his lap, his arms tightening around her, holding on to her as if he would never let go. All this time, all these years, she'd kept everything so tightly woven inside of her, never to be released, but with Harry, she didn't have to hide any more. Finally, she could mourn what they'd lost, *what they'd suffered* together.

"I'm so sorry," he whispered against her shoulder. "I'm so sorry for Adelaide, I'm so sorry for everything."

Elise shut her eyes, breathing him in, committing him to memory in case he was ever taken from her again, her lips never leaving his skin and her arms never breaking their embrace.

Two weeks later, Elise stood at her sister's memorial, admiring the fresh flowers she'd placed there with her little helper. She'd created the memorial beside her parents' graves when she'd returned, but she'd always been void of emotion, too scared to truly think back and remember what she'd lost, what they'd once had. But with Harry home, she'd learnt to grieve for her sister, to stop hiding her tears; she'd broken wide open and yet at the same time was no longer broken like she'd once been.

Louis stood by her side, his pudgy arm around her leg, his hand caught in hers. And this time, when she saw Harry coming up the path, she didn't startle. In such a short time, he'd started to fill out, and he was already looking like her Harry again.

Today he was holding a newspaper, and she smiled as he came closer and scooped Louis up with one strong arm, kissing his cheek before kissing hers. He might have missed out on the early years of his son's life, but he was making up for lost time every hour of every day.

"Look at this," he said, holding the newspaper out. "You won't believe it."

She took the paper from him, her eyes casting over the words as Harry read aloud over her shoulder, starting with the headline. She gripped his arm tightly, staring, not believing his words.

"*Nazi commander charged with war crimes,*" he read.

Elise thought her legs were going to buckle as she gripped the paper, needing to read for herself. Never in a million years did she think there could or would be justice, but perhaps she'd been wrong. Could this really be him?

"*The accused, Commander Wolfgang Schmidt, a highly decorated Nazi soldier, has been nicknamed the butcher of Le Paradis,*" she read. "*Schmidt was found in a prisoner-of-war camp in Sheffield, England, and was picked up by Americans and later transferred to a camp in Yorkshire. The commander is on trial for war crimes committed in the French village of Le Paradis, where he is accused of the massacre of almost one hundred British soldiers. The unit, known as the Royal Norfolk Regiment, were slain in cold blood following their surrender, with Schmidt allegedly giving the order to open fire, killing all but two British soldiers with machine-gun fire and bayonets.*"

Elise glanced up at Harry. His eyes were filled with tears, and she leant against him as she continued to read.

"*The War Crimes Investigation Unit describes Schmidt as a man like his Nazi comrades, well versed in brutality and not showing a hint of remorse. It is understood he is still refusing to acknowledge his actions.*"

Elise shut her eyes, remembering the man, remembering what she'd lost and what he'd been responsible for.

"*Testimony from Private Peter Winston is expected. Despite officials not believing his original account of what had happened at Le Paradis when he returned to London as part of a prisoner exchange, the further written record of Private Harry Cross during his release from a German concentration camp allowed officials to piece together the truth. Investigators appeal to the public to help them find Private Cross, who is believed to be in France still. He is understood to be the only other survivor of the bloody Le Paradis massacre. The trial will be held at the Curiohaus War Crimes Court in Rotherbaum, Germany, and if convicted, Commander Schmidt will be sentenced to death."*

Elise faced her sister's grave again, looking at the fresh flowers and her name carved in the stone. "Justice," she whispered. "I can't believe it. I honestly can't believe it."

"I can't believe Peter survived, either," Harry said. "I was certain he'd be killed as soon as he surrendered, as much to make sure there were no witnesses as anything."

She glanced over the article one more time, letting the news soak in. She could barely believe it.

"Would you be opposed to me going to London so I can give my full account in person to authorities there?" Harry asked, his arms warm around her. "I know I promised I'd never leave you again but . . ."

Elise took a big, shaky breath. "Not at all," she said, relaxing into his chest. "In fact, I've never wanted anything so badly in all my life. You tell them everything, Harry. You tell them what he did to Adelaide, you tell them what he did to all your men. He has to pay for what he did."

Harry's lips were tender as he kissed the top of her head. "Trust me, Elise," he murmured. "This is the last and only time I'm ever reliving what happened, and I'll make sure it counts."

"I love you," she whispered. For a second, she imagined Adelaide there, a flower behind her ear, smiling as she watched their embrace. She could hear her laughter, see her twirling Oscar in her arms and kissing his fur before running through the field by their house where the wildflowers grew.

Goodbye, Addy. She smiled. *You might be gone, but you will never, ever be forgotten.*

CATE
SIX MONTHS LATER

Dear Elise,

I can't believe it's been so long since that fateful day, or that today is the anniversary of Adelaide's death. So much has happened since then, and although I'm sure you've seen this already, I wanted to send you a clipping from the newspaper. He's gone, Elise. After everything he did, after all he took from you, and from Harry and Peter, he's finally gone. Your Harry was so brave, coming to testify and relive it all, but it was worth it. I still can't believe they found him guilty and sentenced him to hang for his crimes; even all these months later, it's still hard to believe that he's taken his last breath. I'm in two minds about the punishment, because I would have preferred he rot for years in jail, but the fact they even caught him is miracle enough.

Speaking of Peter, I bet you were as surprised as I that he survived his ordeal. He testified before the court, as I'm sure Harry's told you, so bravely despite all he's been through. He's still in some pain and has to walk with a stick, but the sweetest thing of all was seeing him with his girlfriend in London when we returned. Well, wife now, because we went to their wedding only last weekend, and it was the most romantic thing, seeing the way she looked at him. I'm so glad that he made it home, and that he had someone so loving waiting.

Peter spoke of Adelaide in his wedding speech, of the brave young woman who accompanied him to the Nazi camp to surrender, and he truly believes that she's the only reason he survived. Without her there, he thinks they would have shot him on sight, and he said he's eternally grateful for her kindness and bravery.

One day, I promise that we'll come and see you, but for now please know that you are always in our thoughts. Oscar is old and grey now, but as happy as could be and sitting at my feet while I write to you, his chin on my toes, and I wonder if he ever thinks of his previous life in France. The sound of his little snore takes me back to being in your home, seeing him nestled on Adelaide's lap. I will never forget your kind, sweet, loving sister for as long as I live.

I wish you love and happiness, Elise. You gave me the chance to live, you saved me when you could have so easily turned me away, and you saved Jack, too. For that, we will always be grateful. In fact, Jack's sitting beside me now, telling me to send you his love. We will see you again soon, I promise.

You are forever in my heart and my thoughts, and on this day, the anniversary of our beloved Adelaide's passing, know that I will never, ever forget your beautiful sister either.

AUTHOR'S NOTE

As with all my books, much of this story is based on fact. It all began when I watched the movie *Dunkirk*, and became fascinated with the story of how British troops waiting on the beach were rescued by so many different vessels. But the more I thought about the movie, the more I asked myself: where were the women?

That was my starting point for this book, as my question led me to research the women who were stationed in France, and how they were evacuated from Dunkirk— if at all. It turns out that many British nationals were evacuated earlier than troops, including nurses, but there were still many women needing to be rescued from Dunkirk.

One of the most alarming things I discovered was about the women of the ATS; some female telephone operators were amongst the last to be evacuated. And there were also many doctors, nurses and orderlies who were still working in clearance hospitals as the evacuation was well underway.

While there are no confirmed cases of nurses being left behind in hospitals after the final evacuations, it's true that doctors and orderlies were required to draw straws or pick numbers to decide their fate. It's also true that they knew what would happen to them—it was a fact that the Germans were coming, but someone had to stay behind to look after the huge influx of soldier patients who couldn't be evacuated. These doctors and orderlies were reminded that it was their duty to continue doing their jobs. Those patients who could get out of bed, called the "walking wounded", made their way to the beach, often so terribly injured they could barely hobble along, but no one wanted to be left behind and they used anything they could find as makeshift crutches and walking sticks. Those doctors and orderlies who drew the short straws and had to stay in France were soon taken as prisoners of war by the Nazis, destined to live behind wire and do their best to survive until they were liberated.

Another part of this story that is based on fact is the massacre at Le Paradis, where ninety-seven members of the Royal Norfolk Regiment were killed. Two men miraculously survived, and after hiding beneath the dead bodies of their fellow soldiers, they crawled to a nearby farm and were concealed there after being discovered hiding in the pigsty. They did eventually surrender again, thankfully to a friendlier German regiment. Due to the severity of his leg injuries, one of the men ended up being repatriated back to London in exchange for some wounded German soldiers, and went on to testify in the war crimes case against the Nazi commander who had ordered the massacre. The commander was convicted and sentenced to death by hanging, and the newspaper article I have Elise reading from in the closing scene of the book is factually accurate on all counts. You can read further about this horrible event by searching for the "Le Paradis massacre" online. It's important to note that although I used this part of history as inspiration for my story, the characters in my book are entirely fictional.

I would also like to mention the character Lilly, who was inspired by one of the last remaining nurses to be evacuated from Dunkirk. Lillian Gutteridge bravely commandeered an ambulance, filled it with her patients, and drove them to the beach. She encountered a Nazi patrol on her way, and when an SS officer ordered her to relinquish her ambulance and his men to throw out the stretcher-bound patients, she slapped him across the cheek and received a dagger in the thigh in response. This might just be one of the bravest nurses I've come across in all the years I've been researching WWII.

Every time I read about a moment in history, I ask myself: What would it have been like to be a woman there? My approach in this book is no different. I can only hope that I have managed to convey the emotions of my characters in an authentic way, by imagining myself in their shoes as they hid from the Nazis and fought to save their own lives, and the lives of others.

ACKNOWLEDGMENTS

As always, I would like to thank a core group of very important people in my life. First of all, my eternal thanks goes to my team at Amazon Publishing, most especially my editor Sammia Hamer for always seeing potential in my ideas, and encouraging me to write the stories of my heart. Thank you also to editor Sophie Wilson, who has now worked on five historical novels with me, and who always manages to bring out the best in me. You two truly are my "dream team"! Thanks to everyone behind the scenes at Amazon Publishing too, including my author relations team—especially Nicole Wagner and Bekah Graham. I would also like to thank my longtime agent, Laura Bradford, for her ongoing support.

I wrote this novel amidst the COVID-19 pandemic, and to say it was a challenging time would be sugarcoating reality. Like many of you, I found it very hard to concentrate on anything, let alone writing. For me, and for my family, I hope that we can remember 2020 as a year that gave us the gift of time together, although I'm mindful of the suffering of so many during this time. Here in New Zealand, we had a very strict period of lockdown while I was writing this book, which meant almost six weeks at home as a family. For my six-year-old son, it was the "best time of his life"; he was at home with us and didn't have to go anywhere, which is his idea of heaven! In the end, we all loved it. We spent time watching movies, playing card games, having fun with our animals and being outside a lot on our property. It made us appreciate what we had, and also reflect on what a hard time it was for many other families. So I'd like to say a huge thank you to my gorgeous boys, Mac and Hunter, for making our stay-home orders so much fun (even if they did make it impossible for me to write!) and to my husband, for indulging my Netflix addiction and staying up late each night with me. I'd also like to thank my parents, Maureen and Craig, for their ongoing support.

Anyone who's ever read one of my books will know I always thank a small group of other authors, and this book is no different. Thank you to Yvonne Lindsay for being my daily writing buddy (I couldn't write without your constant checking in with me!) and to Natalie Anderson and Nicola Marsh for being such amazing, supportive friends. Also, thank you to my fellow Lake Union authors for your regular support.

I love nothing more than hearing from readers, so please do reach out to me if you've enjoyed this book! You can also visit my website www.sorayalane.com for more information about me and my books, and don't forget to sign up to my newsletter while you're there. I'm very active on Facebook if you'd like to find me there (www.facebook.com/SorayaLaneAuthor), and that's where I often share behind-the-scenes photos and information about my current work in progress.

Soraya xx

ABOUT THE AUTHOR

Photo © 2019 Martin Hunter

Soraya M. Lane graduated with a law degree before realizing that law wasn't the career for her and that her future was in writing. She is the author of historical and contemporary women's fiction, and her novel *Wives of War* was an Amazon Charts bestseller. Soraya lives on a small farm in her native New Zealand with her husband, their two young sons, and a collection of four-legged friends. When she's not writing, she loves to be outside playing make-believe with her children or snuggled up inside reading. For more information about Soraya and her books, visit www.sorayalane.com or www.facebook.com/SorayaLaneAuthor, or follow her on Twitter: @Soraya_Lane.

Did you enjoy this book and would like to get informed when Soraya M. Lane publishes her next work? Just follow the author on Amazon!

1) Search for the book you were just reading on Amazon or in the Amazon App.

2) Go to the Author Page by clicking on the Author's name.

3) Click the "Follow" button.

If you enjoyed this book on a Kindle eReader or in the Kindle App, you will be automatically offered to follow the author when arriving at the last page.

LAKE UNION
PUBLISHING